Thomas Codrington

# The Maintenance of Macadamised Roads

Thomas Codrington

**The Maintenance of Macadamised Roads**

ISBN/EAN: 9783742813732

Manufactured in Europe, USA, Canada, Australia, Japa

Cover: Foto ©Andreas Hilbeck / pixelio.de

Manufactured and distributed by brebook publishing software
(www.brebook.com)

Thomas Codrington

**The Maintenance of Macadamised Roads**

# MAIN

# MACADAMI

BY

## THOMAS CODRINGTON,

M. INST. C.E., F.G.S., ETC.,

FORMERLY GENERAL SUPERINTENDENT OF COUNTY ROADS FOR
SOUTH WALES.

*SECOND EDITION, REVISED AND ENLARGED.*

E. & F. N. SPON, 125, STRAND, LONDON.

NEW YORK: 12, CORTLANDT STREET.

1892.

# PREFACE TO THE SECOND EDITION.

THE call for another edition of this work gives the opportunity of adding some new matter relating to road maintenance, and also of modifying or omitting parts relating to management which have become obsolete in consequence of the general abolition of turnpike trusts, and of the transfer of the main roads to the County Councils by the Local Government Act of 1888. The effect of this transfer is to afford scope for road maintenance on a larger scale than has hitherto been possible in England, and may be expected to have good results.

T. C.

*September* 1891.

# PREFACE TO THE FIRST EDITION.

THE maintenance of roads is a subject upon which the published information in this country is remarkably scanty. McAdam and Parnell, while treating of the improvement of old roads, and the construction of new ones, passed over their maintenance with little notice, and those who have since had the charge of road maintenance on any considerable scale have left few records of their practice and experience, beyond what can be gathered from reports, and evidence before Parliamentary Committees.

Information relating to those general principles which should guide the practical work of road maintenance must be sought for almost exclusively abroad, where the State management of roads has afforded facilities for investigation, and for generalising results, which have been wanting in this country. The engineers of the Ponts et Chaussées have been foremost in enquiries of this sort, and the results of their labours are fortunately for the most part as applicable in this country as in France.

At the present time, when opportunities of acquiring practically a knowledge of systematic road maintenance have become rarer as large areas of management under persons of wide experience have become fewer, there is need of a more general acquaintance with the principles upon which good road maintenance depends. The want of this will probably become more apparent when, under the Highways and Locomotives (Amendment) Act of 1878, the incidence upon the county rate of one-half the cost of repairing the main roads leads to a supervision over the expenditure on them, and the mode of their maintenance, by the county authorities.

The following manual is intended to treat of all matters which relate to the systematic maintenance of macadamised roads. The observations and conclusions of foreign engineers are freely used where experience has proved their applicability in this country, and information from other sources not generally accessible has been brought together in, it is hoped, a useful form. The results of enquiries of my own, upon points on which further information seemed desirable, are given, and some experience of the county management of roads enables me to offer suggestions as to the manner in which the control of the county authority over the expenditure on main roads may be exercised with advantage.

T. C.

*January* 1879.

# CONTENTS.

———◆◇◆———

## CHAPTER I.

### PRELIMINARY, AND HISTORY.

## CHAPTER II.

### CONSTRUCTION OF ROADS.

## CHAPTER III.

### ROAD MATERIALS.

## CHAPTER IV.

### COMPOSITION OF ROAD-COATING.

## CHAPTER V.

### DRAUGHT, WHEELS, AND WEIGHTS ON THEM.

## CHAPTER VI.

### WEAR.

a reserve of strength. Surface wear; disintegrating effect of wheels meeting an obstacle, greater as wheels are smaller. Morin's experiments on wear of roads; effect of diameters of wheels, width of tires, weight of the load, springs. Wear from bending and cross-breaking; action of the load on the subsoil; experiments by the author; loaded wheels at rest; area of subsoil affected'; influence of thickness of road-coating, width of tire, and diameter of wheel; wheel rolling forwards; effect of thickness of road on the intensity of pressure on subsoil; on weak roads the load on the subsoil, and not on the wheel tire, should be considered; passage of heavy loads; effects of traction engines; heavy loads on narrow tires; effect of exceptionally heavy traffic on a weak road. Action of the weather, frost, wet, rain after frost, dryness, effects aggravated on a badly kept or weak road, or by heavy traffic; injurious effects of hedges and trees; wear from every cause dependent largely on the nature of the material, and on maintenance, gradient, season, &c. .. *Pages* 69–84

## CHAPTER VII.

### MEASUREMENT OF TRAFFIC AND WEAR. CONSUMPTION OF MATERIALS.

Modes of measuring traffic; in France by collars and tonnage; modification in South Wales. Measurement of traffic in streets of Liverpool and London. Modes of measuring wear of roads, by measuring detritus, and by thickness; composition must be also considered. Process adopted by French engineers, general results obtained, proportion of wear to traffic; instance at Saint-Étienne. Wear as measured by thickness. Consumption of materials, on French roads, on Glasgow and Carlisle, and on Holyhead roads, in streets of London and Birmingham. Quantities of materials used on Metropolis roads, on Edinburgh turnpike roads, on South Wales county roads .. .. .. .. .. .. .. 85–94

## CHAPTER VIII.

### SPREADING ROAD MATERIALS.

Spreading in thin coats. Care required in spreading small quantities of materials per mile; inequality of wear and of strength of road favourable to road maintenance. Mode of laying on fresh materials; small quantities in patches least annoying to the public; hollows and slacks from wear on a good road. Mode of repairing them; form and arrangement of patches; repair of ruts and large hollows one part at a time; stoning from side to side in short lengths; hills not to be stoned from side to side. Metalling not to be laid on more than one stone in thickness; frequent stone heaps necessary; spreading materials by a special man. Picking up the surface not desirable on ordinary thin roads, useful on thick roads, cost of it. Use of a binding material unnecessary, except when large quantities of

materials are laid in streets, &c. Attention to materials after they are
laid, raking, replacing stones, use of a rammer. Season for laying on
materials; commence patching in autumn, and get the greater part on by
the end of the year; stones laid in spring do not consolidate without great
attention. The wear of ordinary traffic can be replaced by patching in
small quantities; with greater traffic, size of patches must be increased;
full quantity to be laid on in sheets after all hollows are covered; danger
of allowing a road presenting a good surface to get weak. Dumas' system;
minute attention to the surface repairs, and excessive manual labour;
results. Spreading thick coats, and consolidating by rolling; advantages
of it under some circumstances; picking up old surface; necessity for
binding, and watering in dry weather; minimum thickness to be laid;
allowance for greater wear in middle of road; length to be undertaken at
once; areas which can be rolled with a horse roller, and with a steam
roller; particulars of steam rollers. Economy claimed for repairs by thick
coats and rolling; particulars of cost given by Graeff; estimated saving in
materials, and in labour; cost of horse rolling and steam rolling; cost of
repairs with a steam roller in Hackney; after attention required; no
economy unless the wear be considerable. Destructive effect of a heavy
roller on weak roads; rolling a coat one stone in thickness only desirable
for public convenience   ..      ..      ..      ..      ..   *Pages* 95–109

# CHAPTER IX.

### SWEEPING AND SCRAPING.   DRAINAGE.   WATERING.   REPAIRS BEYOND ORDINARY MAINTENANCE.

Sweeping; sweeping machines; Whitworth's machine. Scraping; horse
scraping machines; hand scrapers, and hand scraping machines; objections
urged against scraping machines, of little weight; scraping to be done
promptly; collection and removal of road scrapings; amount of scraping
required; often what a badly managed road most requires; most necessary
in early autumn; advantages of keeping a road free from mud; increase
of wear by over scraping, and weakening of road if the wear is not replaced;
caution necessary in some circumstances. Drainage; importance of
attention to it; preservation of cross section; clearing out water-tables
and outlets to ditches; trimming sod bordering; opening side ditches in
spring and summer; examination of covered drains; powers of surveyors
under Highway Act; liabilities of occupiers of adjoining lands; clearing
out ditches by farmers; tendency of ditches on hills to deepen, prevention.
Cutting hedges. Watering seldom necessary for the good of the road, and
often injurious; cost of watering with carts; Bayley's vans; comparative
trials; Willacy's machines; hose and jet system; perforated pipes; use of
sea water, of chlorides. Repairs beyond ordinary maintenance; breaking
up after frost; holes in the crust from heavy loads in wet; traction
engines; provision for recovery of expenses of damage by extraordinary

## CHAPTER X.

MANUAL LABOUR. PROPORTION OF EXPENDITURE ON MATERIALS AND ON LABOUR.

# CHAPTER XI.

### COST OF ROAD MAINTENANCE.

Particulars of cost in London; in Brighton; Metropolis roads, details in 1864 and 1871. Cost of the roads of the Department of the Seine. Edinburgh roads, statement of detailed cost of maintenance; approximate cost of turnpike roads in England and North Wales in 1874 and 1875; cost of roads formerly turnpikes; cost of main roads 1881 to 1888; cost of county roads in South Wales, details; average cost of national roads of France; cost of Calvados roads .. .. .. .. .. *Pages* 143–152

# CHAPTER XII.

### ROAD SURVEYOR'S DUTIES. REPAIRS BY CONTRACT. ROAD MANAGEMENT.

Length a surveyor can superintend; lengths in South Wales; in highway districts; loss from want of proper supervision of road work. Surveyors to keep accounts. System by which no money passes through surveyor's hands. Entries to be made of all measurements; records of the quantities of materials used should be kept, and roads divided into short sections for the purpose; quarterly statements of the quantities of materials; annual statements of tools and other property. Annual estimates, should be prepared in detail. Accounts of expenditure; annual statements of expenditure on South Wales county roads; statements of accounts of turnpike trusts, and highways. Repairs by contract; doubtful advantage of it; terms of a repair contract. Advantage of large areas of management; in France, in Ireland, in Isle of Wight, in South Wales. Control given to the county authority by Highways and Locomotives (Amendment) Act, 1878; provisions of the Act; maintenance of main roads by County Councils; advantages that may result .. .. .. .. 153–163

# CHAPTER XIII.

### RECAPITULATION.

Maintenance a question of wear; conditions under which wear will be reduced to a minimum; good drainage, good materials, well-cared-for road-coating and surface; sufficient strength for the traffic; fluctuations of traffic; extraordinary traffic; economical replacement of wear; importance of removing detritus; necessity for sufficient manual labour; advantages of having men in charge of lengths of road; adjustment of expenditure; care in preparation of estimates and accounts of expenditure; records of the quantities of materials spread; comparisons of various roads as a means of judging of economy of maintenance; means of comparisons in future, and necessity for them .. .. .. .. 164–169

# THE MAINTENANCE

OF

# MACADAMISED ROADS.

## CHAPTER I.

### PRELIMINARY, AND HISTORY.

ROAD maintenance comprises the renewal of the materials worn out by the action of the traffic and the weather, the care of the surface and the drainage, and such casual repairs to the road and works connected with it as may be necessary.

The most obvious feature in road maintenance is the application of new materials, but the prevention of avoidable wear, by keeping the surface and the body of the road in good condition, is hardly less important; and the removal of the materials from the road after they are worn to detritus, the care of the surface, and attention to drainage, are essential parts of a good system of maintenance.

It is plain that if by keeping roads in good order four horses are enabled to do the work of five, or three of four (by no means an unreasonable supposition), the economy in horse labour and wear and tear of vehicles and harness must be considerable; but economy in the actual cost of maintenance generally follows as well. Experience proves that a road with sufficient strength, good surface, and thorough drainage, can be kept in first-rate order with a much smaller quantity of materials than an inferior, ill-kept road requires, and though a greater amount of manual labour may be necessary, a good road on the whole is generally more cheaply maintained than

B

a bad one, especially when there is any considerable amount of traffic.

If the amount spent annually on the macadamised roads in this country be considered, the importance of the application of proper principles and good system to their maintenance will be evident. It appeared from Parliamentary Returns published in 1887, that upwards of 4,000,000*l.** were spent annually on the turnpike roads and highways of England and Wales, exclusive of the metropolis, in which 280,000*l.* was estimated to be annually spent on macadamised roads.† The Annual Local Taxation Returns now show a total expenditure in England and Wales of upwards of 5,500,000*l.* a year on highways, street improvements, and turnpike roads. Of this amount ‡ 2,000,000*l.* are expended by highway authorities in rural districts, almost entirely on macadamised roads. The other 3,500,000*l.* is expended in the metropolis and by urban sanitary authorities, and it is impossible to trace how much of it is spent in macadamised roads. It is certain that a large proportion of this heavy expenditure might be used to much greater advantage with more skill and system on the part of the road surveyors and those who direct their proceedings; and the indirect saving in the cost of traction, and wear and tear of vehicles and horses, which would result from better roads, would probably far exceed any direct saving in expenditure on the roads, considerable as the latter might be.

|  |  | £ |
|---|---|---|
| * *Turnpikes*, 1875, exclusive of payments on account of debts.. | | 383,223 |
| *Highways* in Highway Districts and Divisions, 1875–6, exclusive of payments on account of debts, and payments to turnpike trusts .. .. .. .. .. .. .. | | 1,700,896 |
| *Highways*, in Urban Sanitary Districts (exclusive of the Metropolis) 1875–6 .. .. .. .. .. .. | | 2,036,279 |
| | | £4,120,398 |

† 'Street Pavements,' by G. J. Crosby Dawson, 1876, p. 19.

|  |  | £ |
|---|---|---|
| ‡ Repairs of Highways and Turnpike Roads in 1888–9, exclusive of salaries, &c. .. .. .. .. .. | | 1,994,109 |
| Improvements not defrayed out of loan .. .. .. | | 13,347 |
| | | £2,007,456 |

It is not proposed to touch upon any of the engineering operations connected with laying out a road, nor to enter into details of construction, except so far as they relate to road maintenance. The history of roads, road management, and road repairs, before the time of Telford and McAdam—contemporaries, and in some degree advocates of rival systems—also requires but brief notice.

The earliest roads about which anything certain is known are those of ancient Rome, some of them dating from several centuries before the Christian era. They are characterised by straightness from point to point, and by the solidity of the foundations, which generally consisted of several courses of flat stones, sometimes laid in mortar. In France the Roman method of construction seems never to have been altogether lost sight of, and to have been followed to some extent when new roads began to be made about the beginning of the 18th century. In this country, though Roman roads remain, often visible, and sometimes constituting the foundation of roads now used, there are no traces of Roman influence in roads of later date. The law according to which each parish repaired its own roads by statute labour kept them in an almost incredibly bad state up to the latter part of the last century, and the establishment of turnpike trusts appears not to have effected much improvement up to the beginning of the present century.

What the process of road-making and road-mending was then is thus described by McAdam :—

"The practice common in England, and universal in Scotland, on the formation of a new road, is to dig a trench below the surface of the ground adjoining, and in this trench to deposit a quantity of large stones; after this a second quantity of stone, broken smaller, generally to about seven or eight pounds weight; these previous beds of stone are called the bottoming of the road, and are of various thicknesses, according to the caprice of the maker, and generally in proportion to the sum of money placed at his disposal. On some new roads made in Scotland in the summer of 1819, the thickness exceeded three feet. That which is properly called the road is then placed on the bottoming, by putting large quantities of broken stone or gravel, generally a foot or eighteen inches thick, at once upon it, and from the careless way in which it is done the road is as open as a sieve to receive the water, which is retained in the trench." * With respect to repairs, he says that there seemed to be "no other idea of mending a road than bringing a great quantity of material and shooting it on the ground."

Telford, in his evidence before the Committee on Turnpike Roads and Highways, 1819, describes the shape or cross section of the surface as frequently hollow in the middle, the sides encumbered with banks of mud sometimes 6, 7, and 8 feet high, preventing the water from reaching the side drains, and the gravel or other materials as being laid promiscuously on the road with the clay or soil, with which they were mixed in their native state, and without sorting or breaking them.

Reference to the numerous Parliamentary Reports of that time on the London and Holyhead road, and on the state of the turnpike roads and highways of the country generally, will show that there was no exaggeration in these descriptions.

This state of things arose from general defects of management, and from the ignorance of those entrusted with the repairs of the roads, who were usually farmers, old servants, or broken-down tradesmen. Under Telford and McAdam a regular system of management was established and carried out on the turnpike roads by properly qualified road surveyors.

On the ordinary highways improvement was hindered by the system of statute duty, and by parish management under a person chosen yearly to serve the office of surveyor of highways. Every one who kept a team of horses was liable to be called upon to do six days' team work, and those who did not keep horses paid money instead. The parish surveyor generally had no special knowledge of road repairing, and the team labour and other work were seldom well applied. Statute duty was abolished, and highway rates were substituted by the General

---

* 'Remarks on the Present System of Road Making, &c.,' by John Loudon McAdam, 1820, p. 48.

Highway Act of 1835 (5 & 6 Wm. IV. c. 50), which also permitted the appointment of a paid surveyor, either for a single parish or for a highway district. Another step in advance was made by the establishment of highway districts throughout South Wales by the Act of 1851, and in some other parts of England and Wales under the Acts of 1862 and 1864.

The difference between Telford and McAdam on one point has been more dwelt upon than the similarity of their systems on many other points on which they differed so widely from the practice of their predecessors. Both insisted on the necessity for the thorough drainage of the seat of the road, a thing then utterly neglected, and both made use of materials broken to gauge to form a solid hard surface of uniform cross section, and of curvature just sufficient to throw the rain water off freely to the sides. The distinction usually drawn between the so-called Telford system and that of McAdam is in the foundation, or pavement of large stones upon which Telford generally, but not always, laid the broken stone or gravel, and which he thus describes :—*

"This foundation is a regular close pavement of stones carefully set by hand, and varying in height from eight to six inches, to suit the curvature of the road. These stones are all set on edge, but with the flat one lowest, so that each shall rest perfectly firm. The interstices are then pinned with small stones ; and care is taken that no stone shall be broader than 4 or 5 inches, as the upper stratum does not bind upon them so well when they much exceed that breadth. The pavement thus constructed is quite firm and immovable, and forms a complete separation between the top stratum of broken stones and the retentive soil below."

Sir H. Parnell,† after describing Telford's foundation, of which he was a strong advocate, adds that "this method of making roads with a foundation of pavement is described in French works on roads," and he quotes the description of an altogether similar foundation from the 'Encyclopédie de

* 'First Report on Holyhead Road,' May 1824.
† 'Treatise on Roads,' 1838, p. 137.

l'Ingénieur." It had, in fact, been in use since 1764, when Tresaguet set on edge the foundation stones which had before been laid flat after the Roman manner; and it is interesting to compare with the description of Telford's pavement, Tresaguet's mode of constructing roads, as described by himself in 1764, and adopted generally in France in 1775. He says:—

"The bottom of the foundation is to be made parallel to the surface of the road. The first bed on the foundation is to be placed on edge and not on the flat in the form of a rough pavement, and consolidated by beating with a large hammer, but it is unnecessary that the stones should be even one with another. The second bed is to be likewise arranged by hand, layer by layer, and beaten and broken coarsely with a large hammer, so that the stones may wedge together and no empty space may remain. The last bed, three inches in thickness, is to be broken to about the size of a walnut with a small hammer, on one side on a sort of anvil, and thrown upon the road with a shovel to form the curved surface. Great attention must be given to choose the hardest stone for the last bed, even if one is obliged to go to more distant quarries than those which furnish stone for the body of the road; the solidity of the road depending on this latter bed, one cannot be too scrupulous as to the quality of materials which are used for it."

It was the complete separation of the road metalling from the subsoil by a firm and regular bottoming, rather than accomplishing it by a pavement, that Telford insisted upon as necessary. He says:—"Particular attention should be paid either to find a naturally dry bottom for the roadway or to construct one; and avoid as much as possible suffering the workable materials coming into contact with clay. And this may always be accomplished by means of gravel, sand, vegetable soil, chalk, or bottoming stones, but this bottoming should be made perfectly firm and regular, so as to receive the top workable metal of equal thickness."* Accordingly, where, as on parts of the road between London and Shrewsbury, no stone for a pavement could be got, a bottoming of gravel, or of layers of chalk and gravel, was formed, and thus, although he always advised a

* 'Report on Holyhead Road,' 1819, p. 132.

paved bottom when it could be laid, many pieces of road were made under Telford's direction without the paved bottom with which his name has been associated.

Where the bottom is soft and wet, and the subsoil cannot be made dry by drainage, a bottoming of some sort is very desirable, and where stone can be easily got for a pitched foundation, it will often be found the most economical as well as the most convenient way of making a road if it is required to be of any considerable strength. The cost of a considerable quantity of metalling is saved, and 3 or 4 inches of broken stone laid on 6 inches of pitching consolidates much more quickly under ordinary traffic than the 9 or 10 inches of broken stone alone. The stone used for the pitched foundation may be of a quality unfit for road metalling or building.

McAdam considered a bottoming of large stones useless, and even went so far as to condemn it as mischievous, on the ground that the large stones at the bottom caused motion of the materials, and kept open passages for the water to the subsoil beneath. That motion does take place among large stones thrown down anyhow on to an undrained subsoil, as in the old roads with which McAdam had to deal, is undoubtedly true, but it is not the case with a carefully laid bottoming of stones on edge.

It has also been asserted that the top metalling is crushed between the wheels above and the rough pavement below, but there are no grounds for such a belief if the body of broken stone is kept up to a sufficient thickness; and on a soft subsoil, where a pitched bottoming is most useful, experience proves that even when the broken stone has been reduced by wear to 1½ inch or 2 inches in thickness, there is no sign of such action.

Dispensing with any bottoming, McAdam insisted that it was the native subsoil which carried the road and the traffic, and that, so long as it was preserved in a dry state, it would carry any weight without giving way, and that for this end it must be made dry by drainage, and kept dry by a covering impenetrable to rain. He contended that the thickness of the road should only be regulated by the quantity of material necessary to form this impervious covering, and never with any reference to its *own* power of carrying weight; and that if the water passed through a road, it would go to pieces whatever were its thickness.*

McAdam's doctrines were condemned by the partisans of Telford's system as " contrary to the first principles of science,"† and it cannot be denied that many of his statements are marked by a good deal of exaggeration. He not only condemned a paved bottom as useless, and even mischievous, but he stated that roads upon a hard bottom wore away more quickly than those placed upon a soft soil, instancing a road laid on the naked surface of the soil over a yielding morass, where the water trembled in the side ditches, on which the wear was less than on the adjacent length on limestone rock, in the proportion of 5 to 7. He also said that he preferred a soft substratum to a hard one, provided it were " not such a bog as would not allow a man to walk over it."‡

It is quite contrary to other experience that materials should last longer on a soft bottom, and the small wear in the instance of the road over the morass may have been in spite of its soft foundation, instead of because of it; and it may have another explanation, as will be shown farther on. At any rate, the saving in wear of materials on a flexible road could only have been obtained at the expense of increased draft of vehicles.

His assertion that the thickness of the road-coating should only be such as to form an impervious covering, without reference to its own power of carrying weight, requires modification, as will be shown hereafter. No doubt a water-tight covering, as in limestone roads, is very desirable, but roads of a silicious nature may be very good, although they are always more or less permeable. There are other points upon which the best modern practice is at variance with McAdam's precepts; nevertheless, roads formed on the principle for which he

---

* ' Remarks on the Present System of Road Making, &c.,' by J. L. McAdam, 1820, p. 40.

† Parnell, ' Treatise on Roads,' p. 78.

‡ Evidence, Select Committee on Highways, 1819, p. 23.

contended, of laying broken stone directly on the natural soil, without an artificial foundation, form by very far the largest proportion of the roads of the present day, both in this country and abroad. To McAdam is due the credit of having been the first to direct public attention to the necessity of the proper breaking and preparation of road materials, and to the possibility of forming with them a compact road surface, nearly impenetrable to water, which can be laid so flat as to allow vehicles to pass freely over all parts of the road, and at the same time throw off the water. To him also, though it is generally left out of sight, is largely due the establishment of a regular system of road maintenance under properly qualified surveyors.

# CHAPTER II.

## CONSTRUCTION OF ROADS.

### *Drainage.*

WHETHER a paved bottom be laid or not, it is a matter of the first importance that the seat or foundation of the road should be thoroughly drained. This is usually provided for sufficiently by ditches or drains on each side of the road sunk 2 or 3 feet below the surface, and communicating with the natural watercourses of the country. In ordinary open level districts they are generally on the field side of the fences, and in making a new piece of road, especially where the width of land to be taken is limited, this is the best place for them. They are, however, very often found on the side next the road, and where there is plenty of width, and a footpath or waste ground lies between the metalled surface of the road and the ditch, there are some advantages in having the ditch in that position. The hedge is farther from the road, and leaves it more open to the sun and wind, a matter of importance in promoting the drying of the surface, and the ditch, being nearer, more effectually drains the foundation of the road, and is more easily reached by outlets from the side channels, and is more accessible to the road labourers.

In cuttings, or where the road is below the level of the adjoining land, side drains must necessarily be on the road side of the fence, and they often have to be covered in. They may then be under the water-table or side channel, and should be cut 10 inches or 1 foot below the formation surface, and be filled in with rubble stone up to, and in connection with the road materials. On sidelong ground, where the road is benched into a hill-side, a deep covered drain of the same sort is often required to cut off the land water from the slope above, and prevent it soaking up under the road. The surface water should be carefully excluded from these covered drains and be provided for by catchwater drains and surface channels.

If side-ditches and drains are not enough to lay the foundation dry, cross drains, or mitre drains, must be cut as frequently as may be necessary. The latter are drains meeting in a V in the centre of the road, and running to the side ditches or drains in the direction in which the road falls. An inclination of about 1 in 100 is enough for these drains, which are usually cuts in the formation surface of the road about 6 inches deep and 12 inches wide at top, filled in with broken stone. They may be also drain pipes, or small box drains consisting of dry stone side walls with a flat bottom and cover stone. The latter have the advantage that they can be easily opened from above and cleared if they get stopped. Care should be taken to tap and lead away any springs which may rise under the road.

If necessary, drains can be cut through adjoining land to carry off water from the side-ditches. The General Highway Act gives power to make and maintain drains or watercourses through lands adjoining or lying near a road for the purpose, making satisfaction to the owners or occupiers for damage they may sustain.*

A road on a wet undrained bottom will always be troublesome and expensive to maintain, and liable to serious damage by breaking up in wet weather or after frost. It will be economical in the long run to go to considerable expense in making the drainage of the subsoil as perfect as possible.

Besides the drains required for the road itself, other cross drains and culverts are necessary to convey the surface water of the country from one side of the road to the other. These must be constructed where required, and to suit the particular circumstances of the case. There is an advantage in having culverts under a road sufficiently large for a man to pass through for examination and repairs; smaller ones may be either barrel culverts, earthenware pipes, or box drains. It is not advisable to give much inclination to culverts and drains

* 5 & 6 Wm. IV. cap. 50, sect. 67.

sufficient fall to clear them of water is enough. The scour caused by the too rapid flow of water is destructive, and a drain with a steep inclination is more liable to obstruction than one with a moderate fall.

### Cross Section.

It is essential for the proper and economical maintenance of a road that the rain should flow freely off the surface. Water standing in ruts or hollows is injurious in two ways ; it greatly increases the wear of the traffic, by which the hollow in which it lies is continually deepened and enlarged, and it soaks in and weakens the whole crust of the road and the sub-soil beneath. Such a cross section should therefore be given, and carefully maintained, as will throw the rain water off freely, and a very moderate inclination from the centre to the sides of the road is found to be best for this purpose. On a road too convex, or too high in the centre, there is a tendency for the traffic to follow in the same track along the middle of the road, being the only part where the vehicles can run upright, and hollow tracks are worn by the wheels and the horses' feet, which retain the water, so that such a road is not so dry, and wears more unevenly than one of a flatter section on which the traffic is more evenly distributed over the whole width.

Roads are often made too round in section, with a mistaken notion of keeping them dry, and also to allow for greater wear in the middle, but there is no danger of a road with little con-vexity wearing hollow in the centre, or retaining the water, if the surface is properly attended to. Fairness of surface facili-tates the flowing off of water far more than extreme convexity, and if the surface is neglected and allowed to wear into ruts, no amount of convexity that can be given to a road will clear it of water.

It is necessary to give a somewhat greater convexity to a new road than it is intended to have eventually ; the middle consolidates more by the traffic, and stones are scattered towards the sides, so that, however carefully it is raked and attended to, the road will become flatter as it consolidates.

The section adopted by Telford for the surface of his roads was a flat elliptical curve, differing very slightly from an arc of a circle by being more convex in the middle than at the sides. Walker recommended a cross section composed of two straight lines joined towards the middle of the road by a curve, and falling about 1 in 24 towards the sides. A common form is an elliptical curve flatter in the middle than at the sides, which is apt to be too flat in the middle of the road, though it forms good side channels. Either a flat ellipse like Telford's or an arc of a circle is perhaps on the whole preferable, but regularity of section and evenness of surface is of much more consequence than the slight differences between curves and straight lines. The fall from the centre to the sides need not generally be more than 6 inches on a road 30 feet wide, and should never exceed 9 inches; for a road 18 or 20 feet wide, 3 or 4 inches is enough. On a perfectly level road a rather rounder section is required than on a road with moderate gradients. On hills the fall towards the sides should be enough to lead the water off, and prevent its scouring the surface by running down the hill instead of to the side channels. It has been said that on an inclined road every wheel track becomes a channel for carrying off the water much more effectually than can be done by a curvature in cross section, but this on hills becomes a source of great damage to the road. In heavy rain the wheel tracks are quickly deepened into watercourses, which soon cut into and even through the metalled surface.

When the water-table or side channel has to carry a good deal of water, it may be made deeper by increasing the convexity of the surface for a breadth of 1 or 2 feet at the sides, so that the water may not cover too much of the road. The clearing out of the water-tables has a tendency to deepen them, and to give this increased convexity, and it may generally be omitted in making a new road if the channels are not pitched.

The convexity required for the surface may be given either by diminishing the thickness of the road-coating towards the sides or by forming the seat or bed of the road with a fall from the centre outwards. It was Telford's practice to make the bed of the road level in cross section and to give the convexity by diminishing the thickness of the bottoming of pitching or gravel from the centre towards the sides of the road, and sometimes by reducing both bottoming and metalling at the sides.

On some parts of the Holyhead road the pitched bottom extends on a level bed from side to side, diminishing in thickness from 7 inches in the centre to 3 inches at the sides of a 30-foot road, thus forming a convex surface with 4 inches fall, on which broken stone was laid 6 inches in thickness for a breadth of 18 feet in the middle, and thinning out from 6 inches to 4 inches in the 6 feet of width remaining on the sides of the road, with 1½ inch of gravel over all, so that the finished road had a total convexity of 6 inches. On other parts of this road the pitched bottom was laid over only 18 feet of the middle of a 30-foot road, diminishing from 7 inches to 5 inches in thickness, with a layer of broken metal 6 inches thick over.

On the portions of road made without any pitched bottom the convexity was given partly in the gravel bottoming, which was 7 inches deep in the centre and 2 inches at the sides of a 30-foot road, and partly in the top metalling of broken flint and large gravel, which varied from 8 inches in depth in the middle to 4 inches at the sides, with 1½ inch of binding gravel over all, thus giving 9 inches of convexity in the 30 feet width. Thus, on the Holyhead road, though the sides were made weaker than the middle, there was a width of 18 feet over which the full thickness of top metalling was carried, and the sides had considerable strength.

On roads of ordinary width and ordinary strength it is doubtful whether any good reason can be given for making the sides weaker than the middle, as is commonly done, and which must be the result if the convexity of surface be given by a greater depth of metalling in the middle of a level formation surface. The sides are always the first part of a road to suffer from timber hauling or other heavy traffic, especially on hills, where the softer sides of the road are taken in preference by way of a drag in descending.

In making a new road, it is usually better to form the bed or seat with such a fall towards the sides as will give the desired form of surface with an uniform thickness of metalling over the whole width, or with only a slight extra thickness in the middle to allow for the greater consolidation on that part of the road. This is attended with the advantage that a dry formation surface is prepared for the reception of the road materials, whether bottoming or broken stone.

In forming the seat of a road it is best to leave as much of the original surface of the ground as possible undisturbed, making up inequalities by filling in hollows with material excavated from the side ditches rather than by cutting away the soil. The vegetable soil should always be left on a clay subsoil. After the proper form of cross section has been given, the surface should be rolled, if a roller is available for the purpose.

On a clay subsoil, where small gravel or sand is at hand, a thickness of 2 or 3 inches may be laid on with advantage before the metal is spread, to cut off the body of the road from the clay below. Chalk has been used for the same purpose, but it is a dangerous material unless the road is sufficiently thick to render blowing up in consequence of frost reaching the chalk unlikely.

An uniform width for the metalled surface should be set out, and a shouldering to confine the road materials should be formed either in the solid or by sods backed up by earth. Numerous outlets must be left through the shouldering for surface drainage.

### Road with a Pitched Foundation.

When a pitched bottoming is constructed, the stones must be set with care by hand in a close pavement, with the broadest edges downwards and across the road. If the stones are laid flat, there is a tendency to rock under the traffic, and even to tilt up on edge in soft ground, and the top metalling does not bind upon them so well. The upper edges should not exceed 4 inches in breadth to hold the top metalling well. All inequalities on the upper side should be broken off with the hammer, and small stones or stone chips should be firmly pinned and packed in the interstices with a light hammer, so that every stone may be firmly fixed in place, and a regular convex surface be formed for the top metalling. Carting of materials over the paved bottom should not be permitted until it is covered with a coating of broken stone, as the stones are thereby displaced. Three or 4 inches of the top metalling should be first put on, and carefully attended to by raking in the ruts while it is consolidating under the traffic, and the remainder of the thickness should be added when the first layer has nearly consolidated. With ordinary traffic, 4 inches of broken stone over a pitched foundation will consolidate in about three months.

A road with a pitched bottom must have at least 4 inches thickness of pitching, over which it is not desirable to have less than 4 inches of broken stone metalling. The pitching will often be made thicker, without any increase of cost, and it may be, as in the Holyhead road, as much as 7 inches thick. The broken stone metalling over a pitched bottom need never be thicker than in the Holyhead road, viz. 6 inches when consolidated.

When a pitched foundation is laid in a level street, its upper surface must have a fall at the side channels towards the gullies, otherwise the metalling will be too thin near them when the proper form has been given to the surface.

### Concrete Foundations.

A foundation of concrete was introduced by Macneill, when acting under Telford, on the Highgate Archway road in 1828. It consisted of a bed of Roman cement concrete, 6 inches thick, the upper surface of which was indented across with angular channels to hold the metalling and to drain off any water that might pass through it. The broken stone over the concrete was 6 inches thick, and the annual wear of the road is stated[*] to have been half-an-inch, all actual wear of the surface, under very considerable traffic. Afterwards a bed of common lime concrete, 6 inches thick, was used by Penfold on the Brixton

---

[*] Macneill's evidence, Committee on Steam Carriages, 1831.

and Kennington roads. The gravel or broken stone was laid on in two thicknesses, the lower 3 inches before the concrete was set, by which a union between the metalling and the concrete was effected. The upper 3 inches were added when the lower layer had been partly consolidated by the traffic.

Lias lime concrete has more recently been used for the same purpose under the macadamised roadways of the Victoria and Chelsea Embankments. In each case the concrete foundation is 12 inches thick on a slightly convex formation surface, and extends from side to side of the road, and under the kerbs of the footways. When the concrete was thoroughly set, 6 inches of granite was laid over it in two courses, each consolidated by rolling.

## Broken Stone Road.

If the road be made entirely of broken stone, a thickness of from 3 to 6 inches should be laid first, choosing, if possible, dry weather for the operation. When that has partly consolidated under the traffic, care being taken meanwhile to rake the ruts as soon as they appear, other coats may be added until the full thickness is reached. The layers after the first will work in better if laid in wet weather. If the materials are laid on too thickly, there is very great wear and waste before they consolidate; but it is necessary where the traffic is heavy, especially if the bottom be soft, to lay on a good thickness at first to prevent the wheels cutting through to the formation surface.

In considering the thickness of metalling to be given to a new road, due regard must be had to the diminution which will take place in consolidating, and also to the danger of the road being cut up by the traffic, or weather, before it is thoroughly consolidated. It is consequently best to give a new road a stronger coat than would be enough for an old road under the same conditions of traffic and situation, and it is seldom advisable, even on the best bottom, to make a new road less than 6 inches thick. On a good well-drained bottom this will make an excellent road sufficient for a considerable country traffic. McAdam considered that 10 inches of well-consolidated material was enough to carry the heaviest traffic on any sub-stratum, and experience has proved this to be true with a well-drained and properly kept road, and even in the macadamised streets of London. It is seldom necessary to give more than 8 or 9 inches of thickness, and it is better to add gradually by successive coats of metalling to a road made at first rather too weak for very heavy traffic than to give the whole thickness at once.

### Breadth.

The breadth of the metalled surface of the road should be enough to accommodate the traffic, and it will consequently be a matter to be determined by circumstances. It may be from 12 or 15 feet in country roads to 30 or 50 feet in roads of importance near towns. A breadth of 15 feet between the sod borders admits of the easy passage of two vehicles, and it has been said that the breadth should be a multiple of that required for one vehicle, so as to allow of two, three, or more abreast. Practically this is quite unnecessary; more than two vehicles are so seldom abreast that a few feet of extra width, without any reference to the multiples of the space taken up by one vehicle, often gives great accommodation to the traffic. The breadth decided upon should be uniformly preserved, except where some local cause, such as a hill, renders an extra breadth desirable, and it should be well defined on each side in straight lines or fair curves. Uniform breadth and well-defined side channels not only give a finished appearance to a road, but render it easier to keep in good order, and diminish the cost of maintenance.

### Water-tables or Side Channels.

When the road occupies the whole width between banks or walls, the metalled surface abuts against them, and the water-table or side channel is formed by the sloping surface of the road meeting the bank or wall. There is, however, usually space on each side of the metalled surface of the road occupied by footpaths or waste, and where this is the case, a sod bordering or kerbing should always, when possible, define the road and form the water-table. A sod bordering is formed by laying two sods, about 12 inches wide and 4 or 5 inches thick, one on the other, and backing them up behind with earth to form a footpath or a flat mound for the reception of road scrapings and materials, and it can generally be formed for about 1*d*. to 1½*d*. per lineal yard. The wastes should be levelled and covered with turf or sown with grass seed.

Instead of a sod bordering, a kerbing may be used by the side of the footpath when the situation justifies the increased expense, and the water-table may be pitched, or a paved channel may be laid consisting of flat stones 9 or 10 inches wide abutting against the kerbstone, and slightly inclined towards it. Too great an inclination tends to throw the wheels against the kerb. Local circumstances will of course influence the cost considerably. When a flat-bedded local stone is at hand, a rough kerb costs little, and a channel may often be cheaply formed of asphalte made of gas tar, gravel, and road scrapings.

A limestone or sandstone kerb about 1 foot deep and 4 inches wide costs from 2*s*. 6*d*. to 3*s*. 6*d*. per lineal yard, and a channel 10 inches wide by 6 inches thick rather more. Granite kerbs 12 inches wide and 9 inches deep, suitable for towns, cost 6*s*. 6*d*. to 7*s*. per lineal yard, and granite channel stones, 12 inches wide and 6 inches deep, about 4*s*. 6*d*. per lineal yard. A channel 12 inches wide formed of granite cubes, 4 inches by 7 inches, costs about the same.

In villages, or where the road is bordered with houses, it is often impossible to form a water-table in either of these ways, as it would interfere with the passage of vehicles to the houses ; and a shallow gutter must be formed by a slope inclining towards the road and meeting the edge of the metalling in the line of the water-table. This may be pitched or channelled.

At junctions and cross roads the side channels require careful arrangement and attention to the form of the surface, so that the water from one road may not be thrown upon another. Cross drains are often required at such places to get rid of the surface-water.

## Outlets.

There must be ample means for the water to escape from the side channels, in which it should never be allowed to run along very far, or to stand and soak into the road. Numerous outlets to the ditches, so placed as to suit the configuration of the surface, must be made. They may be open cuts through the sod bordering and waste, but drain pipes or stone drains will be required under footpaths; and where the road is bordered with houses and becomes street-like in character, iron gully-gratings and cesspits will be necessary.

On hills it is especially necessary to provide frequent outlets for the escape of water from the side channels, or it will break out over the road and do great damage in storms.

## Footpath.

If a footpath is constructed, it may be 5 or 6 feet or even more wide, and 9 inches or 1 foot above the water-table; it should slope towards the road with an inclination of about 1 in 30, and it should be bordered with a sod edging along the outer side as well as along the road side, if not close to a bank or wall.

## Fences.

Fences as a rule do not belong to the road, and there is no obligation on the owners of adjoining lands to fence roads. It is sometimes desirable for the safety of the public to fence places on the road side which would otherwise be dangerous, such as the top of an embankment, or other steep slope, or the edge of a river, stream, or ditch. A post-and-rail fence would be the best for the road, as it does not screen it from the sun and wind, but its liability to decay is a disadvantage. On the whole the best fence is a bank and a live hedge kept low, as it costs little to keep it in order. A bank or mound alone is often sufficient. It may be made of scrapings from the road, and when 2 feet or 2 feet 6 inches high, it answers all purposes of safety as well as, or even better than, a post-and-rail fence. Where there is room for it, a mound of scrapings may be accumulated between the posts of a post-and-rail fence, to take its place when it goes to pieces. Where stone is plentiful, walls of stone either laid dry or with mortar form a good fence. They may be well and economically coped with sods, which grow together and cannot be so easily displaced as stones.

## Stone Depots.

When there is no room for stone heaps on the waste by the roadside, receptacles for materials for repairs, called "stone depots" or "metal holders," should be provided. They may be walled recesses in the bank or fence, or independent masonry structures. They are sometimes constructed to hold a certain number of cube yards of stone, but the advantage of this is doubtful. Some trouble in measuring is saved to the surveyor, but when filled up, there is considerable difficulty in ascertaining that the depot contains nothing besides properly broken stones. The depots should be close enough together for the roadmen to wheel out the materials to the intervening portions of road.

## Rolling.

Whenever it is possible, a new road should be finished with a roller. The metalling is by that means at once consolidated together without the grinding and crushing caused by the displacement of the loose materials by the wheels of vehicles. There is less wear and waste of materials, and the public is also spared the labour of consolidating the road by the traffic, which can only be effected at great inconvenience and wear and tear of horses and vehicles. The advantages of rolling newly made roads were pointed out by the late Sir J. F. Burgoyne, in a paper written in 1842, in which the practice in France and Germany was described, and its extension to the roads in Ireland and this country was advocated.

Horse rollers usually consist of a single cast-iron cylinder 3 feet to 4 feet 6 inches or even more in diameter and 4 feet to 5 feet long, or of two or more narrower cylinders arranged side by side. The weight, when not loaded, may be 2 to 3 tons, and by loading a box provided for the purpose, or by filling the roller with water, the weight can be increased, so that rolling can be commenced on freshly laid stoning with the roller light, and as the road consolidates and the draft becomes less, the load may be increased.

Horse rollers have the disadvantage that, to obtain sufficient weight, they must be rendered cumbersome and difficult to draw. Too light a roller only consolidates the materials after many passages, and then not so thoroughly as one of sufficient weight. It is desirable that the pressure should reach to a ton or a ton and a half per foot of width of roller, and for this a roller 4 feet wide must be loaded to 6 tons, and will require six horses to draw it. Turning becomes awkward, and an arrangement for drawing in either direction is required, but even then so many horses are difficult to manage, and their feet tear up the loose materials if the draft is heavy.

For these reasons, and because of the superiority and economy of the work done, steam rollers have in a great degree superseded those drawn by horses. A roller weighing 10 tons or 15 tons, and rolling a width of 6 feet or 7 feet, such as those of Aveling and Porter, gives $1\frac{3}{4}$ or $2\frac{1}{4}$ tons pressure per foot of width, and compresses the stones far more rapidly than a horse roller. It can roll in either direction and turn easily, and is capable of thoroughly consolidating 1000 to 2000 square yards of newly laid stones per day.

When a road is to be rolled, the metalling must be put on to its full thickness at once if it does not exceed 4 or 5 inches; if thicker, it is better to roll two coats separately. When the materials have been carefully formed to the proper cross section, any large stones on the surface should be broken. The roller, if one drawn by horses, is then to be passed over several times unloaded, and any hollows from unequal settlement must be filled in with materials. When the materials begin to set, the roller may be partly loaded, and finally the fully loaded roller must be used until it produces no movement among the stones. With a steam roller the weight is of course the same from the first. Unless the rolling be done in wet weather, artificial watering is necessary from the commencement. The number of times that the roller has to be passed over depends on the nature of the soil and of the materials, and very much on the thickness of the coat to be rolled. Four or 5 inches generally consolidate more readily than either a thicker or thinner coat. It is best to commence rolling at the sides, and work towards the middle, as the form of the road is better preserved. After the rolling is thoroughly completed, the road presents a mosaic-like surface, made up of the flat sides of the stones wedged together, on which loose stones are crushed by the roller instead of being forced into the road. When the stones are thoroughly wedged together, but not before, binding must be added. This may consist of fine gravel, road scrapings, or sand. When the road materials are silicious, a binding of limestone detritus or road scrapings is the best, and with limestone materials sand may be used, but a chalky or clayey binding should be avoided. The binding should be spread dry with a shovel, uniformly, and in not too large quantities, and be rolled into the interstices between the stones with the help of watering and sweeping, fresh binding being added when that first applied has worked in.

It is necessary that all the interstices in the upper stratum of the road should be filled when the stones are perfectly consolidated, and provided that this is done, the less binding that is used the better. The closer the stones are wedged together the greater will be the proportion of surface of stone to resist wear. By the process of rolling, the interstices which were at first 45 to 50 per cent. of the whole body of the metalling can be reduced to 30 per cent. or even less, but binding sufficient to fill this amount of void is not required. About one quarter the bulk of the stones is a proportion sometimes used in France, and one-sixth is laid down in the Hanoverian official instructions as the proper proportion, but as little as possible is the best quantity to use. With a larger quantity of binding material, less rolling is required, but the road will not be so sound and durable. When more binding has been used than is necessary to fill the voids, it is sometimes the practice to water plentifully, and then by rolling to squeeze out the excess as mud. This must be swept off, or the road will be left very muddy. There is danger of softening the foundation of the road by excessive watering, and more especially in the early stages of rolling.

The effects of using a binding material in Liverpool is thus stated by Mr. Deacon :— *

"Under a 15-ton steam roller, preceded by a watering cart, 1,200 yards of trap-rock macadam, without blinding, can only be moderately consolidated by twenty-seven hours' continuous rolling. If blinded with trap-rock chippings from a stone breaker the same area may be moderately consolidated by the same roller in eighteen hours. If blinded with sicilious gravel from $\frac{3}{4}$ inch to the size of a pin's head, mixed with about one-fourth part of macadam sweepings obtained in wet weather, the area may be thoroughly consolidated in nine hours. Macadam laid according to the last method wears better than that laid by the second, and that laid by the second much better than that laid by the first."

### Use of a Binding Material.

It is undoubtedly necessary to make use of a binding material when a roller is used to consolidate a road, but when the ordinary traffic is left to do this, the employment of a binding has been by many considered mischievous. Telford provided a binding material in the $1\frac{1}{2}$ inches of gravel spread over the broken stone, but it has been contended by McAdam and others that most of the material put on for the purpose has to be re-moved again by scraping, and that what remains lessens the compactness of the road, which is consequently more affected by wet and frost than it would have been had the broken stone been left to work in and unite by its own angles without any other material. On the other hand there is no doubt but that broken stone consolidates more quickly under the traffic, with-out losing its angular form, and with far less labour to the horses, when binding is used; and though an unsound rotten road may be made by the admixture of a quantity of clayey matter or other improper material with the broken stone metal-ling, under the pretence of binding it together, the proper use of a binding on a new road is founded on reason.

* Proc. Inst. C.E., vol. lviii. p. 18.

Examinations made by the Author of the structure of the best roads * prove that from one-fifth to one-fourth of the whole coating consists of a fine muddy cementing matter, and that probably one-third of the whole is such small stuff as would be removed as ordinary scrapings. This is the result of the wear of the stones by crushing and grinding in the road, and in a new road as much as one-third of the weight of the stones forming it must be reduced to the character of road scrapings before the composition can become that of a well-consolidated road in which the stones are bound together by their own detritus. It is evident, therefore, that if this detritus, or a portion of it, can be provided at first, much wear of materials will be avoided, and the stones will consolidate together with their sharp angles preserved.

The binding material should be spread over the surface of the stone after it is laid, and its incorporation into the road-coating may be aided by raking. A mixture of the binding material with the broken stone before it is spread results in a large proportion of the former sinking to the bottom of the road-coating, where it is least required.

### Cost of Macadamised Roads.

The cost of constructing macadamised roads varies greatly, according to the price of materials and other circumstances. With materials close at hand, a good road may be formed and coated for 1s. or 1s. 3d. per square yard, and a London street, constructed in the best manner with 9 inches of Guernsey granite, may cost as much as 6s. or 7s. per square yard.

The following particulars of the construction of roads in the neighbourhood of London were given by Sir James McAdam.†

For a road of the first class, sufficient for a street with the heaviest traffic, 4 inches of gravel, riddled and broken so that no piece exceeded 3 ounces, was laid on a well-drained and prepared surface having a fall of an inch in a yard from

---

* See table, p. 54.
† 'Annales des Ponts et Chaussées,' 1850, vol. xx. p. 28.

the centre towards the sides. When partly consolidated by traffic or by a roller, 2 or 3 inches more was laid, and over this, when sufficiently consolidated, 3 inches of granite or other hard stone. The furrows were kept raked, and the cross section maintained in true form until the whole was consolidated, but no binding was used. The second class roads required 4 inches of gravel and 3 inches of hard stone or granite ; and the third class 3 inches of gravel and 2 inches of granite or hard stone. Taking the gravel at 5s. per cube yard, the granite at 14s. per cube yard, the drainage and preparation of the surface, and spreading and raking, each at 2d. per square yard, a first class road was estimated to cost 2s. 6d. per square yard.

Prices are now higher, and the cost of such a road may be as above stated, 6s. or 7s. per square yard. About London, instead of the gravel, hard core, clinker, brick or stone rubbish is often used for the bottom 9 or 12 inches, over which 3 inches of Thames ballast is laid, and then the granite or hard stone, which is often thicker than 3 inches. The bottoming, the ballast, and the top metalling are generally now rolled separately. Roads suitable for suburban or country traffic, consisting of 9 inches of hard core, 3 inches of gravel, and 4 inches of granite or other hard stone, or of 6 inches of rough stone, and 6 inches of road metal, covered with 1 inch of gravel, may be constructed for 2s. 9d. to 3s. per square yard. A road with a pitched foundation 7 to 10 inches thick, with 4 to 6 inches of broken stone over it, and an inch of binding, costs from 4s. to 7s. per square yard.

## *Re-forming an Old Road.*

An operation required more commonly than making a new road is that of putting in order an old neglected one which has gone too far out of shape to be put right by ordinary repairs. The objects should be the same as in constructing a new road, namely, to provide sufficient drainage both of the foundation and the surface, a good and regular cross section, and sufficient strength.

The side-ditches should be cleared out and lowered if necessary, and any other drains that are required for the thorough drainage of the road must be constructed. Before proceeding to re-form the surface, the thickness of the road should be ascertained by sounding or pitting, i.e. by digging small holes in the surface, as the amount and nature of the materials in the road will, in a great measure, determine the proper mode of treatment.

When the road is thin, it is generally best to leave the old surface undisturbed as much as possible, and to give the proper form by adding fresh materials, only lowering the sides, cutting down the high places, digging out earth and putting in broken stone where necessary, and taking up and breaking large stones, or breaking them in place with a heavy sledge-hammer when they appear on the surface. A uniform breadth should be determined on, a regular transverse section with a proper fall towards the sides should be given, and the water-tables or side channels should be brought to the same level on either side of the road, regulated, and defined by a sod bordering laid in straight lines or fair curves, wherever the width admits of it. Any metalling there may be outside the new side channels may be taken up and used to form the middle, and any useless material from the road may be laid behind the sod bordering. The waste on the sides of the road should be levelled and put in order, either by covering it with turf or sowing it with grass seeds, so that the feet of horses, cattle, &c. may not work it into mud in the winter. On one side, if required, a footpath may be formed behind the sod bordering. It is not desirable to have the footpath or the edge of the waste alongside the road higher than the sod bordering, i.e. more than 9 inches above the water-table, as if higher, the edge is troublesome to keep in order, being liable to moulder away and clog up the water-table. Outlets from the water-table through the sod bordering and mound behind must be made as frequently as required to carry off the water from the road.

A good deal of the work attending the regulation of the sides may be done gradually after the metalled surface of the road has been put in order, but the road should not be con-

sidered as thoroughly in order until the whole width between
the fences has been attended to.

If the road contains a large quantity of mud and detritus,
they should be removed by continual scraping until they are
reduced to a proper proportion. The hollows and flat places
should be patched with fresh materials as they appear, until a
sound surface has been formed, which can be gradually thickened
by the ordinary processes of maintenance. By these means
the road is improved generally and gradually without being
unnecessarily pulled to pieces.

### Lifting a Road.

Picking up a rough road, unless it is thick, does not generally
succeed without the addition of a considerable quantity of
materials, as the whole road is broken up and left open to the
action of the weather. But when a road has been made of large
stones, which have become mixed with the subsoil or with
other useless materials, it often happens that the road contains
in itself sufficient, or nearly sufficient, materials to make a good
road when properly used. The process of *lifting* described by
McAdam, and perhaps too often practised since, then becomes
applicable.

The whole body of the road is to be loosened with the pick,
and all stones exceeding 6 ounces in weight, or which will not
pass through a 2½-inch ring, are to be raked off to the sides by
a strong heavy rake and broken to 2½ inches gauge. By removing the old materials to the sides of the road and breaking
them there, the stone is separated from the dirt with which it
was mixed in the old road, and proper breaking is ensured, both
likely to be imperfectly done on the road itself. When the
large stones have been removed, the road is to be put into
shape, a rake which brings the remaining stones to the surface
being used for the purpose. The stone that has been broken by
the side of the road is then to be spread on the surface thus prepared. A layer of quarry rubbish, or some other dry material,
may be spread upon the foundation before the stone taken out
is replaced, and fresh materials may be added if required. It is

generally preferable to lift the surface to the depth of about 4 inches, rather than to the foundation, as in the latter case a large quantity of dirty and inferior stone is unprofitably moved. Only a small length of road should be lifted at once; two or three yards at one lift is enough. Of a gang of five men, two may be employed in picking up the road, raking off the large stones, and forming the surface, while the other three break the stones; or where there is less breaking to be done, these proportions may be reversed. It is always possible by proper management to carry on the operation in short lengths without stopping the road, but the inconvenience to the traffic is of course great, and after being relaid, the broken stone presents the same surface as on a new road, and requires the same attention until consolidated by the traffic.

McAdam stated that the price of lifting a rough road 4 inches deep, breaking the stones, reforming the surface, and cleaning out the watercourses was found to be from 1$d$. to 2$d$. per square yard lifted.*

McAdam's description of the condition of the roads with which he had to deal has been already quoted. It is clearly one to which the process of lifting is especially applicable. There was plenty of stone, imperfectly broken, badly arranged, and mixed with the soil, and by taking it up and re-making the road with care, a successful result was obtained. He pointed out, however, that in many cases it would be wrong to lift a road, and in the present day it is so in a great majority of cases. With the mistaken notion of following McAdam's directions, roads are often pulled to pieces which would be better dealt with by a less violent process.

* 'Remarks on the Present System of Road Making,' p. 41.

## CHAPTER III.

### ROAD MATERIALS.

THE materials used for road-metalling must of necessity vary very much. The haulage from any distance forms so large a part of the total cost that stone from local sources must generally be employed. The best material available should be chosen, and if not very strong, it will suffice where the traffic is moderate, a greater quantity making up for want of durability; but more labour will be required to keep the surface of the road in proper order with a weaker material under the same traffic. With heavier traffic the use of a better material, even at a higher price, becomes more advantageous, and in or near large towns the best material at almost any price is generally the most economical in the end. This is especially the case when the dirt arising from wear must not only be scraped off constantly, but be removed altogether from the road. Sometimes a stronger and more costly material may be used only for the surface, the body of the road being made of inferior local stone. For repairs the better material may be laid only on the middle of the road, where the wear is the greatest.

A good road material should be hard, tough, and not affected by the weather. These three qualifications are by no means always found together. Thus flint, though hard, is often brittle, and some schistose or slaty rocks, although hard and tough when quarried, often disintegrate when exposed to the weather. Another quality of importance is that of binding well, and this is rarely found in combination with extreme hardness and toughness. Materials well consolidated together and united in a mass resist crushing much better than when loose, and good binding property enables a stone comparatively weak to wear better than a harder stone which does not bind. The igneous and silicious rocks as a rule have but little binding property. The sandy detritus which is formed from their wear, and in which the individual stones are bedded in the road, has no cohesion or elasticity beyond that which moisture gives it, and which it consequently loses when dry. The materials, therefore, work loose in dry weather, and stones at the surface are displaced. Limestones, on the other hand, furnish a mortar-like detritus which has considerable cohesion, except when softened by excessive moisture.

For very heavy traffic, hardness and toughness are of more importance than good binding properties, and the best road materials are traps, basalts, and greenstones, such as whinstone, Clee Hill stone, Rowley rag, Mount Sorrel, Nuneaton, and Hartshill stone, and syenitic granite, such as the Guernsey stone used in London. Ordinary granite is generally an inferior road material, from the brittleness of the feldspar, and gneiss is no better.

Hard quartzose grits and cherty sandstones from the Silurian and other formations make excellent road materials, but sandstones, unless they are cherty, or contain a considerable proportion of iron, are generally inferior. An irony sandstone sometimes met with in the coal measures, the Ightham stone, and the iron sandstone of Sussex, are examples of sandstones very good for road purposes.

Copper slag, and furnace cinders from iron works, may be used with advantage where they are procurable, and when no stone strong enough to stand heavy traffic can be got. They are both very durable, but care is required in the selection of the tougher sorts. They have no binding properties, and on this account are sometimes used with limestone; a rough surface will, however, always result from the unequal wear of two materials so different in hardness. Limestone scrapings or red ashes, laid on as a binding material, aid consolidation very much, and also prevent the injury to horses' feet from the sharp edges of the fresh-laid slag, which is so much complained of.

Chalk flints and flint gravel are extensively used on the

roads of the south of England. The former, though brittle, especially when freshly obtained from the chalk, make an excellent road, but one rather liable to work loose in dry weather. Flints obtained from the surface of the ground, or from gravel-pits, are tougher, and chert gravel is tougher than flint gravel.

Flint gravel generally contains a large proportion of rounded pebbles mixed with loam. All the pebbles above 1 inch in diameter should be broken, or they will not set, but it is a mistake to make a gravel of rounded pebbles too clean. A certain amount of adhering loam is useful as a binding material; and if too much is left, it will be scraped off the road as mud, but if there is too little, the pebbles will never form a firm and solid surface. By raking together the larger stones—those exceeding 1 inch or 1½ inch in size—in the pits as the gravel is thrown out, the expense of riddling will generally be saved, the smaller stuff is useful for footpaths and other purposes, and the larger stones can be broken for the roads.

Penfold recommended * that flint pebble gravel should be first cleansed from dirt and useless matter by sifting or screening, and then that the stones above 1 inch in diameter should be separated by another sifting and then broken. The small unbroken pebbles are to be laid first with about one-fifth the quantity of chalk if it can be obtained, and when worked together for a while, the broken pebbles are to be laid on. The chalk should be small, and thoroughly mixed with the pebbles before they are spread. A very hard surface is thus made, but it is liable to blow up in frost. This liability may be preferred, however, to a loose pebbly road.

Field stone gathered from the surface of the land and river stone from the beds of streams and rivers are largely used in districts where quarries do not furnish a stone fit for road purposes. They both consist of the harder parts of stones derived from various and often distant sources, which have withstood the weathering and wear by which the softer portions have perished. Stones thus derived are not of uniform hardness, and, from their unequal wear, roads made

* 'Practical Treatise on Roads,' p. 12.

of them are not so smooth as when a material of one quality is used.

The pebble stones scattered over much of the surface of Warwickshire, Staffordshire, and Shropshire are an excellent road material.

For traffic not very heavy, the harder limestones have great advantages, from their binding properties, in which the igneous and silicious rocks are deficient, and which enables a comparatively weak stone to wear better than harder stones which do not consolidate so well. The best limestones are the carboniferous or mountain limestone, the Devonian, and some from the older Silurian rocks. Lias limestone is inferior to these, and makes a muddy road, and the oolitic and most of the newer limestones have little strength or power to resist the weather, and should not be used for roads if anything else can be obtained.

Limestone binds quickly and well, the detritus producing a sort of mortar which cements the whole together and forms a very smooth road. The wear takes place almost entirely on the surface, and although it may be considerable, the road shows no signs of weakness until the thickness is so far reduced that it is no longer able to bear the weight of the traffic. An unusually heavy load then breaks up the crust, and the road goes to pieces with little warning.

The relative strength and durability of various road materials is a difficult matter to determine. No test but actual wear in the road can be fully relied on, and though it is easy to see that one stone wears twice or three times as long as another, it is almost impossible to take into account all the circumstances under which they are exposed to wear. The nature of the traffic has a considerable effect on the relative wear as well as on the actual wear of different materials, and the moisture or dryness of the road has often a great effect on the wear of the same material.

The French Administration des Ponts et Chaussées endeavoured to obtain a comparative numerical value of the qualities of the materials used on the national roads. The quality was assumed to be in inverse proportion to the quantity

consumed on a given length of road with the same traffic, and
the coefficient 20 was given to trap, basalt, &c., of which the
consumption is 15 metres cube per kilometre per 100 collars of
traffic, and the coefficient 5 to stone, of which the consumption
is 60 metres cube per kilometre per 100 collars. A scale was
thus arrived at which is here reduced to English measures.

| Consumption per mile and per 100 collars in cubic yards. | Coefficient of Quality. | Signification of Coefficient. |
| --- | --- | --- |
| 30 | 20 | excellent. |
| 40 | 15 | very good. |
| 50 | 12 | good. |
| 60 | 10 | sufficiently good. |
| 80 | 7·5 | passably good. |
| 100 | 6 | mediocre. |
| 120 | 5 | bad. |

The mean coefficient of quality was determined in this
manner for the materials used in each department. The following list has been compiled from a return for 1876.* It will
be observed that materials of the same character bear widely
different coefficients of quality.

### Coefficients of Quality of Road Materials.

| | | |
| --- | --- | --- |
| Granitic gravel .. .. .. .. | 23·8 | |
| Quartz gravel .. .. .. .. | 21·4 | |
| Trap .. .. .. .. .. .. | 20 | |
| Quartz .. .. .. .. .. .. | 10 to 25 | (in one instance 4·8). |
| Basalt .. .. .. .. .. .. | 12 to 20 | |
| Porphyry .. .. .. .. .. | 10 to 20 | (in one instance 5). |
| Quartzite .. .. .. .. .. | 11 to 18 | |
| Devonian schist .. .. .. .. | 16 | |
| Schist .. .. .. .. .. .. | 4 to 12 | |
| Sandstone .. .. .. .. .. | 12 to 16 | |
| Granite .. .. .. .. .. .. | 6 to 20 | (generally 10 to 12). |
| Syenite .. .. .. .. .. .. | 12 | |
| Gneiss .. .. .. .. .. .. | 9 to 12 | |
| Silicious pebbles and gravel .. | 8 to 19 | (in one instance 6). |
| Silex .. .. .. .. .. .. | 8 to 16 | |
| Chalk flints .. .. .. .. .. | 7 to 11·6 | |

* État indiquant la Décomposition par Département des Dépenses d'Entretien
des Routes Nationales en 1876.

| | | |
|---|---|---|
| Silicious limestone .. .. .. | 6 to 18 | (generally about 10 to 12). |
| Compact limestone .. .. .. | 14 | |
| Magnesian limestone .. .. .. | 12 | |
| Carboniferous limestone .. .. | 9 | |
| Oolitic limestone .. .. .. .. | 5 to 12 | |
| Lias limestone .. .. .. .. | 5 to 10 | |
| Jurassic limestone .. .. .. | 5 to 8 | |
| Limestone .. .. .. .. .. | 5 to 12 | |
| Mean of all France .. .. .. | 10·63 | |

The accuracy of the coefficients depended on the exact determination of the quantity of materials consumed by a certain amount of traffic, a process requiring great care and a considerable amount of time before correct results could be arrived at. It was, therefore, resolved to determine by direct experiment the quality of samples of materials from every department. These experiments were commenced in 1879 and were directed to the determination of (1) resistance to wear and collision, and (2) resistance to crushing. The apparatus used to determine the former consisted of cylindrical boxes of iron about 8 inches in diameter, and 13 inches long, mounted on an axle revolving horizontally, and so cranked as to hold the axes of the boxes at an angle of 30° with the axis of revolution. In each box was placed 5 kilogrammes of the broken materials to be tried, carefully cleansed from dust by washing, and the apparatus was put in motion at a rate of 2000 revolutions per hour. The stones rolled against one another, and were thrown from one end of the box to the other at each revolution. After 5 hours or 10,000 revolutions, the boxes were opened, the detritus resulting from the rubbing and collision was carefully collected and sorted, and the weight of all of less diameter than $\frac{1}{16}$ inch, compared with that of the original sample, gave the degree of wear. It was found that the best materials seldom gave less than 20 grammes of detritus per kilogramme, and the coefficient of 20 was, therefore, adopted for materials having that proportion of wear. For other materials the coefficient was derived from the proportion—

Grammes of detritus : 20 = 20 : coefficient.

Resistance to crushing was determined by means of an hydraulic press. Experience having shown that cubes of the

D 2

hardest materials rarely resisted more than 3000 kilogrammes per centimetre square (equal to about 19 tons per square inch, or the resistance of soft iron), the coefficient of 20 was given to materials presenting that degree of resistance, and other coefficients were derived from the proportion—

3000 : crushing weight per square centimetre = 20 : coefficient.

637 samples were experimented on, with every precaution to ensure accurate results. When the materials were already rounded, as pebbles, they did not wear much in the machine, and obtained a coefficient far above their value, and there were anomalies with a few other materials, such as chalk flints with a softer coating, and stones with cavities. The size to which the stones were broken did not seem to have much influence on the wear. Generally the coefficients obtained agreed fairly well with those attributed to the materials from experience on the roads. The following table gives a summary of the results of these experiments :— *

| Materials. | Coefficient of Wear. | Coefficient of Crushing. |
|---|---|---|
| Basalt .. .. .. .. | 12·5 to 24·2 | 12·1 to 16 |
| Porphyry .. .. .. | 14·1 „ 22·9 | 8·3 „ 16·3 |
| Gneiss .. .. .. .. | 10·3 „ 19 | 13·4 „ 14·8 |
| Granite .. .. .. | 7·3 „ 18 | 7·7 „ 15·8 |
| Syenite .. .. .. .. | 11·6 „ 12·7 | 12·4 „ 13 |
| Slag .. .. .. | 14·5 „ 15·3 | 7·2 „ 11·1 |
| Quartzite .. .. .. | 13·8 „ 30 | 12·3 „ 21·6 |
| Quartzose sandstone .. | 14·3 „ 26·2 | 9·9 „ 16·6 |
| Quartz .. .. .. .. | 12·9 „ 17·8 | 12·3 „ 13·2 |
| Silex .. .. .. | 9·8 „ 21·3 | 14·2 „ 17·6 |
| Chalk flints .. .. | 3·5 „ 16·8 | 17·8 „ 25·5 |
| Limestone .. .. | 6·6 „ 15·7 | 6·5 „ 13·5 |

*Powers to get Materials.*

Under the General Highway Act, surveyors of highways may get materials for the repairs of roads from any waste land or common ground, river, or brook, in the parish within which

* Détermination directe de la qualité des matériaux d'entretien. Paris, 1880.

they are to be used, and in case sufficient cannot be conveniently had within the parish, in any other parish; and may likewise gather stones lying upon any lands or grounds within the parish, making satisfaction for all damages done to the lands or grounds by carrying them away. A month's notice in writing, signed by the surveyor, must be given to the owner of any enclosed land or ground from which materials are intended to be taken, that he may attend before the justices to show cause why such materials should not be had therefrom, and the justices may give the surveyor licence in writing to dig, get, and carry away materials (if sufficient cannot be had conveniently from waste land, common grounds, rivers, or brooks) in and through enclosed grounds within the parish where the same shall be wanted; or within any other parish adjoining or lying near the highway for which the materials shall be required, if it shall appear that sufficient materials cannot be conveniently had in the parish where such highways lie, or in the waste lands, &c. of such adjacent parish; the surveyor making such satisfaction for the materials and for the damage done as shall be settled by order of the justices at a special sessions for highways.* Gardens and ornamental grounds cannot be thus entered for materials, and any pits made must be fenced off, filled up, or sloped.

These powers are, by the South Wales Highway Act of 1860, transferred to the surveyors of highway districts, and by the Highways Act of 1864 are vested in the highway boards constituted under the Act in other parts of England and Wales. The powers of a highway board are vested in County Councils, for the maintenance of main roads, by the Local Government Act, 1888.

### Supply of Road Materials.

The materials for road repairs may be supplied by contract, and delivered ready broken, or the stone may be delivered unbroken, by the side of the road, to be broken by the road labourers; or the obtaining and preparation of the material may be done altogether by the road labourers.

* 5 & 6 Wm. IV. cap. 50, sects. 51–54.

Whether broken or unbroken, the stone should, if possible, be delivered on the roadside in the summer or early autumn, when the roads are best able to bear the carting, and as most good stone hardens by exposure after being broken, the materials are improved by lying for some time before they are used. There are, however, generally local circumstances which must be considered, as to get materials cheaply the cartage must be done by those who undertake it when they have no other use for their horses, and ill-considered conditions in the terms of a contract may raise the price without any corresponding advantage to the roads.

Road materials, whether broken or unbroken, are sometimes paid for by the ton, but more generally by the cube yard. They should not be purchased by the load, as the quantity delivered is uncertain when thus reckoned. When the quantity required is considerable, it is generally best to obtain it by contract, ready broken. The contractor should be required to deliver materials at such times, at such points, and in such quantities, as the surveyor may direct, not exceeding the amount of his contract. Where there are stone depôts, or room on the sides of the roads for stone heaps, it is best that the materials should be stacked on the roadside, where they are to be used, in regularly shaped heaps on a levelled bed, where they can be measured by the surveyor. If the heaps are all made of a uniform cross section, their contents can be obtained by measuring the length only, a method convenient both to the surveyor and contractor, when the quantity in a yard run is agreed upon between them. Thus, heaps 6½ feet wide at base, 2½ feet wide at top, and 2 feet high, will contain 1 cube yard for every yard of length. Disputed measurements may be settled by means of a measuring box. A bottomless box 3 feet square and 1 feet 6 inches deep, holding half a cube yard is convenient for the purpose. The heaps should not be allowed to encroach upon the road or to interfere with the side channels. They should be so close together that the materials may be wheeled out on to the intervening parts of the road by the roadman in such quantities, and at such times, as they are wanted.

Where there are no convenient places for stone heaps on the roadside, or they are too far apart for the roadman to wheel out the material, the contractor may be required to cart the material to the road after it has been stacked up and measured. Unless very carefully looked after, this tends to waste. It is the interest of the contractor that large quantities of stones should be put on at one place, and at one time, while economy in the use of materials often requires small-sized patches, perhaps not containing one-eighth or one-fourth of a cube yard in one place. With a contractor looking after his own interests, and a roadman after those of his road, the latter too often suffer, and materials are extravagantly used.

When carting from the heaps to the road is unavoidable, as it sometimes is, if it is done by contract, a certain fixed distance, say 50 yards, should be stipulated beyond which the contractor is to cart materials in such quantities as he may be required on receiving notice, and under which distance the roadman is to wheel them out. This prevents the roadman from wheeling to long distances to which the contractor should cart, and prevents disputes and jobbery. A far better way is to employ team labour, that is, to hire a horse and cart by the day for the purpose.

When stones are carted to the road and shot down, all the small stuff and dirt remains where the load was shot, and instead of being useful, as it would be if it were used from the bottom of a heap by a good roadman where required, it only makes a dirty place on the road. To avoid this, it is better that the stones required should be shot down clear of the place where they are to be used, and spread uniformly from the heap with the shovel.

### Size of Road Materials.

The size to which road materials should be broken was laid down by McAdam as not to exceed 6 ounces in weight, the difference in the specific gravity of the various stones not making any appreciable difference in the size. Telford adopted this weight, and also 8 ounces, for making new roads, but a stone that would pass in its largest dimensions

through a 2½-inch ring soon became, and has since remained,
a recognised size.   A cube of rather less than 1½-inch,
containing 3 cubic inches, and about 6 ounces in weight,
will pass this gauge, and it is a size sufficiently small for
road-making.   For surface repairs a smaller size may be used
with advantage, especially when the material is hard, as it
covers a larger surface, consolidates sooner, and makes a
smoother road.   The metalling, called "medium" in London,
not exceeding 5 ounces in weight, will pass through a 2-inch
ring, and a 4-ounce size is sometimes used.   On the South
Wales county roads the stones were specified to be broken to
a ring gauge of 2¼ inches, or sometimes 2 inches, the latter
giving stones not much more than half the cubic content and
weight of a stone of 2½-inch gauge.

The tougher the stone is, the smaller it may be broken with
advantage to the road, but of course at an increase of cost.
On roads where the traffic is of a heavy character, breaking
the materials to a small size is an expense not attended by
any advantage, and if the stone is not very tough, too large
a proportion of small stuff is produced, which is of little use
in the road, and can only be separated by screening at an
extra expense.   Metalling to be laid with a roller need not
be broken so small as it should otherwise be.   When stones
are once well bound together, as they are by a roller, they are
the stronger for being larger.

Considerable care should be taken to ensure the proper
preparation of road materials.   The stones should be able to
pass the gauge in every way, so as to be neither long, flakey,
nor flat, but as nearly cubical in form as possible.   Uniformity
of size within certain limits is desirable, especially with
harder descriptions of materials, as stones of the same size
resist wear and crushing much better than a mixture of large
and small, and a large stone makes a point in the road surface.
It is seldom necessary, when stone is properly broken by hand,
to screen out the small stuff, as the proportion is not greater
than is useful, but clay and dirt of all sorts should be rigorously
separated.   It is sometimes of advantage to separate materials
of very uneven size by screening, and to use the smaller and
larger separately.

It is generally considered that a cube yard of materials broken to a gauge of 2 or 2¼ inches will cover 30 square yards, if carefully spread one stone in thickness, or that 300 cube yards will coat a mile 5 yards wide.

## Stone-breaking.

According to McAdam, the only proper method of breaking stones, both for effect and economy, was by persons sitting, as more stones were broken, and with a lighter hammer. The hammer he recommended was about a pound weight, with a face the size of a shilling, well steeled, and with a short handle. Among the road tools figured in the "General Rules for Repairing Roads" issued by the Parliamentary Commissioners in 1819, and often reproduced since, is a hammer of this sort, 1 pound in weight, and 5¾ inches long in the head, with a handle 1 foot 6 inches long, and also a heavier hammer, 2 pounds in weight, and 2 feet 6 inches long in the handle. A heavy hammer is required to break large stones into pieces which can be afterwards reduced by a few blows from a light hammer to the proper size, but a light hammer with a short stiff handle is not used by the more expert stone-breakers, nor in the sitting posture generally preferred by them. The blow from a small head, on a long flexible handle is much more effective than that from a short-handled hammer, but great quickness of eye and long training are required to give the blow at once exactly in the right place.

A good stone-breaker will break 2 cube yards of hard limestone to the ordinary gauge in a day, and some men will break more. Hard silicious stones and igneous rocks can only be broken at the rate of 1½ or of 1 cube yard per day. Of some of the toughest, such as Guernsey granite, a man can only break on an average half a cube yard per day. River gravel, field stone, or flints, which are already of a small size, can be broken at the rate of of 3 or 4 cube yards per day.

Stone-breaking by road labourers can only be done to advantage when their proper work is not sufficient to keep them otherwise fully employed throughout the year. It is then useful to employ their spare time in stone-breaking by the cube yard, and this may be done through the summer months, when the roads require less labour, but when it is still very desirable to have a man in charge of a length of road, and ready to attend to it at once on any emergency, such as a heavy storm. Road labourers are often not expert stone-breakers, and are consequently disinclined to undertake the work. They expect to make at least as much as their usual wages by it, and to do so they must often have a higher price per cube yard than the practised stone-breaker.

### Stone-breaking by Machinery.

The increased cost of labour and the difficulty of procuring a sufficient number of stone-breakers have led to the introduction of stone-breaking machines. The original and best-known machine is that of Blake, an American crushing machine, in which modifications have been made in this country to fit it for breaking road metalling. There is also a similar machine patented by Hope, and a machine known as Archer's.

In the two first-named machines the stone is broken between powerful jaws opening upwards, one fixed, the other hinged at its upper end and actuated by an eccentric. As the fragments are reduced in size by successive strokes, they fall lower and lower in the jaws until they are sufficiently small to pass through into a revolving cylindrical screen of wrought iron pierced with holes, by which the useful stone is separated from the small.

The cost and results of working a Blake machine at Barrow are given by Mr. Arthur Jacob,[*] from which it appears that the cost of breaking hard greenstone pebbles 4 inches to 6 inches diameter to the size for road metalling, including every expense of unloading from a vessel by a steam crane,

* Proceedings of the Association of Municipal and Sanitary Engineers, vol. ii. p. 76.

labour, coal, oil, repairs, wear and tear, &c., was 1s. a ton. The machine was 15 inches by 9 inches at the mouth, and broke on an average 60 tons a day of a hard and tough stone. The wear and tear was very great. During twelve months the loose jaw had to be replaced nine times, the fast jaw eight times, the cylindrical screen once, the toggle plates four times, and the side cheeks six times, at a cost of 124*l*., or 62½ per cent. of the original cost of the machine. The "improved jaw," intended to break long pieces across, into a more cubical form, did not appear to have any advantage over the ordinary jaw; it presented so many angles that it soon wore away, and became inferior to the ordinary fluted jaw.

It is stated * that at Birmingham a Blake's stone-breaking machine broke on an average 40 tons of Rowley ragstone (a basalt) per day, at a cost of 10½*d*. per ton, exclusive of the wear and tear of the machine, the cost of breaking the same stone by hand being 1s. 9*d*. per cube yard. It is stated that 16 per cent. of dust or fine stone was produced, and of the remainder one-fifth had to be broken by hand. It was very irregular in size, and flakey in comparison with hand-broken stone. The machine was more efficient in breaking granite, or pebbles, than the Rowley rag.

All three of the above named machines—Blake's, Hope's, and Archer's—were thoroughly tried at Barnton, at Ravelrig, and at Blackford quarries, worked under the trustees of the Edinburgh turnpike roads. The stone is a hard whinstone (trap) in the two last-named quarries, and an excessively hard syenite at Barnton, and therefore well calculated to test the powers of a stone-breaking machine. Archer's machine was found to produce the best quality of road metalling, but in smaller quantities, and at such a cost for repairs and renewals as to prohibit its use. The Hope machine, the peculiarity of which is in its cubing jaws, was found to produce metalling very nearly as good as, and with much less wear and tear than, the Blake machine. The quantity of whinstone broken by a 16-inch by 9-inch Hope

* Report of the Borough Surveyor, 1874. p. 11.

machine was about 40 tons a day, and the cost was as
follows :—

|  | £ | s. | d. |
|---|---|---|---|
| Wages, 5 men and 1 boy | 0 | 17 | 10 |
| Coal, ½ ton | 0 | 7 | 6 |
| Oil, cotton-waste, &c. | 0 | 3 | 6 |
|  | **£1** | **8** | **10** |

equal to 9d. per ton, screenings included, and the total cost,
including wear and tear and all expenses, was about 1s. a cube
yard for breaking by the machine a stone which costs 1s. 10d.
per cube yard to break by hand. The amount of small stuff
separated by the screen averaged about one-sixth of the
whole, or twice as much as would result from hand-breaking.
At Barnton, where the stone is syenite and much harder, an
average of about 32 tons a day was broken by a machine of the
same sort, at a cost, for wages, coal, oil, &c., of 1s. 1d. per
ton. Including all expenses, the total cost was about 2s. per
cube yard of road material, which it would cost 3s. 6d. to 4s.
per cube yard to break by hand.

In France a commission appointed to experiment on stone-
breaking by machines found that an American machine,
similar to Blake's, produced one-fifth of screenings compared
with one-sixth produced by hand-breaking. There was, however, less dust and more small stone in the screenings from
the machine, the proportion varying with the nature of the
stone. The machine broke about 22 cube yards per day, and
the cost including interest, depreciation, &c., was found to be
1s. 7d. per cube yard, when the price paid to contractors for the
same stone was 3s. 3d. An economy of 50 per cent. was thus
shown, supposing that the machine was kept in regular work,
which can very rarely be realised in practice.

The following particulars of the cost of stone-breaking by
machines of various sorts, including all charges, compared with
hand-breaking, are extracted from a table given by Mr. Hall.*

* Trans. Soc. Engineers, 1879, p. 65.

| Locality. | Material. | Gauge. | Cost of Breaking by Machine, per ton. | Cost of Breaking by Hand, per ton. |
|---|---|---|---|---|
| | | in. | s. d. | s. d. |
| | Flints .. .. .. .. | 2¼ | 0 7 | Flints .. 1 0 |
| Sussex .. .. | Purbeck stone .. .. | and | to | Purbeck 2 0 |
| | Boulders .. .. .. .. | 1½ | 0 10 | Granite . 2 0 |
| Great Ayton.. | Blue whin .. .. .. | 2 | 1 3 | 1s. 6d. to 2 0 |
| West Coast .. | Trap, syenite, Welsh granite .. .. .. .. | 2¼ | 1 4 | 1 10 |
| Warwickshire. | Rowley rag .. .. .. | 2½ | 0 10½ | 2 3 |
| Somerset .. | Carboniferous limestone. | 2½ | 6 | 1 0 |

At Mount Sorrel, Leicestershire, the stone, a hard trap, is passed through an improved Blake machine, and then through riddles separating the gravel from the 2¼ inch Macadam, the residue which will not pass the 2¼ inch mesh being passed through fluted rolls. Leaving out the cost of getting, &c., which is the same whether the stone is broken by machine or by hand, the costs of breaking in the two ways as obtained by taking quantities of 50,000 to 100,000 tons is as follows :—

| | By Machines, Cost per ton. | By Hand, Cost per ton. | |
|---|---|---|---|
| | s. d. | | s. d. |
| Loading .. .. .. .. .. | 0 7 | | |
| Breaking .. .. .. .. .. | 0 6 | Labour and tools .. .. | 2 2 |
| Stores .. .. .. .. .. | 0 5 | Loading up .. .. | 0 2 |
| Repairs .. .. .. .. | 0 1 | Locomotives .. . .. | 0 2 |
| Locomotives .. .. .. .. | 0 4 | | |
| | 1 11 | | 2 6 |

There is here apparently 7d. per ton in favour of machine breaking, but when the interest on capital and depreciation of machinery are added, there is really a very small gain by the use of machinery. The great drawback is the large amount of gravel and chips produced, which at Mount Sorrel amounts to more than one-fourth of the rough stone broken.

Stone broken by machines is not so durable as if hand-broken. There is always, even with the hardest stone, a certain amount of crushing, which is greater when the jaws become worn. A stone not so hard, such as mountain lime-stone, suffers so much from the crushing as to stand very little wear on a road afterwards. The stones are not so cubical in form or so uniform in size as if well broken by hand.

To use stone-breaking machines to advantage, they must be kept pretty constantly at work, and an annual turn-out of 12,000 to 18,000 cube yards of road metalling cannot under ordinary circumstances be used within a short distance of a fixed machine. There must therefore be a siding and railway communication to convey away the broken stone, and the cost of carriage by railway and carting soon adds to the price. A stone-breaking machine and its engine may be moved from place to place, but the former, when mounted on wheels, weighs 6 or 7 tons, and the engine which works it must be capable of drawing it from one place to another.

Generally speaking, stone-breaking machines can be used to the greatest advantage when the material is difficult to break, and where there are facilities for distributing large quantities from one, or a small number of sources of supply. The loss of durability resulting from machine-breaking can be compensated for by the use of an increased quantity of mate-rials, and the economy of substituting machines for hand labour will generally be almost entirely a question of transport of the broken stone to the roads. Where stone is obtained here and there in small quantities, and is broken on the spot, or in the stone depôts, a machine is not applicable.

### Cost of Road Material.

Quarrying stone for road metalling usually costs, at ordinary rates of wages, 6d. to 1s. per cube yard, according to the difficulty of the work, and stacking the stone for measurement, 2d. per cube yard. Breaking by hand costs from 1s. 3d. or 1s. 4d. to 1s. 10d. per cube yard for ordinary silicious rocks and the harder limestones, and 2s. to 2s. 6d. for harder silicious and igneous rocks. Igneous rocks are sometimes difficult and costly to quarry, and can then be broken at a comparatively cheap rate, owing to the small size of the fragments. Thus some hard basalts and traps cost no more than 1*s.* 3*d.* per cube yard to break, after having been raised from the quarry at 1*s.* or more per cube yard.

The cost of carting of course varies very much according to the distance. It can generally be done at about 6*d.* per ton per mile, equal to about 6½*d.* per cube yard, by arranging for it at the time of year when work for horses is slack. On 290 miles of county roads in Carmarthenshire the cost of hauling stone from local sources was found to be a little less than one-half the total cost of the materials, or on an average 1*s.* 10*d.* per cube yard, out of a total cost of 3*s.* 9½*d.* On 130 miles in Radnorshire the cost of haulage bore nearly the same proportion to the total cost. The conveyance of a good material by railway soon increases the cost to 6*s.* or 8*s.* per cube yard, and it is sometimes well to go to 12*s.* or 13*s.* per cube yard, or even to the London price of 16*s.* or 18*s.* per cube yard for first-rate material exposed to heavy traffic. The cost of wheeling out materials from depôts or heaps about 100 yards apart, and spreading them in sheets, is about 5*d.* per cube yard, or a man can wheel out and spread 7 cube yards per day. When laid in small patches, the cost per cube yard is higher.

In the county of Edinburgh, the average cost of a cube yard of materials for the turnpike roads in 1877 was made up as follows in the different districts:—

| | Lesswade and Wrights-houses. | | Dalkeith and Post Road. | | Cramond. | | Calder, Slateford, and Corstorphine. | |
|---|---|---|---|---|---|---|---|---|
| | *s.* | *d.* | *s.* | *d.* | *s.* | *d.* | *s.* | *d.* |
| Quarrying and quarry expenses .. | 1 | 5¾ | 1 | 4¼ | 1 | 3¾ | 1 | 7¾ |
| Breaking .. .. .. .. .. .. | 2 | 0¼ | 1 | 7 | 1 | 10¼ | 1 | 3 |
| Carting to depôts.. .. .. .. .. | 2 | 7¾ | 2 | 4 | 1 | 5 | 1 | 1¾ |
| Carting from depôts to road .. .. | 0 | 11¼ | 0 | 7½ | 0 | 4¼ | 0 | 4½ |
| Cost before being spread .. | 7 | 1 | 5 | 10¾ | 4 | 11¼ | 4 | 5 |
| Spreading .. .. .. .. .. .. | 0 | 7¼ | 0 | 5¾ | 0 | 5¾ | 0 | 9½ |
| Total cost on road .. .. | 7 | 8¼ | 6 | 4½ | 5 | 5 | 5 | 2½ |

The materials were whinstone (trap), in the first, second and last-named districts, and syenite of a very hard nature, in the Cramond district, and they were principally machine-broken. The distance to which they were conveyed to depôts, in many cases by rail, and thence to the road, was often considerable.

# CHAPTER IV.

## COMPOSITION OF ROAD-COATING.

STONE, when broken to a size fit for road material, is more bulky, weight for weight, than either the solid rock or the quarried stone from which it is derived. The late Mr. C. W. Merrifield, F.R.S., noted that, assuming that none of the faces are concave, and that there are no built up hollows, broken stone cannot lie looser than when all the pieces are of the same size and shape and are regular tetrahedrons, and when that is the case he showed that half the space is filled and half void.* Experiments confirm the conclusion thus arrived at. Herr Bolkelberg states† that he found that broken stone, averaging in size from $3\frac{3}{4}$ cubic inches in some experiments to from 4 to 6 cubic inches in others, consisted very nearly of half solid and half empty space, that rounded stones packed closer than angular ones, and left less void, and that by packing irregularly shaped broken stone in a chest the empty space could be reduced to as little as 40 per cent. of the whole. As a general result the size of the stones was without sensible influence on the proportion of the empty space if the stones were of an even size, but stones of various sizes mixed together gave a smaller proportion of void, which diminished as the variety in the size of the stones was greater.

The last observation as to the effect of various-sized stones on the proportion of solid to void explains the difference between the results of other observers.

M. Berthault Ducreux states‡ that stone broken to pass a

---

* A plane can be completely covered with tetrahedrons, of which the volume will be as one-third of the height. A complete set of tetrahedrons cannot be inverted on the first so as to fit in, but half a set can be made to fit in with a whole set. This gives $\frac{1}{3} + \frac{1}{6} = \frac{1}{2}$ of space filled, and the other half empty.

† Zeitschrift des Architecten- und Ingenieur-Vereins für das Königreich Hannover, 1856, p. 225.    ‡ Annales des Ponts et Chaussées. 1834, vol. vii.

E

gauge of $1\frac{2}{3}$ inch to 2 inches, and separated from the small stuff which breaking produces, contains 54 per cent. of solid stone and 46 per cent. of void. M. Gasparin gives * the proportion as 55 per cent. solid and 45 per cent. void. Mr. Leahy† gives as the result of experiment that 100 cube feet of stone, when broken to pass through a ring—

> $1\frac{1}{2}$ inch in diameter, measured 205 cube feet.
> 2    „      „      „     190    „
> $2\frac{1}{2}$   „      „      „     170    „

which gives the following proportions of solid stone to void :—

> Stone broken to $1\frac{1}{2}$-inch gauge : solid 49, void 51 per cent.
> „     „     2   „     „     „   53, „ 47   „
> „     „     $2\frac{1}{2}$ „     „     „   59, „ 41   „

In this case it would seem that the stone must have been more even-sized when broken to the smaller gauges.

It appears from the weights per cubic metre, and the specific gravities of the 637 samples of broken materials used on the national roads of France, which were experimented on as already described, that the proportion of solid ranged from $49\frac{1}{2}$ to $57\frac{3}{4}$ per cent. of the whole, and was generally 52 or 53 per cent.

Mr. J. Mitchell,‡ by beating down screened broken stone metalling of ordinary size in layers of 6 inches in thickness, obtained a proportion of rather more than 59 per cent. of solid stone, thus agreeing closely with Bolkelberg's result with packed stone.

The following are the weights of a cube foot of some of the stones generally used for road metalling :—

> Clee Hill stone .. .. .. ..    $179\frac{1}{2}$ lbs. per cube foot.
> Other basaltic rocks.. .. ..    173 to 187   „     „
> Syenite (Guernsey granite) ..    $173\frac{1}{2}$ „     „
> Limestone.. .. .. .. ..    154 to 172   „     „
> Sandstone .. .. .. .. ..    156 „ 165   „     „

Taking 55 per cent. as the amount of solid stone contained in broken stone metalling, the weight of stone in pounds per

---

* Annales des Ponts et Chaussées, 1853.
† Practical Treatise on Roads, p. 186.
‡ New Mode of Constructing Streets, &c., p. 14.

cubic foot, multiplied by 27 × 0·55, or 14·85, will give the weight of a cube yard of the same stone when broken to road metalling. Thus, a cube yard of broken road metalling of compact mountain limestone weighing 172 lbs. per cube foot will weigh 172 × 14·85 = 2554 lbs. or 1 ton 2 cwt. 3 qr. 6 lbs. A simple proportion will show that in this case a ton of stone will produce rather less than $\frac{9}{16}$ cube yard of broken road metalling. Lighter stones will give a rather less proportion of broken road material per ton, but in taking account of materials used, tons may be reckoned at $\frac{9}{16}$ of a cubic yard.

Gravel, though made up of a lighter material, contains a larger proportion of solid, and weighs heavier. A coarse flint gravel was found by the author to weigh 1 ton 5 cwt. per cube yard as it came from the pit.

According to Mr. Leahy's experiments, stone, when broken to a 1½-inch gauge, measured nearly one-fourth more than when broken to a 2½-inch gauge. It thus appears that there is less of solid stone, as well as a proportion of small useless stuff, in a cube yard of stone broken unnecessarily small.

In road maintenance a coating of materials has to be dealt with which has been modified by wear into something very different from the broken stone originally spread, and a knowledge of its constituent parts is necessary for its proper treatment.

On pulling to pieces a specimen cut out of a good limestone road, kept in first-rate order, the author found that the stone in it which would not pass a $\frac{3}{4}$-inch ring, and which consisted of all sizes, from $\frac{3}{4}$ inch up to the gauge of 2¼ inches, to which the stone had been broken, contained 55 per cent. of solid to 45 of void, being the proportions which broken stone has already been stated to contain. The stone of all sizes in the same specimen after everything that would pass through a cheese-cloth having twenty threads to an inch had been washed away, weighed, when not perfectly dry, 68 per cent. of an equal bulk of solid stone, thus giving a proportion of 68 solid to 32 void.

In a consolidated road all interstices are filled up either with small detritus or mud, and the author has found that specimens of consolidated limestone roads weigh from 161 to 163½ lbs. per cube foot when the limestone of which they are made weighs 171½ to 172 lbs. per cube foot, the consolidated road thus being from 93½ to 95½ per cent. of the weight of an equal bulk of solid stone. The same proportion was found to prevail in consolidated road surfaces composed of igneous rocks. These results agree with those recorded by M. Bardonnaut,[*] giving the specific gravity of a road 2·40, when that of the limestone of which it was composed was 2·57; and with a statement by M. Gasparin,[†] that the density of consolidated road to solid stone is as 240 to 255, which gives for the weight of consolidated road from 93½ to 94 per cent. of the weight of an equal bulk of solid stone.

Assuming, as experiments show, that broken road materials contain 55 per cent. of solid stone, a cube foot composed of broken stone which weighs in the solid 172 lbs. per cube foot will weigh 172 × 0·55, or 94½ lbs. By the process of consolidation in the road it is crushed and compressed together till it weighs, as in the roads above referred to, say 162 lbs. per cube foot, and the bulk it then occupies must be in the inverse proportion, i. e. $\frac{94½}{162}$ = 0·583, or 58 per cent. of its bulk before it was spread on the road. Or put in another form, it takes nearly 1¾ of road metalling measured by bulk or thickness before it is spread to make 1 of consolidated road surface.

These proportions may be expected to vary with the amount of solid stone in the materials, and of detritus contained in the road. M. Berthault Ducreux[‡] states that as a mean result he found that 1 cubic metre of limestone, broken to 1⅜-inch to 2-inch gauge, gave 0·71 cubic metre of consolidated road, or that 1·41 of broken stone was required to make 1 of consolidated road. M. Bardonnaut[§] gives as the result of experiment that 1 cube metre of a consolidated limestone road contained 1·64 cube metre of materials when pulled to pieces and sorted in various sizes. M. Graeff[‖] found that with schist the proportion was from 1·30 to 1·55 and the mean very nearly 1·41 of materials to 1 of consolidated road.

* Annales des Ponts et Chaussées, vol. xvi. 1838.
† Ibid., vol. vi. 1853.        ‡ Ibid., vol. vii. 1834.
§ Ibid., vol. xvi. 1838.        ‖ Ibid., vol. ix. 1865.

It may be assumed therefore that it takes from 1·3 to 1·7 by bulk or thickness of road materials, as measured before they are spread, to make 1 of consolidated road, or that materials, when consolidated in a road, occupy from 0·77 to 0·58 of the space they did before they were spread. A proportion of $1\frac{1}{2}$ of materials to 1 of road, or $\frac{2}{3}$ of road-coating to 1 of materials, will generally not be far from the truth.

So long ago as 1834* experiments were made by M. Berthault Ducreux to ascertain the composition of consolidated road surfaces by separating the different sizes of the materials. Taking 2 centimetres (= 0·8 inch), which was the size of the mesh used to separate the small gravel from the road materials, as the gauge for stone, he found that the proportion of stone above 2 centimetres in the coatings of different roads was generally from 18 to 31 per cent. of the whole, rarely over 35 or less than 9 or 10. The proportions of the smaller sizes appear also to have been ascertained, but are not recorded. The gauge of 2 centimetres or 0·8 inch has since been generally adopted by French engineers as that above which the material in a road is ranked as stone, and below which it is called detritus. Though the general result of wear must be gradually to reduce the materials from the size at which they were put on the road to the mud and small detritus scraped off, it is difficult to draw any line between stone and detritus, or to say at what size a stone ceases to be useful. The proportion of large stone would often be a fallacious measure of a road's strength. The author has found portions of road which always go to pieces in wet weather to have an unusually high proportion of large stone, the reason being that large quantities of materials are continually laid down on a soft, wet subsoil, and the road is weak and bad for want of drainage, though full of stone. On the other hand, in a dry situation, the proportion of large stone may be but small, and the road perfectly good under traffic which would convert a more stony but ill-drained one into a bog. Nevertheless, under the same conditions, a road with an undue proportion of small detritus and mud is less able to resist the wear of heavy traffic, and

* Annales des Ponts et Chaussées, vol. vii. 1834.

ANALYSES OF THE COMPOSITION OF ROAD-COATINGS.

| No. | LOCALITY. | PERCENTAGES. | | | | |
|---|---|---|---|---|---|---|
| | | STONE. | | | | MUD, &c., under $\frac{1}{10}$ in. |
| | | Over $\frac{7}{8}$ in. | Over $\frac{1}{4}$ in., under $\frac{7}{8}$ in. | Over $\frac{1}{8}$ in., under $\frac{1}{4}$ in. | Over $\frac{1}{16}$ in., under $\frac{1}{8}$ in. | |
| 1 | Pembrokeshire mail road, west of Canaston Bridge—Mountain limestone 8 inches thick, as good as a road can be ; upper 4½ inches .. .. .. .. .. | 40·6 | 12·9 | 7·1 | 20·2 | 19 1 |
| 2 | Do.   do.   do. ; lower 3½ inches | 53·5 | 13·2 | .. .. | 33·3 | .. .. |
| 3 | Kidwelly road, near 6 m.—Mountain limestone 3¼ inches thick, on strong clay subsoil  .. .. | 45·0 | 12·7 | 6·3 | 14·5 | 21·5 |
| 4 | Kidwelly road, near the same place—Mountain limestone 1½ inch to 2 inches thick ; road not metalled for three years at least | 20·5 | 17·4 | 9·9 | 22·6 | 20·4 |
| 5 | Brecon and Crickhowell road, east of Bwlch—Bwlch limestone 7 inches thick, then subsoil, very good road ; chosen as the cleanest and driest part of the road  .. | 33·5 | 14·9 | 8·1 | 18·5 | 24·8 |
| 6 | Brecon and Crickhowell road, near Scethrog—Bwlch limestone 5½ inches thick, on field stone 6 or 7 inches ; chosen as the softest and muddiest part  .. .. .. | 21·5 | 16·0 | 10·5 | 28·0 | 24·0 |
| 7 | Brecon and Hay road—Mountain limestone 2 to 3½ inches thick, on a pitched foundation .. .. | 23·5 | 14·9 | 9·0 | 32·4 | 20·2 |
| 8 | Near Presteign toll-gate—Nash silurian limestone 4¾ inches thick .. .. .. .. .. .. | 36·9 | 11·9 | 7·5 | 17·9 | 25·8 |
| 9 | Pembrokeshire mail road on embankment near Cock's Hill—Camphill stone 1½ inch to 2½ inches, on grey stone, 8 inches thick altogether; upper 2 inches | 32·4 | 16·9 | 8·8 | 20·9 | 20·9 |
| 10 | Llandore road — Copper slag, silicious and limestone ; lower 3¼ inches of road 6½ inches thick .. .. .. .. .. .. | 52·1 | 10·5 | 4·2 | 9·9 | 23·4 |

ANALYSES OF THE COMPOSITION OF ROAD-COATINGS—*Continued.*

| No. | LOCALITY. | PERCENTAGES. | | | | |
|---|---|---|---|---|---|---|
| | | STONE. | | | | MUD, &c., |
| | | Over $\frac{7}{8}$ in. | Over $\frac{5}{8}$ in., under $\frac{7}{8}$ in. | Over $\frac{3}{8}$ in., under $\frac{5}{8}$ in. | Over $\frac{1}{16}$ in., under $\frac{3}{8}$ in. | under $\frac{1}{16}$ in. |
| 11 | Llandore road—Nearly all copper slag; upper 3¼ inches of the same specimen as 10 .. .. .. | 44·3 | 10·4 | 6·1 | 19·1 | 20·0 |
| 12 | Llansamlet road—Copper slag on furnace cinders .. .. .. .. | 40·1 | 9·1 | 6·1 | 30·2 | 14·4 |
| 13 | Newtown road, Radnorshire—river stone 5½ inches thick, on strong clay, drainage bad, much cut up in wet weather .. .. .. .. | 36·2 | 17·5 | .. .. | 45·0 | |
| 14 | Ditto ditto near same place.. | 40·5 | 10·5 | .. | 49·0 | |
| 15 | Penybont Common—Graig stone (igneous) 5¼ inches thick, on dry clay .. .. .. .. .. | 47·0 | 11·7 | .. 20·7 .. | | 20·5 |
| 16 | Near New Radnor—Gore stone (basalt) 3½ inches thick, on a dry bottom; stood timber hauling well in bad season .. .. | 46·8 | 14·3 | 6·3 | 10·7 | 21·9 |
| 17 | Near Penybont station—Llanfawr stone (igneous) 8¼ inches thick. | 44·0 | 11·8 | 7·5 | 14·8 | 21·9 |
| 18 | Mail road, 2½ m. S. of Llandegly—Eddw stone (igneous) 3½ inches thick, on dry subsoil.. .. .. | 45·9 | 11·7 | 6·1 | 17·4 | 18·9 |
| 19 | Between Llandegly and Penybont—Graig stone (igneous) 6 inches thick, on dry subsoil.. .. .. | 43·9 | 11·8 | 8·0 | 16·8 | 19·5 |

the action of wet or frost, than one with a large proportion of stone.

Generally the materials are smaller in size, and there is a larger proportion of detritus, near the surface than in the lower part of the crust of a good road.

When road metalling is put on in great thickness at once, the proportion of large stones remaining in the consolidated surface is greater than when thin coats are applied, and

80 or even 90 per cent. of the whole may be found to be over $\frac{3}{4}$ inch or $\frac{7}{8}$ inch in diameter in a road newly made of materials broken to the usual gauge, and consolidated with a roller.

The above table shows the results of some of the experiments made by the author, and under his directions, on the constituent parts of different roads. Blocks of the whole thickness of the macadamised coating were cut out and pulled to pieces. The stone was sorted by sieves to the various sizes, and the mud, &c., was separated by washing through a cheesecloth having twenty threads to an inch, which allowed everything under $\frac{1}{30}$ inch to pass away. Newly stoned portions were avoided in taking the specimens, and the points chosen were such as to give a fair sample of the composition of the road. The materials employed had been in all cases broken to the gauge of $2\frac{1}{4}$ inches or $2\frac{1}{2}$ inches, and the roads were maintained on the same general system with thin coats of stone.

It will be observed that of stone above $\frac{7}{8}$ inch, a gauge rather larger than the 2 centimetres of the French engineers, the proportion varies from $21\frac{1}{2}$ to $53\frac{1}{4}$ per cent., and only exceeds 50 per cent. in the lower portions of two roads. Of stone above $\frac{5}{8}$ inch, the proportion varies from $37\frac{1}{2}$ to $66\frac{3}{4}$. The weakest in stone of the larger size, either above $\frac{5}{8}$ inch or $\frac{7}{8}$ inch, is No. 6, a specimen from a point chosen as being by reason of its situation the softest and muddiest on a very good limestone road from which No. 5 was taken at a clean and dry spot for comparison. A specimen almost as poor in large stone is No. 7, from a road having a pitched foundation, over which the broken stone had worn thin. The roads composed of igneous rocks, traps, and basalts, appear always to abound in large stone. The stones probably do not split up when once in the road, either from the action of the traffic or the weather; but are reduced more gradually by attrition. The constituent part which exhibits the most constant proportion is the mud and other small stuff washed out, which in all specimens but one is from 19 to $25\frac{3}{4}$ per cent. of the whole. Two specimens in which extreme proportions of mud

appear, viz. No. 1 and No. 5, are from roads both excellent, and
between which it is hard to say which was the better. No. 12,
in which only 14½ per cent. of mud, &c., was found, is from
a road made of copper slag, on a foundation of furnace cinders,
and covered with a binding of red ashes. This piece of road
was constructed under the author's directions, two years and
a quarter before the sample was taken; and as No. 11, which
is also of copper slag, but an old road, contains 20 per cent. of
mud or small stuff, it may be presumed that the new road will
ultimately reach a proportion not different from the rest.
It appears from the author's examinations that, whether the
road be a strong good road 7 or 8 inches thick, a thin worn
coating over a pitched foundation, a road reduced to 1½ inch to
2 inches of limestone on a clay subsoil, a road from its situation
requiring a great deal of scraping, or one requiring very little,
and whatever may be the material, or the traffic, the proportion
of mud, &c., which can be washed out, and which forms the
binding material, is about the same. For this to be the case,
it is no doubt necessary that the mud should be constantly
removed as soon as it is formed and appears on the surface,
otherwise the proportion would be far higher in many roads.
As an instance of this, the analysis by Mr. Joseph Mitchell of
the crust of the road in the Mall, St. James's Park,* may be
cited, which shows as much as 40¾ per cent. of mud, 9 per
cent. of sand and stones up to $\frac{3}{16}$ inch in size, 24½ per cent.
of stones between $\frac{3}{16}$ inch and ½ inch, and only 26 per cent. of
stones over ½ inch diameter.

An examination of the scrapings removed from the limestone roads from which samples 5, 6, and 7 were taken, proved
that about two-thirds consisted of mud, &c., which would wash
out through a cheese-cloth having twenty threads to an inch,
the remaining third being grit of about the size of small shot,
and up to ¼ inch in diameter, and it appeared that of the
whole body of the road about one-third consisted of mud and
grit of the same composition as the scrapings.

When in the condition of a stiff mud, such scrapings consist
of about 70 per cent. by bulk of dry detritus, and 30 per cent. of

* New Mode of Constructing the Surface of Streets, p. 15.

water, and these proportions are the same when the road material is silicious. Water to the extent of 30 per cent. adds nothing to the volume of the dry detritus, but a greater proportion increases the bulk and renders the mud more or less liquid.

The large proportion thus found to exist in the coatings of the best roads, of small stuff which only requires water to make it mud, shows the strong necessity for keeping roads dry, and this necessity must be the greater as the proportion of detritus is allowed to increase in the road beyond the amount absolutely necessary to fill the voids between stones closely wedged together. In the latter case an excess of moisture will destroy all coherence in the binding material, by which alone motion among the stones in the road-coating is prevented.

# CHAPTER V.

## Draught.

THE resistance of wheeled vehicles to traction is made up of two parts, the friction of the wheel on its axle and the rolling and rubbing resistance between the wheel tire and the surface of the road. The former has nothing to do with the road, and may be passed by with the remark that it is nearly the same at all velocities, and is, in wheels of ordinary construction and proportions, equal to $\frac{1}{130}$ to $\frac{1}{100}$ of the weight on the axle, or 17 to 22 lbs. to a ton of load. The resistance between the tire of a cylindrical wheel and the road depends on the roughness of the surface and its compressibility. If the roughness of the surface be considered as small obstacles in the path of the wheel, the force necessary to overcome them can be shown to be nearly in the inverse proportion to the square root of the diameter of the wheel.

Edgeworth,* and others after him, considered that the resistance from compressibility of the surface under the wheel was of the same character, and that the whole resistance between the tire and the road was in the inverse proportion to the square root of the diameter of the wheel. This view was strongly maintained by Dupuit, in opposition to Morin, whose experiments led him to the conclusion that the resistance to rolling varies inversely as the diameter. The difference between these two ratios is very great. If the draught increases inversely as the diameter, it would be reduced to one-half by doubling the diameter of the wheel, while, if it increases only in inverse proportion to the square root of the diameter, the same

---

* Roads and Carriages, 1817, p. 18.

result would only be attained by making the diameter of the wheel four times as great.

From experiments made at the Royal Agricultural Show at Bedford in 1874, with Easton and Anderson's horse dynamometer, it appeared that 1 lb. of draught was expended on moving every 35·1 lbs. of weight resting on the fore-wheels of a waggon, 3 feet 5 inches diameter, as compared with 58·7 lbs. on the hind-wheels, of 5 feet diameter.* This gives an increase of draught in rather a greater ratio than inversely as the diameter, and is consequently even more favourable to large wheels than Morin's proportion.

Other experimenters have arrived at results giving intermediate ratios, and it is natural to suppose that on different roads there may be influences by which the total resistance may be modified in either direction. At any rate, there is no doubt that large wheels are favourable to draught, and cause less wear of the road.

Both Dupuit and Morin considered that the width of the wheel tire had only an unimportant influence on the draught of vehicles. Dupuit concluded that on even surfaces, whether soft or hard, the resistance to draught was independent of the width of tire. Morin's experiments showed that on solid macadamised roads in a good state of repair, the resistance to rolling was almost independent of the width of tire, while on compressible surfaces, such as earth, sand, or gravel, it decreased as the tire was wider, in a proportion depending on the nature of the ground. On rough uneven surfaces, such as a stony road, Dupuit considered that draught was lessened by wider tires, and Morin that tires 3 or 4 inches wide had an advantage, but that beyond that width the resistance to draught was nearly independent of the width of the tire. Experiments by other observers show that on a gravel road in good order, there is no sensible difference in the traction, whether the tires are narrow, or nearly 4 inches wide, but that the latter have an advantage on an earth road, or on clay soil.

The resistance due to gravity on inclined roads must of course be allowed for in all considerations of draught. It is very

* Journal of Royal Agricultural Society, 1874, p. 683.

nearly equal to the gross load divided by the rate of gradient, thus, on a gradient of 1 in 20 the increase of draught due to gravity will be $\frac{1}{20}$ of the gross weight of the vehicle and its load.

All observers agree that the draught is less as the road is smoother, harder, more solid, and less compressible or flexible under the load. There is not sufficient elasticity in the coating of a road to give back to a wheel from behind the force expended in compressing or pushing down the surface before it. On a yielding road the wheel is thus always in a hollow which it never gets out of, and the horses are always drawing up hill. With respect to excessive draught arising from irregularity of the surface, Morin says* that experiments with the same waggon running over various parts of the same road, maintained with the same materials, in the driest season of the year, showed that, while upon portions in good condition the tractive force exerted was from $\frac{1}{35}$ to $\frac{1}{36}$ of the load, on parts badly maintained, having ruts and hollows, it rose to $\frac{1}{25}$ and $\frac{1}{21}$; that is to say, that three horses would be required on the badly maintained road to do the work of two on the well-maintained road.

The results of two series of experiments made by Morin on macadamised roads in good condition, maintained with silicious pebbles and limestone, gave a mean draught of $\frac{1}{34 \cdot 7}$ and $\frac{1}{35 \cdot 6}$ of the gross load. On some parts in a perfect state the draught was as little as $\frac{1}{48}$. The waggon employed had fore-wheels 2 feet 11 inches and hind-wheels 4 feet 7½ inches in diameter, with tires 4 inches wide, and was loaded with about 5⅓ tons. The trials were made in the end of summer, when the roads were in their best condition, and the draught is the actual tractive force employed, including of course the axle friction.

The proportion of draught to load with large wheels is stated by other observers to be from $\frac{1}{30}$ to $\frac{1}{40}$ on a dry and level macadamised road in first-rate condition, increasing to $\frac{1}{18}$ or $\frac{1}{20}$ when the road is covered with mud and loose stones, and to $\frac{1}{10}$ or even more on freshly laid unconsolidated stones.

The trials at the Royal Agricultural Show at Bedford in 1874 gave the average draught of single horse carts having wheels

* Mécanique Pratique, p. 349.

4 feet 6 inches to 5 feet 2 inches in diameter, and tires $3\frac{1}{4}$ inches and 4 inches wide, loaded to about 30 cwt., as about $\frac{1}{35}$ of the gross load on a level macadamised road at a walking pace. With other carts, having wheels 4 feet 9 inches to 5 feet 1 inch in diameter, and tires 4 inches and $4\frac{1}{2}$ inches wide, and a gross load of 41 to 45 cwt., the draught was on the average $\frac{1}{31}$ of the gross load under the same circumstances. With waggons having fore-wheels 3 feet 4 inches to 3 feet 5 inches in diameter, and hind-wheels 4 feet 9 inches to 5 feet $1\frac{1}{2}$ inch in diameter, tires $2\frac{1}{2}$ inches to $4\frac{1}{2}$ inches wide, and a total weight of $61\frac{3}{4}$ to 103 cwt., the average draught was $\frac{1}{45}$ of the gross load.

The draught is less with carts than with waggons, because in carts the whole load rests on large wheels, whereas in waggons, one-third or more of the load rests upon the fore-wheels of smaller diameter.

These trials may be assumed to have been made with vehicles in the best possible condition to give favourable results.

The tractive force required on every part of the road between London and Shrewsbury was measured by Sir J. Macneill with an instrument devised by him for the purpose. The results are recorded in elaborate tables,* which give the force exerted to draw a common four-wheeled waggon, empty, weighing about 21 cwt., during dry weather in March, at about $2\frac{1}{2}$ miles per hour. A correction is applied to the draught actually shown by the instrument, to give the tractive force on a horizontal road. The general results of the experiments, as given by Telford,† are as follows :—

Draught on a well-made pavement .. .. .. .. .. 33 lbs. $= \frac{1}{71}$

,, ,, broken stone surface on old flint road .. 65 ,, $= \frac{1}{36}$

,, ,, gravel road .. .. .. .. .. .. 147 ,, $= \frac{1}{16}$

,, ,, broken stone road upon a rough pavement foundation .. .. .. .. .. .. 46 ,, $= \frac{1}{51}$

,, ,, broken stone surface on a bottoming of concrete .. .. .. .. .. .. .. 46 ,, $= \frac{1}{51}$

These results have been often quoted, but it does not appear in what way they were deduced from the recorded observations. They can only be looked upon as averages from which many of

* Appendix to 7th Report of the Holyhead Road Commissioners, 1830.

† 7th Report, &c., p. 13.

the observations differ widely, and without apparent cause. According to these figures, the draught on a broken stone road over a paved foundation or over a bottoming of concrete was $\frac{1}{71}$, and on a broken stone surface on an old flint road $\frac{1}{36}$ of the load drawn, while on a gravel road it rose to $\frac{1}{16}$.

With respect to the traction on roads of different materials, Sir J. Macneill states* that he found from his experiments that granite gave the best road surface in wet and limestone in dry weather, while gravel was always very imperfect.

The effect of springs in reducing draught is that they enable the wheels to rise and fall over inequalities of the road, while the load on them moves forward without being sensibly raised. The more perfect the elasticity of the springs is in a vertical direction, the greater is the reduction of draught, but any elasticity in the direction of the traction tends to increase the draught. The good effect of springs is much greater at high than at low velocities. Morin considered that at a walking pace the resistance was the same for vehicles with or without springs on roads of all sorts. The trials at Bedford before alluded to gave 10 lbs. per ton less draught with a spring waggon, compared with one without springs, on a hard road, and the difference was also noticeable, though in a much less degree, on arable land.

The general conclusions arrived at by Morin from his experiments on draught are as follows.†

The resistance to rolling of vehicles on solid metalled roads and pavements is proportional to the weight and inversely proportional to the diameter of the wheels.

On solid roads the resistance is very nearly independent of the width of the tires when it exceeds 3 to 4 inches, but on compressible surfaces it decreases in proportion to the width of the tire.

The resistance increases with velocity on hard roads, but is independent of velocity on soft surfaces.

Springs diminish resistance at high speeds, but not at slow speeds.

* Evidence, Committee on Turnpike Roads, 7833, p. 128.
† Expériences sur le Tirage des Voitures, p. 187.

*Wheels, and Weights on them.*

The regulation of the form and construction of wheels has been the subject of legislation ever since the beginning of the century. In this country one of the early results was to bring into use an excessively broad conical wheel with a tire considerably rounded or barrelled, and often with a middle tire projecting so far beyond the others that it constituted the wheel on a hard road, and which was on the whole about the worst form of wheel that could have been devised. The rounding of the tire and the projecting bands were of course adopted to give the semblance of a broad wheel without the reality, but to some extent they were attended with advantage. A conical wheel can only be made to travel in a straight course by a constant twisting action at the surface of the road, and the wider the bearing surface of the tire, the greater the grinding and dislocating of the materials must be, and wheels 12 and 16 inches wide bearing fairly over their entire width would have been worse for the roads, as well as for the horses. A cylindrical wheel, having a tire bearing flatly on the ground, and of the same diameter on each side of the wheel, which would roll fairly on the road, was strongly advocated, and on some turnpike trusts was encouraged by lower tolls. The conical or dished wheel has, however, practical advantages which have kept it in general use, and cylindrical wheels are still the exception. The inclined spokes of the dished wheel give it strength to resist lateral shocks, and afford greater room for the body of the vehicle, and the objections to the conical form diminish with the breadth of the wheel. When the tire is flat, or only slightly rounded, and with the nails entirely countersunk, there is little to be said against the dished wheels of the moderate breadth at present in use.

The General Turnpike Act (1823) (3 Geo. IV. cap. 126), regulated the weights to be allowed to waggons, carts, &c., having wheels of the breadth of 9 inches, 6 inches, $4\frac{1}{2}$ inches, and under $4\frac{1}{2}$ inches, in winter and in summer, according to the following table :—

| Description of Vehicles. | Weight of Carriage, and Loading. | | Pressure per Inch of Width of Tire. | |
|---|---|---|---|---|
| | Summer. | Winter. | Summer. | Winter. |
| | Tons cwt. | Tons cwt. | Cwt. | Cwt. |
| Waggon with 9-inch wheels .. .. .. | 6 10 | 6 0 | 3·6 | 3·3 |
| Cart „ „ .. .. .. | 3 10 | 3 0 | 3·9 | 3·3 |
| Waggon with 6-inch wheels .. .. .. | 4 15 | 4 5 | 4·0 | 3·5 |
| Cart „ „ .. .. | 3 0 | 2 15 | 5·0 | 4·6 |
| Waggon with 4½-inch wheels .. .. | 4 5 | 3 15 | 4·7 | 4·1 |
| Cart „ „ .. .. .. | 2 12 | 2 7 | 5·8 | 5·2 |
| Waggon with wheels less than 4½ inches. | 3 15 | 3 5 | 2½-inch tires. {7·5 | 6·5 |
| Cart „ „ .. .. .. | 1 15 | 1 10 | {7·0 | 6·0 |

Additional toll was chargeable for overweight above these weights, and the use of broad tires was encouraged by rendering vehicles with wheels of less breadth than 4½ inches chargeable with one-half more toll than those with 6-inch wheels, and those with wheels of 4½ inches breadth and less than 6 inches with one-fourth more toll than those having 6-inch wheels. A vehicle having upright cylindrical wheels, with the nails countersunk, was charged two-thirds the toll otherwise payable. These regulations did not extend to coaches and carriages, and applied only where the Turnpike Acts were in force. They were repealed in South Wales in 1844, and the width of wheels was subject to no restrictions.

It will be observed from the above table of weights that all wheels of less width than 4½ inches were treated alike, so that a cart or waggon having wheels 2½ inches wide could carry as heavy a load as one with wheels 4¼ inches wide, and that the pressure per inch of width is far greater on these narrow tires than with wheels 4½ inches wide and upwards. Increased tolls on narrow wheels did not prevent their use, nor the carrying of heavy loads on them, and as tolls were abolished they became more general, and it seemed unlikely that fresh regulations would take the place of those expiring with the Turnpike Acts. The Highways and Locomotives Act of 1878, however, gave power to the County Authorities to make bye-laws regulating

F

the width of wheels in proportion to the weight carried, and the power has been generally exercised. Usually the weights allowed by the General Turnpike Act have been followed with some modification, and sometimes with additions to provide for heavier loads, or to restrict the weights to be carried on wheels of a less width than 4½ inches. It is doubtful, as will be shown further on, whether there is any advantage in limiting the loads to be carried on wheels of 4½ inches and upwards, and while it is certain that narrow wheels with heavy loads cause the greatest damage to roads, it is difficult to enforce bye-laws against them and to put new restrictions on existing vehicles.

The following average weights of coaches and waggons, with the load on each wheel, and the pressure per inch of width of tire, were given by Sir J. Macneill in 1831 : —*

| Description of Vehicles. | Weight on the Average. | Breadth of Wheel. | Pressure of each Wheel. | Pressure on each Inch of Breadth. |
|---|---|---|---|---|
| | Tons. | Inches. | Cwt. | Cwt. |
| Mail-coach .. .. .. .. .. | 2 | 2¼ | 10 | 4·40 |
| Stage-coach.. .. .. .. .. | 2½ | 2 | 12·5 | 6·25 |
| Van .. .. .. .. .. .. | 4½ | 2½ | 21·25 | 8·29 |
| Waggon .. .. .. .. .. | 6 | 9 | 30·0 | 3·33 |
| „ .. .. .. .. .. .. | 4½ | 6 | 22·5 | 3·75 |
| „ .. .. .. .. .. .. | 3½ | 4 | 17·5 | 4·37 |

To which may be added the particulars given on the following page, of some of the heaviest loads that now usually come upon roads.

It will be observed that the pressure per inch of tire is much greater in the case of heavy vans and waggons with narrow wheels than in the case of traction engines and trucks with wide tires, and it must be remembered that the effect of wear is to round the edges of tires, so that the pressure on the narrow tires is generally greater than the tables show.

The pressure per inch of width of tire cannot, however, always be taken as a fair measure of the load on a road ; a good deal

* Evidence, Committee on Steam Carriages, p. 95.

will depend upon the sort of road. A strong hard road, on a good foundation, may bear a considerable load on narrow tires without perceptible damage being produced, while a more yielding road will break down under a traction engine, although the pressure per inch of tire is far less.

| Description of Vehicles. | Breadth of Tire. | Load on Wheel. | Load per Inch of Width of Tire. |
|---|---|---|---|
| | Inches. | Cwt. | Cwt. |
| Cart : weight 10 cwt., load 32 cwt. .. .. | 4 | 21·0 | 5·25 |
| Cart : weight 10 cwt., load 35 cwt. .. .. | 2½ | 22·5 | 9·0 |
| Pickford's waggon : weight 1 ton 1 cwt., load 2 tons .. .. .. .. .. .. | 2 | 15·25 | 7·62 |
| Pickford's waggon : weight 1 ton 7¼ cwt.. load 3 tons .. .. .. .. .. .. | 2½ | 21·87 | 8·75 |
| Railway van : weight 1½ ton, load 3½ tons.. | 3 | 25·0 | 8·33 |
| Waggon : weight 1½ tons, load 5 tons .. | 3¾ | 32·5 | 8·66 |
| Waggon : Weight empty .. .. .. .. 21 cwt.⎫<br>„ when loaded, on forewheels, 46 „ ⎬<br>„ „ „ hind „ 56 „ ⎭<br><br>Total .. 102 „ | 4 | 28·0 | 7·0 |
| 11-ton traction engine, weighing 12 tons with coal, water, &c., two-thirds weight on driving wheels .. .. .. .. .. | 18 | 80·0 | 4·44 |
| 8-ton traction engine, weighing 9 tons with coal, water, &c., two-thirds weight on driving wheels .. .. .. .. .. | 16 | 60·0 | 3·75 |
| Waggon for steam traction : weight 1 ton 10 cwt., load 6 tons .. .. .. .. | 8 | 37·5 | 4·69 |
| Waggon for steam traction : weight 1 ton 8 cwt., load 4 tons .. .. .. .. .. | 6 | 27·0 | 4·5 |
| Waggon for steam traction : weight 1 ton 5 cwt., load 3 tons .. .. .. .. .. | 4 | 21·25 | 5·31 |
| 15-ton steam road roller .. .. .. .. | 20-24 | 75·0 | 3·12-3·75 |

The crushing action of heavy loads on narrow tires is of course severe at the surface of the road, and such as only the strongest materials can withstand. Sir James McAdam, speaking from experience of the Metropolis roads, considered that 2 tons was the maximum load that should be allowed on any one wheel 4½ inches broad, which gives a pressure of nearly

9 cwt. per inch of width. For the generality of roads this is undoubtedly too much. Telford was of opinion that the weight should not exceed a ton upon each wheel,* and Sir J. Macneill, taking the road from London to Shrewsbury as a criterion to judge by, considered that a wheel ought to be an inch in width for every ton that a carriage and its load would weigh, thus giving 1 inch of tire for every 5 cwt. of load on the · wheel.†

The diameter of the wheel, as influencing the pressure on the road, may be left out of account for wheels of common size, on ordinary road surfaces. It is, however, necessary to consider the causes of wear of materials in roads before proceeding further with this subject.

---

* Evidence, Committee on Highways, 1819.
† Evidence, Committee on Steam Carriages, 1831, p. 95.

# CHAPTER VI.

## WEAR.

THE wear of material in roads is due to two causes, the traffic and the weather, which react on each other, so that it is not easy to distinguish their effects. Sir J. Macneill, who as resident engineer under Telford, on the London and Holyhead and Liverpool roads, had considerable experience of road maintenance, estimated* that, of the total wear, 80 per cent. on the average was due to the traffic, and 20 per cent. to atmospheric causes, and of the 80 per cent. due to the traffic, 60 per cent. was due to the wear of the feet of the horses drawing and 20 per cent. to the wheels in the case of fast coaches, and 44½ per cent. to the horses' feet, and 35½ per cent. to the wheels in the case of waggons. Telford and Sir J. McAdam † both agreed with Sir J. Macneill that the injury done to a road by the feet of the horses drawing was greater than that from the wheels, since the former tore up the surface, and displaced the materials, while the crushing and grinding action of the latter was comparatively small on a hard smooth road. With fast coach traffic on a strong road no doubt this was true, but it is otherwise when heavy loads travel on a comparatively weak road.

The wear from horses' feet will of course be increased by anything which increases the draught, such as unevenness of surface, or a yielding road.

Sir J. Macneill considered that the wear due to atmospheric causes might be less than 10 per cent. of the total wear on a properly made road, in an open situation, and might be more than 30 per cent. on a weak road, on a clay subsoil, and shaded by trees. The grounds on which the estimates of the wear from

* Evidence, Select Committee on Steam Carriages, 1831. † Ibid.

atmospheric causes were based are not stated. The relative
wear to the road from horses' feet, and from wheels, was deduced
from the wear of iron in the horses' shoes and in the wheel tires.
The total wear as well as the relative proportions caused by
the traffic and by the weather are influenced by the nature of
the materials, the subsoil, drainage, situation, strength of the
road, the care with which it is maintained, the traffic, and other
circumstances which may vary almost from yard to yard. Any
general estimate, therefore, by however good an authority, must
not be considered as even approximately true for any particular
case, and there are sometimes wider differences in the proportion
of wear due to traffic and weather than the above.

The passage of vehicles over a road produces several effects,
which it is important to distinguish. There is, first, the grinding and crushing action of the wheels and horses' feet on the
surface, and there is, secondly, the effect of the load in giving
rise to bending and cross-breaking strains throughout the
whole thickness of the road-coating. When the materials are
loose and unconsolidated, either because they are freshly laid,
or from having been disintegrated, there is a third action,
namely, a displacement of them by the wheels and horses' feet,
accompanied by a rubbing together of the stones among themselves. This is the cause of great wear and waste of materials
laid in thick coats.

On a thick strong consolidated road, or on one of less thickness on a hard foundation, the bending and cross-breaking
tendency of the load produces no sensible effect; there is no
movement in the body of the road, and the wear is confined to
the grinding and crushing of the materials at the surface. This
is the most favourable condition under which road materials
can be subjected to wear, and it rarely occurs without the
addition to some extent of the third-named effect, namely, a
movement and rubbing among the materials, extending to the
small depth to which the wheels affect the surface. In proportion, however, as it is confined to the surface and approximates
in character to that on a paved roadway will the wear be small
and gradual.

A good limestone road, strong enough for the traffic it has

to carry, sometimes affords an instance of wear confined to the surface, even on a yielding subsoil. The cementing nature of the limestone detritus gives the crust enough transverse strength to resist bending and cross-breaking under the loads to which it is exposed, and it may be compared to thick ice bearing heavy weights on water. It is possible that the case of the limestone road over the morass referred to by McAdam,* on which the wear was small, may be thus explained, and that, although the subsoil was a bog, the coating was so strong that there was no cross-breaking or bending, nor any wear except at the surface of the road. Cases have come under the author's observation where the cohesive strength of a limestone coating has enabled it to carry the ordinary traffic on a wet undrained subsoil without excessive wear, until bending and cross-breaking was set up by heavier loads or some unfavourable circumstance. When this happened, the break-up was serious, and was due to the badness of the subsoil as much as to the thinness of the coating. The latter would have been thick enough on a dry subsoil, and a thicker coating would have saved the road from damage on a soft subsoil.

On a weak road, such as one of insufficient thickness or cohesion on a yielding foundation, bending and cross-breaking produce the effects which were accurately described by Sir J. Macneill : " If the road be weak or elastic and bend or yield under the pressure of the wheels, the particles of which it is composed will move and rub against each other, or perhaps break by the action of the heavy wheels over them."† It is by a process of this sort that a very large proportion of the wear of roads is occasioned. In consequence of want of drainage, or of insufficient strength on a bad bottom, continual bending and cross-breaking goes on under passing loads. The wear of materials thus caused takes place throughout the whole thickness of the road-coating, and is of course all in addition to the surface wear. It is aggravated by the softening action of the water which finds its way through the cracks which must attend bending in the road-coating, and the displacement of materials at the surface by the wheels and horses' feet is much greater than on a strong

* *Ante*, p. 8.    † Evidence, Select Committee on Steam Carriages, 1831, p. 97.

road. Stones are forced down into the subsoil, and the latter rises up and becomes mixed with the metalling, so that it is sometimes difficult to make out where the road-coating ends and the subsoil begins.

Such a road can only be kept in tolerable order by an excessive outlay for maintenance, which would be avoided, and money in the end be saved, if the wear were lessened by proper drainage of the subsoil, and by giving the road-coating sufficient thickness to carry the traffic. Macneill says that "where an accurate experiment was made, the wear was found to be 4 inches of hard stone where it was placed on a wet clay bottom, while it was not more than half an inch on a solid dry foundation, or with a pavement bottom on a part of the same road where it was subject to the same traffic,"* and instances might be given where the quantity of materials required to keep a piece of road in order has been reduced to one-third or even less by drainage alone.

On roads of all sorts a reserve of strength, in the shape of a greater thickness of materials than is absolutely necessary, is always very desirable. The wear is less under the same traffic on a stronger road, which is better able to stand heavier traffic should it come upon it, or to bear a reduction in the quantity of materials to be laid should it be necessary to make it.

### Surface Wear.

When a wheel meets with an obstacle in passing along a road, the force necessary to overcome the resistance to the forward motion of the wheel may be resolved into a pressure acting vertically tending to compress the obstacle into the road, and a force parallel to the surface tending to push forward the obstacle in the path of the wheel. The latter force is the greater in proportion as the diameter of the wheel is smaller; it tends to disintegrate the road-coating, and is far more destructive than the vertical pressure, or than the greater impression which smaller wheels make. Morin points out † that a simple experi-

---

* Evidence, Committee on Steam Carriages, 1831, p. 97.
† Mécanique Pratique, p. 355.

ment will confirm this. If one takes stones about 3 inches in diameter, and puts them on a somewhat wet and soft road before the wheels of a vehicle, they will be pushed forward by the small fore-wheels, and plough up the surface of the road, while the large wheels will press them down, and generally pass over without displacing them. The greater disintegrating effect of small wheels holds good equally when the obstacle is a compressible surface.

Morin's investigations on draught having established a connection between the tractive force exercised and the destructive effects produced, a series of experiments having more especial reference to the wear caused by vehicles to macadamised roads was undertaken by him.* Vehicles in other respects the same, but with diameters of wheels, breadth of tires, or load, different in different experiments, were made to pass and repass over the same tracks, which were sometimes kept watered to accelerate the wear. The state of the tracks or ruts produced by the wheels was carefully examined and compared from time to time. The roads experimented on were nearly level, about 13 inches thick, of a silicious gravel, in good condition, without hollows or ruts or newly laid materials. The loaded vehicles represented traffic of a heavy nature, but the roads were so strong that the wear may be assumed to have been limited to the surface.

The effect of the diameter of the wheels on their destructive effects on roads was shown by experiments with three vehicles loaded with equal weights of 4 tons 17 cwt. each, having wheels 4·6 inches wide in the tire, but with diameters 2 feet 10½ inches, 4 feet 9 inches, and 6 feet 8 inches respectively. After 980 tons had been transported, the tracks of the smallest wheels had deep ruts of unequal depth, the next size well-marked ruts almost as deep, while there was only a slight trace of the passage of the large wheels of 6 feet 8 inches diameter. The road was 1 foot 2 inches thick, and was watered freely.

The effects of the width of the wheel tires on the road were shown in the same series of experiments. Three similar vehicles with four wheels of the same diameter, having cylindrical tires of 2·4 inches, 4·6 inches, and 7 inches respectively,

* Expériences sur le Tirage des Voitures.

were equally loaded to 5 tons 8¾ cwt. After the vehicles had made a number of passages equivalent to the transportation of about 5300 tons, it was found that the track of the vehicles with 2·4-inch tires presented deep ruts, and was too bad for further experiment. The passages of the vehicles with 4·6-inch and 7-inch tires were continued until the weight transported equalled about 8200 tons, when it was found that there was no difference between the conditions of the two tracks, but both were less worn than that of the 2·4-inch tires, after transporting 5300 tons. Thus it appeared that on a strong gravel road a load of nearly 5½ tons on four wheels did much more damage with 2·4-inch tires than with 4·6-inch tires, but that there was little or no advantage to the road in having tires beyond the latter width. Some of the stones of which the road was made up took nearly all the bearing, and the weight was not distributed equally over a wide tire. This result entirely confirmed the opinion given by Sir J. McAdam* some years before, that no increase of breadth of tire above 4½ inches is useful, as a greater width cannot at one time touch the surface of a well-formed road.

The transport of 8200 tons on 4·6-inch tires did less damage than 5300 tons on 2·4-inch tires, the loads in each case being 5 tons 8¾ cwt., so that, speaking roughly, the narrower tires caused double the wear to the road. This is quite in accordance with the experience of the excessive wear caused by heavy loads on narrow tires.

A load of 5 tons 8¾ cwt. on four wheels having 2·4-inch tires gives a pressure of 11½ cwt. on each inch width of tire, which exceeds by 2½ cwt. per inch that on the wheel of a Pickford waggon with 2½-inch tires loaded with 3 tons. With loads not so excessive, although narrow wheels may appear to do no more harm to a hard road than wider ones with the same weight, a close examination of the surface will show that more crushing has taken place. On the 4·6-inch tires the pressure was at the rate of rather less than 6 cwt. per inch of width, still a heavy load, and exceeding by nearly one-fifth the 5 cwt. per inch which Sir J. Macneill considered should be the maximum load for the generality of roads; nevertheless, the greater width of

* Evidence before Select Committee on Steam Carriages, 1831.

tire, 7 inches, reducing the pressure to less than 4 cwt. per inch of width, did not appear to be of any advantage to the road.

On a weaker road, the greatest useful width of tire would have been found to have been more than 4·6 inches. Instead of the weight being borne, as on a hard road, on a few points, it would have been more equally distributed over the whole tire. Nevertheless, as will be shown farther on, the advantages of a wide tire to carry a heavy load on a soft and yielding road are not so great as might be supposed.

The wear resulting from the transport of a given weight was found to be diminished by dividing it on two or more pairs of wheels. About 6900 tons transported in loads of about 36 cwt. on four wheels having 2·4-inch tires, equal to 3¾ cwt. per inch of width, produced less wear than when transported in loads of 8 tons on four wheels having 6·6-inch tires, equal to 2 tons on a wheel, and nearly 6 cwt. per inch of width. The same weight transported in loads of about 5 tons on two wheels having 6·6-inch tires, equal to 2½ tons on a wheel, and upwards of 7½ cwt. per inch, caused greater wear to the road than in either of the preceding cases.

When three similar vehicles were loaded with weights proportioned to the breadth of tire, equal to nearly 5 cwt. per inch of width, and amounting to about 2·4, 4·5, and 6·9 tons respectively, it was found that the heavier loads on the wider tires were more damaging to the road than the lighter load on 2·4-inch tires, which made 3107 passages—equal to about 7370 tons transported—without producing any trace on the road, while the load of 6·9 tons on the 7-inch tires caused far more damage than the 4·5-tons on the 4·6-inch tires. A slight trace without apparent disintegration was produced by the transport of 7878 tons in 4·5-ton loads on the 4·6-inch tires, while the transport of 6924 tons in 6·9-ton loads on 7-inch tires produced well-marked ruts, the bottoms of which were completely disintegrated for a thickness of several centimetres. The draught of the vehicle with 7-inch tires and 6·9 tons load was found to increase with the number of passages much more rapidly than that of the other two. The draught increased also, but in less proportion, with the 4·6-inch tires, while with the vehicle with tires 2·4 inches wide it remained the same. The road was 14 inches and upwards thick, and if it had been thinner and weaker the comparison would no doubt have been still more unfavourable to the heavier loads on wider wheels.

Springs were found to diminish the wear of roads, more especially at speeds beyond a walking pace. Vehicles on springs going at a trot were found not to cause more wear than vehicles without springs at a walk, all other circumstances being the same. The concussions arising from irregularities of surface affect the road as well as the vehicle, and though springs to a considerable extent neutralise concussions, from the way in which they are fixed, they do so much more effectually in a vertical direction than in that parallel to the surface of the road, and it is in the latter direction that concussions are more destructive to the road-coating. Smoothness of surface, even with springed vehicles, conduces greatly, therefore, to diminish the wear from passing wheels, as well as that from horses' feet in consequence of the lessened draught.

*Wear from Bending and Cross-breaking.*

When bending or cross-breaking takes place, there must be a yielding of the subsoil, as well as of the road-coating, under the passing load. The subsoil has always eventually to support the load, and its ability to do so depends on its nature and condition, which can be much influenced by drainage, and on the area over which the load is distributed. The latter depends chiefly on the thickness, but also to some extent on the cohesive strength of the road covering by which the weight is transmitted from the surface to the subsoil.

The weight on a loaded wheel, supported on the small part of the road surface in contact with the tire, is distributed over an area which increases with the depth below the surface, and in such a manner that the pressure on the subsoil is greatest beneath the wheel, and diminishes towards the outside of the area affected by the load. If the subsoil yields, the road-coating yields with it to a certain extent without visible cracking, but it ultimately breaks under the shearing and cross-breaking strains to which it is exposed. The road is forced upwards round the depression caused by the loaded wheel, and as the latter moves forward, an undulation of the surface in advance of the wheel may be observed, accompanied by cross-breaking of the road-coating. Along the sides of the hollow track left by the passage of the wheel the elevations of the surface remain as low ridges in which cracks are visible which can be traced towards the subsoil by cutting into the road.

These effects may be watched during the passage of a heavy load over a weak road, but to illustrate further the manner in which a road on a weak bottom gives way under excessive loads, the effects have been reproduced on a small scale by the author with model wheels on a model road-coating composed of partially set plaster on a subsoil of soft tempered clay. The models were one-eighth of real size, but in giving the results it will be convenient to speak of the full size intended to be represented. Thus the wheels represented were, one 34 inches in diameter with a rounded tire $1\frac{3}{4}$ inch wide, and others from 33 to 60 inches in diameter with cylindrical tires $3\frac{1}{2}$, $5\frac{1}{2}$, and 6 inches wide. The road-coatings represented varied from 2 inches to $4\frac{1}{2}$ inches in thickness, and were of different degrees of cohesive strength and hardness.

When a wheel at rest was loaded until the road-coating began to crack, there was a bulging out of the underside in a roughly shaped oval, and a depression of the subsoil, which beneath the wheel was nearly equal to the depth to which the wheel sank in the surface, and which was surrounded by an elevation of both subsoil and road surface. On making sections, it appeared that, besides smaller cracks, there were two pairs of principal cracks, originating at the edges of the tire, one pair approximately vertical, and another pair spreading outwards at an angle of 35° to 55° towards the sides of the bulged part of the road-coating. With an increased load the latter cracks extended at about the same angle to the margin of the bulge round the ends of the oval, and an irregularly shaped truncated cone was separated from the rest of the road-coating. The area of the base of the conical piece thus, as it were, punched out may be taken to be that on which the load was ultimately supported by the subsoil, and its shape and size was apparently influenced in several ways.

The width of the oval depended on the breadth of the tire, the angle at which the cracks spread outwards, and the thickness of the coating they had to traverse before reaching the subsoil.

The length of the oval depended on the length of wheel tire in contact with the road, and on the angle of the cracks and the thickness of the coating.

Thus the width, other things being the same, was determined by that of the tire, but the length was influenced by the size of the wheel, and also by the breadth of tire. A larger wheel, having a greater part of its circumference bearing on the road, and a narrower tire, by making a deeper and longer impression in the surface, both tended to make the oval longer. Thus a wheel 6 inches wide in the tire and 42 inches diameter ultimately rested on an oval area of subsoil 12 inches wide and 16 inches long, containing 153 square inches; and a wheel of the same width of tire and 58 inches diameter, on an area 12 inches wide and 18 inches long, containing 166 square inches; the thickness of the road-coating being in each case about 3½ inches. A pair of wheels 42 inches in diameter with the tire of one wheel 3½ inches wide, and of the other 6 inches, when equally loaded, were ultimately carried by a larger area of subsoil under the narrow wheel than under the broader, in consequence of the deeper impression and longer oval made by the narrower wheel. The narrower rounded tire, when the surface was hard enough to prevent its cutting in, was often borne by a considerable area of subsoil, the cracks originating on the surface of the road around and quite clear of the impression made by the wheel.

The influence of the thickness of the road-coating, in increasing the area of subsoil over which the load is distributed, becomes apparent if we consider that, if the cracks spread outwards at an angle of 45°, which is an average inclination, an additional inch of thickness would give an additional inch all round the margin of the bulge and increase the areas above given for a thickness of 3½ inches by nearly one-third for a road-coating 4½ inches thick.

When a heavily loaded wheel was made to roll forwards, the bulging of the underside of the road-coating moved forward also, and the cracks extending round the margin and meeting in advance of the wheel formed a succession of conical fractures, which were followed up by the more vertical cracks beneath the edges of the wheel tire; and as the weight came on them, the conical pieces formed by the inclined curved crack in advance were successively broken off by transverse fractures.

After the passage of a wheel, the surrounding portion of the road-coating could be removed, leaving a roughly shaped prism slightly embedded in the subsoil, its top being generally the wheel track, its base the subsoil, and its sides sloping outwards at an angle of 35° to 55°. It was divided by numerous longitudinal and transverse fractures, in some of which there was considerable dislocation and grinding together of the fragments, and in those cracks which opened downwards the subsoil rose and became mixed with the road material.

The surface of the road alongside such a wheel track, even if apparently uninjured, would of course be undermined and weakened by the loss of support from the prism-shaped piece forced downwards under the wheel, and loads which the road could have borne before would be quite sufficient to cause further damage. This is often proved by experience; the single passage of a heavy load does apparently little harm, but repeated passages soon tell on a road.

The way in which thickness of road-coating increases the area of subsoil over which the load on a wheel is distributed has been pointed out. It has of course also an important influence on the intensity of the pressure of the load on the subsoil which is independent of the width of the tire; and other considerations tend to show that the weight per inch of width of tire affords no true measure of the pressure on the subsoil. Assume the weight on a tire 4 inches wide to be 5 cwt. per inch of width, and to be distributed over an oval 16 inches long and 10 inches wide, containing 138 square inches. By adding 2 inches of width to the tire, loaded as before with 5 cwt. per inch, the breadth only of the oval bearing on the subsoil will be effected, and it will be increased by 2 inches, and the area by 2 × 16 = 32 square inches, or less than one-fourth, while the load on it would be 30 cwt. instead of 20 cwt., or one-half greater. There is reason to suppose further that, when tires are loaded in proportion to their width, the pressure on the subsoil is greater immediately under the wheel with wider tires, though to what extent it is difficult to say.* Another most important point is that wide tires cannot bear uniformly on a road, and a large proportion of the whole weight on a wheel is borne on a small part of the surface and a proportionately small area of subsoil.

When weak and yielding roads are concerned, it is the load on the subsoil, and not on the tire of the wheel at the surface of the road, that should be considered, and that depends far more on the total weight on the wheel than on the weight per inch of width of tire.

It is plain both from experiment and observation that on roads of all descriptions it is the passage of heavy loads that causes the greatest injury, and that even on strong thick roads an increase of breadth of tire in proportion to the heavier load does not prevent a considerable increase of wear, while on weak, yielding roads an increased width compensates still less for an increased load on the wheel.

The observed effects of heavy traction engines, and the trucks drawn by them, illustrate this. A reference to the tables of weights before given (p. 67) will show that the loads per inch

---

* If a road-coating be supposed to be made up of smooth spheres of the same size, each sphere pressing equally on four spheres underneath it, it can be shown that the area over which a weight on the surface is distributed increases with the depth below the surface, the portion affected spreading out on all sides at an angle of 54° 44' with the horizon. The area over which the full surface pressure is borne decreases with the depth, at the same angle of 54° 44', so that at a depth from the surface of rather more than two-thirds of the width of the loaded area no part of the road-coating would sustain the full surface pressure; and at a depth equal to a little more than $1\frac{1}{3}$ of the width of the loaded area of surface the pressure at the centre would not exceed three-quarters of that on the surface, and would diminish towards the edges of the area affected.

Unequal-sized spheres under the conditions here supposed would somewhat modify the result, and the cohesive strength in a road-coating, and sinking of the subsoil, would also have some effect, but it appears probable from experiments that it is very much after this manner that the load is distributed through a road-coating to the subsoil. If so, when tires are loaded in proportion to their width, the depth to which the full surface pressure extends is about two-thirds of the width of the tire.

of width of tire in the case of traction engines and trucks are less than in the case of many waggons, carts, vans, and coaches, though the weight on the wheels of the former may be three or four times as great. Experience, however, shows that roads which are able to bear heavy coaches and waggons with 6 or 8 cwt. of load per inch of tire, with no injury beyond some crushing of material at the surface, are squeezed out of shape and broken down by the heavy engines with far less weight per inch of width of tire.

When heavy loads are carried on narrow tires, the damage is far greater on all roads, but more particularly on those that are weak from want of thickness or a yielding subsoil. This cause of excessive wear has long been recognised. When the wear is chiefly confined to the surface the crushing action of heavy loads on narrow tires is such that only the strongest materials can resist, and when, besides, there is cross-breaking of the road-coating, the wear is largely increased.

Unfortunately, excessive weights, whether on broad or narrow wheels, come upon roads without any reference to their strength to bear them. It often happens that a road on a weak foundation, kept in a good state of repair, will stand the weather and carry a certain traffic for years with a material not very strong, and of a thickness, though small, sufficient for the traffic, showing no signs of weakness, and presenting a hard, smooth surface to which the wear is almost entirely confined. But should exceptionally heavy traffic, such as hauling of timber or building materials, or a traction engine, come upon it, and tax it beyond its strength, it will at once suffer, perhaps only to an extent which is not noticed except by the surveyor, but which demands a large increase in the outlay for maintenance; or it may be cut up and destroyed to such an extent that repairs become more of the nature of reconstruction than of ordinary maintenance. As much material may be required in a short length as would have been enough for the maintenance of a mile or more of the road with its former traffic, or of a road originally stronger under the heavier traffic.

It may be, and no doubt it often is, the case that better drainage of the subsoil would have enabled the road to resist the action of the heavier loads, and the importance of drainage cannot be too much insisted upon. But the least thickness of road required on a naturally bad bottom is only learned by experience, and a surveyor will naturally suit the strength of his road to its situation and traffic, strengthening those parts that show signs of weakness, by successive additions of materials, until they are well able to bear the traffic, and the road has a certain reserve of strength ; but he will not incur useless expenditure by putting on more materials than the traffic requires, or can work in without inconveniencing the public, to provide strength for heavy loads that may never come on his road.

## *Action of the Weather.*

The weather acts to some degree directly on the materials, but to a much greater extent indirectly, by increasing the wear from the traffic. Frost expands the moisture in the crust of the road, and perhaps in the road material itself, and when the thaw comes, a general disintegration takes place, converting the surface into a stratum of loose materials into which the traffic cuts, and the surface water soaks.

Wet weather, by softening the muddy binding matter, which, as it has been already shown, forms so large a proportion of the best road-coatings, destroys the solidity and coherence of the road, rendering it less capable of supporting the traffic, and increasing the wear from crushing and rubbing together of the materials. Rain following frost and thaw is very damaging, and alternations of these, frost returning when the disintegrated surface has been saturated by rain, will break up the thickest road-coating if the surface is once destroyed, and the drainage be defective.

Violent rain on exposed situations, especially where the materials are silicious, washes out the binding portion, and often the smaller stone as well, leaving the road loose and porous. On hills the scouring of the surface, from water breaking out of the side channels in heavy rains, causes great damage. The amount of materials washed away from the surface, and even from the body of a neglected road, is often much greater than that fairly worn out by traffic.

Excessive dryness has the effect of loosening the surface of roads made of silicious materials, the detritus of which has little or no binding property when dry.

The extent to which these various effects may be injurious will depend on the nature of the road materials, on the drainage, subsoil, situation, and on many other accidental circumstances. Frost and thaw have but little effect on a dry, well-kept road, especially when the materials are igneous or silicious. A limestone road will always suffer more, and severely if, owing to its situation or bad drainage, it holds the wet. When the frost is severe enough to reach the subsoil, if it be boggy or wet, the road-coating will be blown up from the bottom, whatever be the nature of the stone composing it. On a chalky subsoil great injury is often done on the breaking up of frost, whatever may be the material of the road or the care taken of its drainage and general condition.

On a road subjected to cross-breaking and cracking arising from traffic beyond its strength, all atmospheric causes of wear are greatly aggravated. Rain and frost easily penetrate it, and through it to the subsoil.

Heavy traffic coming on a road disintegrated by frost or softened by wet increases enormously the mischief originally caused by the weather.

Hedges and fences which obstruct the sun and wind, hinder the road from drying, so that a road sheltered by trees or high hedges is always softer, and more liable to be injuriously acted upon by the weather and the traffic, than one well exposed to the sun and air. Trees have been supposed to add 25 per cent. to the cost of maintaining a road, and high hedges, especially on the southern side of the road, are very injurious, particularly on a heavy clay soil, or where drainage is imperfect.

*Circumstances which influence Wear.*

The amount of wear from every cause depends, of course, largely on the nature of the road material. Materials of a fairly good quality, such as flints or hard field stone, wear two or three times as fast as Guernsey granite, whinstone, and other traps and basalts ; and when the material is weak and the traffic heavy, the wear may be four or even five times as great as it would be with the best material.

Generally speaking, the wear from every cause is less in proportion as the road is kept in good condition as to surface, solidity, thickness, and drainage. It is less on slight gradients than on a dead level, because of the better drainage, but on hills it is increased by the use of skidpans or drags, and from the effects of running water. The surface on a hill is washed clean, and looks better than the flat below on to which the mud is carried down, and this often leads to the neglect of a hill until it is worn down to the rough bottom stones. There is more wear in winter than in summer, in wet situations than in dry, and where sheltered by hedges and trees than where open to the sun and air. When traffic follows in the same track, which it has a strong tendency to do, particularly where the surface is soft and the tracks are visible, there is a great increase of wear.

# CHAPTER VII.

### *Measurement of Traffic and Wear.*

IN experiments like those of Morin, vehicles with loads well ascertained were employed, and the amount and nature of the traffic which caused the wear were accurately known. Unfortunately, any measure of the ordinary traffic on roads can only be obtained with difficulty and imperfectly.

In France, the number of "collars," or animals drawing loads, was formerly counted, four animals drawing empty vehicles being counted for one collar. The imperfection of this way of reckoning traffic is evident. All draught animals rank alike, whatever loads they are drawing, so that two horses with three tons on one pair of wheels count for no more than a pair of ponies in a light carriage, though the wear they occasion is many times as much. Horses not drawing, cattle, sheep, &c., are not taken into account at all—in some districts an important omission. Afterwards an account was taken of the weights carried as well. In 1876, the mean daily number of collars counted in this way on all the national roads was 156, and the average daily weight 182 tonnes,* ranging from 1159 collars or 1589 tonnes in the department of the Seine, to 100 collars and tonnes or even less in some departments. In 1882 a new plan was adopted; vehicles were counted in three categories :—(1) those loaded with produce and merchandise ; (2) those used for the transport of travellers, and (3) private carriages and empty vehicles. Animals not drawing were counted, and the value to be given to them and to empties in "collars" was left to the engineers. The gross and net weights of the vehicles were also ascertained, and the traffic on all the national roads is now given in "collars"

---

* Tonne = 2205 lb.

and in "tonnes" per day. The traffic is indicated on a map by a band along the roads proportionate in breadth to the traffic.

In taking account of traffic in South Wales, under the author's direction, the light collars drawing carriages, &c., paying a higher toll, were kept distinct from the heavy collars drawing carts and waggons; and horses not drawing, cattle, sheep, &c., were valued at fractions of collars in rough proportion to the tolls payable on them. The object of this was to arrive at a value, in collars of traffic, of the tolls paid at the various gates, as well as to separate the light and heavy traffic for the purpose of estimating the wear.

Where, as in a street, the traffic is so considerable that it is spread nearly uniformly over the whole width, the width of the road must be taken into account, though in the most crowded streets the traffic is greater in the middle than at the sides. Mr. Deacon, in measuring traffic in the Liverpool streets, ascertained :—

(a) The tonnage passing over the carriage-way in twelve months.

(b) The width of the carriage way.

(c) The number of wheels on which the traffic in borne.

Thus $\frac{a}{b}$ = the weight of traffic per unit of width,

and $\frac{a}{c}$ = the number of tons per wheel.[*]

A method adopted in London by Mr. Howarth, consists in obtaining the average weights per unit of width, by observations taken for half hours at fixed periods throughout the day of 16 hours, from 7 a.m. to 11 p.m., and repeated at the same points on different days, and in different conditions of the weather. The traffic on some of the principal macadamised thoroughfares of the Metropolis in November, 1878, as thus ascertained, may be given, though wood pavement has since superseded the macadamised surface.

The average weight per wheel was 0·26 tons in Piccadilly and 0·30 tons in Parliament Street.[†]

---

[*] Proc. Inst. C.E., vol. lviii. p. 21.

[†] Ibid., p. 33.

| | Average Number of Vehicles per day of 16 hours. | Gross Weight. | Average per Vehicle. | Average Width of Roadway. | Weight per foot of Width. |
|---|---|---|---|---|---|
| | | tons. | tons. | feet. | tons. |
| Regent Street .. | 10·796 | 9,668 | 0·900 | 52 | 186·0 |
| Piccadilly .. .. | 10·776 | 9,358 | 0·868 | 37 | 252·9 |
| Parliament Street | 14·306 | 14,380 | 1·005 | 45 | 321·7 |
| Victoria Street.. | 6·040 | 5,780 | 0·957 | 40 | 144·5 |

The difficulties in the way of measuring the ordinary wear of roads are considerable. M. Bardonnaut, M. Dupuit, and other French engineers, have endeavoured to deduce the wear arising from traffic to a certain extent known by measuring the amount of detritus collected in the form of mud or dust. Many precautions are necessary to avoid measuring matters not proceeding from the wear of the part of the road under experiment, and to prevent the loss of any part of the detritus by its being washed away by rain, or blown away, and it is only in special circumstances that the results can be thoroughly relied on.

Cross sections of the surface carefully taken at the same points at intervals of time, sometimes combined with soundings or pittings to measure the thickness, have been employed both in France and in England, as a means of ascertaining the wear.

It is not, however, enough to measure the wear, as shown by loss of thickness; regard must be had as well to the composition of the road-coating. One result of wear is that materials are consumed and removed from the surface as mud or dust, another result is a breaking up and grinding down of the stone remaining in the road, so that the proportion of detritus to stone increases as wear goes on. The variation in the proportion of stone found in different specimens of road-coatings has already been pointed out, and it is stated * that a road in good order, of the same materials, and exposed to heavy traffic, may contain proportions of stone above 2 centimetres (= 0·8 inch) in diameter, varying from 87 to 37 per cent. To ascertain, therefore, all the effects of wear, it is

* Annales des Ponts et Chaussées, vol. vi, 1853.

necessary to learn how far the proportion of stone to detritus has diminished, and how far it has been maintained by the addition of fresh materials.

The process adopted for this purpose by the engineers of the Ponts et Chaussées is as follows : Trenches are cut across the road, and, from the thickness observed, the quantity of materials which the road-coating represented is deduced, regard being had to the relative bulk of new materials and of consolidated road. The contents of the trenches are sorted into stone above 2 centimetres (= 0·8 inch) in diameter and detritus below that size, and the proportions are noted. After an interval of several years, during which the quantities of fresh materials laid are carefully recorded, the same process is repeated. A comparison of the quantities of materials in the road at the two periods, making allowance for the fresh materials which have been added, gives the quantity consumed by wear and removed as mud or dust in the interval, and the proportion of stone and detritus at the beginning and end of the trial shows to what extent the road-cutting has deteriorated or improved in composition. The traffic must be observed also, if any deductions as to the amount of wear caused by traffic are to be attempted.

By observations and experiments of this sort the French engineers have endeavoured to ascertain the actual wear of roads, and its relation to traffic as measured by collars and by tonnage.

Some engineers have maintained with M. Dupuit that the wear increases in the same proportion as the traffic when the nature of materials and other circumstances are the same, while others have contended that the wear increases in a much greater ratio than the traffic. It is probable that with ordinary traffic the former view may be not far from the truth, but when the loads represented by collars are different, it must obviously be otherwise if, as is undoubtedly the case, heavy loads cause more wear than light ones, even when the same total weight is transported.

An instance is recorded * of two pieces of the same road

' Annales des Ponts et Chaussées, vol. vi. 1843.

maintained with materials of the same quality, on one of which, where three-quarters of the traffic consists of very heavy loads, the consumption was ascertained to be 287 cube yards per mile, while on the other piece, where one-quarter of the loads were heavy, and the rest light or empty, it was only 81 cube yards per mile per annum for a mean daily traffic of 100 collars. In this case the wear of 100 collars of heavy traffic was three and a half times as great as that of the same number of collars with light loads.

The effects of an increase of traffic measured by tonnage on the wear of materials are illustrated in a memoir by Mr. Graeff.* Owing to the falling in of the Saint-Etienne tunnel, the traffic on a road was suddenly increased from its usual amount of 1378 tons per day to 2264 tons, 3150 tons, and to 5315 tons on different portions, at which rates it continued for 74 days, after which it fell on all the portions of the road to 1772 tons per day. The consumption of materials, i. e. the amount removed from the road, and that reduced to detritus below 2 centimetres in diameter, was measured in the manner which has been above described, and the results were as follow :—

| Daily Traffic. | Annual Consumption of Materials per Mile. | Annual Consumption per Mile per 100 Tons of Daily Traffic. |
|---|---|---|
| Tons. | Cube yards. | Cube yards. |
| 1378 | 724 | 52 |
| 1772 | 1857 | 104 |
| 2264 | 2780 | 122 |
| 3150 | 4615 | 146 |
| 5315 | 9886 | 186 |

These figures show a nearly uniform increase of wear, at a much higher ratio than the increase of tonnage, less than four times the traffic, measured by tons, consuming more than 13½ times the quantity of materials. The case was no doubt an extreme one. The road was from 20 to 23 feet wide, and 5315 tons per day represents 250 tons per foot of width, in this case carried mostly in heavy loads on narrow wheels. The material

* Annales des Ponts et Chaussées, vol. ix. 1865.

was schist, the subsoil clay, and the thickness of the road-coating, which was less than 9 inches at the outset, appears to have been only $7\frac{1}{4}$ inches under the heaviest traffic.    All the conditions were thus unfavourable.  Both in the nature of the material and in thickness, the road was altogether insufficient for such a traffic, and the annual consumption of materials was equal to a thickness of more than $1\frac{3}{4}$ inch over the whole surface, before the excessive traffic was thrown on it, and under the traffic of 5315 tons per day the consumption was at the rate of more than 2 feet of thickness in a year.

On another part of the same road, with the same material, where the wear was measured by the loss of thickness on the surface, an increase of traffic from 1200 to 1500 tons per day caused an increase of wear from 464 to 896 cube yards per mile per year, or from 38 to 60 cube yards per 100 tons of daily traffic, or an increase of traffic in the proportion of from 4 to 5 nearly doubled the wear.

It will be unsafe to draw any general conclusion as to the increased rate of wear from these cases.   There is no doubt that when the road or the materials are too weak for the traffic the wear is augmented, and that it increases enormously when the limit of strength either of the road material or of the road itself is approached.   Here both limits must have been nearly reached before the exceptionally heavy traffic was thrown on the road.

The observations at Saint Etienne, by M. Graeff, appeared to show that with an equal traffic the wear of materials increased with the proportion of detritus in the road, and in a more rapid ratio, and that with greater traffic the rate of increase of wear appeared to be more rapid.   This would probably have shown itself in a more marked way if, instead of considering everything under $0 \cdot 8$ inches diameter as " detritus," a much smaller gauge had been adopted.

### Consumption of Materials.

The annual wear of a road as measured by thickness has been seldom found in France to exceed $\frac{1}{2}$ inch, or on the most frequented roads 1 inch, and to be not more than $\frac{1}{8}$ inch on roads

10 or 12 feet wide, with an average traffic of about 30 collars per day.

Several observers agree in considering about 100 cube yards per mile per year to be an average consumption of good silicious or calcareous materials by 100 collars of traffic per day. Some give as little as 58 cube yards per mile for quartz gravel, 43 cube yards for muschelkalk, and 33 cube yards for granite gravel,* and 65 cube yards per mile is stated to be the consumption of a middling silicious material by 100 collars per day of the light carriage traffic of the Avenue Neuilly, Champs-Elysées.† The average consumption of materials on all the national roads of France in 1869, and in 1875, is stated to have been at the rate of 49½ cube yards per mile per annum for 100 collars of daily traffic.‡

In 1876 it appears§ that the mean consumption of materials on the whole of the national roads of France was 78 cube yards per mile, being at the rate of 53 cube yards per mile per annum for every 100 collars of daily traffic, and 50 cube yards per mile per annum for every 100 tons carried daily. In the different departments, the average quantity of materials per mile of road varied from 22 cube yards in Corsica to 390 cube yards in the department of the Seine, seldom falling below 40 cube yards, or exceeding 150 cube yards per mile. The consumption per 100 collars and per 100 tons of daily traffic was generally below the averages above given when the traffic was considerable, and this is very observable in those departments where the traffic was very heavy. The influence of the weather is shown by the high average consumption of materials compared with the traffic in some departments where the traffic is small, and the effect of a good material is also observable in a small consumption under considerable traffic where igneous rocks were used.

There are no means of knowing, even approximately, the

---

* Annales des Ponts et Chaussées, 1834, vol. viii. p. 190.
† Crinier, Annales des Ponts et Chaussées, 1843.
‡ Annales des Ponts et Chaussées, 1869, vol. xviii. p. 366 ; 1877, vol. xiii. p. 229.
§ État indiquant la Décomposition par Departement des Dépenses d'Entretien des Routes Nationales en 1876.

quantities of material used on the roads of England, whether turnpikes or highways. It is impossible from the returns made of annual expenditure even to get at the cost, and information of any kind on the subject is almost entirely wanting.

The number of cube yards of materials per mile usually required for the annual repairs of the Glasgow and Carlisle road constructed by Telford are stated* to have been from 60 to 120 cube yards per mile on different parts of the road, the material being whinstone; and on the the Holyhead road, 96 cube yards per mile in Anglesey, 73 cube yards per mile between Bangor and Cernioge, and 162 cube yards per mile between Cernioge and Chirk, where the materials were softer, were used for repairs in 1835.†

The annual wear of the macadamised streets of London has been given as from 1 inch to 4 inches in thickness of granite coating, and as much as 5½ inches on Westminster Bridge, and that of the streets of Birmingham as on an average 2 inches, in some cases as much as 4 inches, and in one street nearly 6 inches of hard pebblestone, ragstone, and basalt (Hartshill stone).‡  It is doubtful whether the wear was measured, and what is given as such is probably the thickness of materials laid.

On the Metropolis Roads north of the Thames, which up to 1864 comprised about 121 miles of the main roads through the suburbs of London, extending to Hounslow, Uxbridge, Harrow, Edgware, Hampstead, Highgate, Enfield, and Snaresbrook, an average of from 470 to 580 cube yards per mile of granite, hard stone, flints, and gravel was used annually.  On the 53 miles of these roads lying within the district of the Metropolis Local Management Act, 650 to 700 cube yards, principally of granite, were used annually per mile.  After 1864, when the latter roads were given up to the parishes, the average on the 67 miles of road which remained was from 380 to 470 cube yards per mile per year of granite, hard stone, gravel, and flints.

In the county of Edinburgh, where 441 miles of turnpike

---

* Life of Telford, p. 485.
† Mr. Provis's evidence, Select Committee on Turnpike Trusts, 1836.
‡ Proc. Inst. Civil Engineers, vol. xii. p. 228.

road were kept in excellent condition under one management for many years, the following average quantities of syenite, trap, and whinstone were used annually :—

In the Lasswade district .. .. .. .. .. .. 41 cube yards per mile.
„ Dalkeith and Post Road district .. .. .. 98 „ „
„ Cramond district .. .. .. .. .. .. 170 „ „
„ Calder, Slateford, and Corstorphine district 67 „ „

The quantities varied considerably on different portions of road; while near Edinburgh 500 or 600 cube yards per mile were used, 15 or 20 were enough for remote country districts.

In South Wales, where the turnpike roads were under an uniform system of management from 1845 to 1882, the quantities of materials used on about 86 lengths of road, amounting in all to about 1000 miles, have been recorded in the quarterly returns made by the surveyors, and form the best data which as yet exist in this country for judging of the amount of materials required to keep roads in good order under different conditions.

In Glamorganshire, in the suburbs of Swansea and Cardiff, the traffic is that of the streets of large and busy seaport towns. On one mile at Swansea, 500, 600, and 800 cube yards of materials, consisting of copper slag and mountain limestone, were spread for many years in succession on a road 8 yards wide, having a traffic of about 550 collars per day with very heavy loads; 600 cube yards per mile would give a coat of an average thickness of 1½ inch of unconsolidated materials for the whole width and length, and represent about 1 inch of consolidated road surface. At Cardiff 800 to 1000 cube yards of limestone per mile were used for many years on a road of the same width, giving a greater average thickness of coating.

These large quantities of materials were only required for a mile or two, and the rate soon fell to 200 and 150 cube yards per mile. The average on the whole 235 miles of turnpike roads in Glamorganshire was about 110 cube yards of materials per mile, many miles having been maintained with 60 cube yards, and some roads at as low a rate as 30 cube yards per mile.

In Carmarthenshire, the average on 290 miles of road was

during ten years, 73 cube yards per mile ; some lengths of road
having required upwards of 200 cube yards, while other roads
were kept well with 20 cube yards, but the majority being
nearer the average of 73 cube yards per mile.

In Pembrokeshire, the average on 85 miles of turnpike road
was 64 cube yards per mile, one road requiring 120 and all the
others from 90 to 40 cube yards per mile.

In Cardiganshire, the average on 134 miles was 58 cube yards
per mile, varying on different roads from less than 20 to upwards
of 100 cube yards per mile.

In Breconshire, the average on 127 miles of turnpike road
was 51 cube yards per mile, varying on different roads from 30
to 100 cube yards per mile, and exceeding 200 cube yards per
mile on a short length.

In Radnorshire, the average on 130 miles was 48 cube yards
per mile, the quantities on different roads varying in a corresponding degree.

The materials consisted of carboniferous, silurian, and lias
limestone, coal-measure sandstone, the grits and slates of the
silurian rocks, and very largely of river and field stone.
Igneous rocks are obtained only in small quantities in Radnorshire and Pembrokeshire. Copper slag has been used either
alone or with mountain limestone in the neighbourhood of
Swansea.

On some of these roads the traffic is light, and on many of
them more materials would have been used if the funds at com-
mand had permitted it. Though the strength of the roads was
in these instances suffered to fall below what was desirable, they
were kept in very good condition with the amounts of materials
stated above.

# CHAPTER VIII.

NEW materials may be added to a road either in thin coats and small patches year by year, or in a thick coat consolidated by rolling. In the first method the wear is replaced annually, and the traffic is depended upon to work the materials into the road. Where the traffic is not excessive this can be accomplished under proper management with excellent result, and at no serious inconvenience to the public. Considerable care in the use of materials is necessary to ensure their proper application. Sixty or 70 cube yards per mile amount to less than ¼ inch of consolidated road surface, supposing the materials to be spread uniformly over a mile of road to a width of 4 or 5 yards. It is impossible so to spread it, even if the wear were so uniform over the whole surface as to render it desirable. A cube yard of stones broken to a 2-inch gauge, when carefully spread, will cover 30 square yards, so that 60 cube yards would only coat about a quarter of a mile 4 yards wide, or 70 cube yards a quarter of a mile 5 yards wide. With such quantities each part of the road would be coated once in four years, and it must have sufficient strength to stand the wear of four years without being coated. If only 30 cube yards per mile of materials were used, it would be eight years before every part of a road 4 yards wide were covered, and the road must be able to undergo eight years wear without giving way, while waiting the turn for each part to be coated.

In actual practice both the wear and the thickness of roads is irregular, and if large pieces of the surface of a road on which the wear is small, and the quantity of materials to be laid is limited, are coated all over, it is tolerably certain that thickness is added to perhaps one-half or two-thirds of the area which is already thick enough to bear the traffic, while other parts, including weak places, must be left until their turn comes to be coated, which may be as just shown, from four to eight years. The ordinary wear on weak portions thus neglected is considerably greater than it would be on a stronger road, and if from the effects of heavy traffic or bad weather they break up, the extra quantity of materials required for their repair may be very large. Instead of thus always contending with a road which is in many parts too weak, the irregularity of wear and of strength in different parts of the coating and the consequent reserve of strength in some parts of the road should be taken advantage of. Materials should be laid only on the places that require them, and the whole road should be brought as far at practicable to a uniform strength throughout. Thus no part of the surface is neglected and no materials are wastefully applied to portions already quite thick enough to stand the traffic, and a better road is obtained with a less expenditure of materials.

In laying on new materials, the old-fashioned way of waiting till the road has lost its shape, and then spreading a thick coat over a large surface and leaving it to be worked in by the traffic without further care, should never be followed. A good deal of the new material is thus wasted by being ground up and crushed before it is consolidated, and when at length, and at great inconvenience to the traffic, consolidation has been effected, the surface of the road will be left irregular and out of shape. The materials necessary to replace the wear of any ordinary traffic can be laid in comparatively small quantities, where hollows or weak places appear, or where required to keep the cross section of the road in good form. If they are laid in small patches, and with care, the inconvenience to the traffic will be scarcely perceptible. It should be remembered that until the newly laid stones are consolidated, the operation is not completed, and if the task of working them in is left to the public, it is only right that the process should be rendered as easy and speedy as possible, by good arrangement and care in laying the materials, and by attention to them after they are laid.

On a road maintained in good repair on a good system,

there are no holes or ruts or long hollows worn by the wheels or the horses' feet, but only irregular depressions or "slacks" of the surface, which show where fresh materials should be applied. They are more or less rounded and undefined in outline, less than an inch deep in the middle, and shallowing gradually towards the edges. Considerable care is required in determining the size and shape of the patches of materials to be laid to repair these hollows, as both a good result and economy of materials and labour depend upon it. Unskilled labourers are inclined to lay stones in rectangular patches, with more regard to the neat appearance of the newly laid stones than to the needs of the road. Parts of the round or oval-shaped hollows must thus be left uncovered, or fresh materials must be laid where they are not required. The angles of a square patch are, besides, very liable to be knocked away, and if the stones are not wasted in this way, they do not set so quickly as if laid in a rounded form. If the ends of a patch be made in the form of an oval more or less pointed, the traffic will wear it in from the sides, and on a hill the water will be diverted towards the sides of the road, instead of running into the stones, as it does with a square-ended patch. Care should be taken to cover the whole surface of a hollow, so as to leave no place where water may lodge.

The object should be to give the surface, after the consolidation of the new materials, as nearly as possible the regular form due to the cross section of the road. With stone broken to the usual gauge, and giving a thickness of ¾ inch to 1 inch of consolidated coating, this can only be done approximately and by using the smaller stuff at the edges, and requires a good deal of aptitude on the part of the roadman. The patches seldom need be more than 3 or 4 yards long and 2 yards wide. Too many hollows on the same part of the road should not be covered at once, the deepest may be coated first, and when the stones have partly set, the shallower ones may be attended to ; and if, meanwhile, the water lodges in them, it may be led off by cutting small grooves with the pick.

It is generally easy to leave a winding track along the road free from stones, by arranging patches sometimes on the

H

sides, and sometimes on the middle, so that the horses' feet may avoid the stones, which will be worn in from the sides of the patches by the wheels. When this has been partially effected, other patches may be so laid as to divert the traffic into another track. The curious tendency of horses drawing vehicles to follow in the same track must be checked by inducing them by means of small patches to change the track. This, of course, must be done with due regard to the places that require strengthening, and demands more contrivance than is to be expected from an ordinary roadman, unless trained by the surveyor.

If, from neglect or bad management or other cause, long ruts or large hollows have been allowed to form, they should be repaired in short lengths, and one part at a time. Vehicles avoid long strips of stones laid in a hollow worn by wheels, and soon make another rut alongside. Laying a long strip of materials on the middle of the road diverts the traffic to the sides, which are sure to suffer a good deal, and may be entirely cut up before the stones in the middle are worked in. If, after all hollows have been covered, there is still material that ought to be laid, it should be spread in sheets one stone thick over the whole width of the road, up to, but not including the water-tables. The sheets should not be more than 6 or 8 yards long, and with intermediate lengths at least two or three times as long as the stoned portions, and when the stones first laid have worked in, other patches may be laid in the intermediate spaces till the whole has been covered. On steep hills, coating from side to side is an unnecessary inconvenience to traffic. One side should be coated first, and the other left until the stones are partially consolidated by the descending vehicles.

A thick coating of metalling should never be laid on; a layer one stone in thickness, the stones being laid sufficiently close to support each other, is almost always enough, and if not, one layer put down upon another when it has almost worked in will give any thickness required.

The practice of using trestles, logs, or stones to force the traffic over newly laid stones to work them in is one to be avoided. It is generally but a clumsy way of doing that which can be accomplished by good arrangement in laying materials, and by after attention to them. The legal right to use trestles on highways has been held to exist, though it has been disputed.

That materials may be spread in small quantities, they should be at hand in depots or heaps, from which they can be wheeled out by the roadman as he requires them. There is generally no difficulty in arranging this; room can almost always be found on the roadside for stone depots or heaps about 100 yards apart, when the distance to be wheeled will never exceed 50 yards. Stone should be kept in reserve on the roadside, so that it may not be necessary to deposit small heaps at short intervals every year, when the consumption is small. If there are no places for stone heaps, or depots, close enough together for the materials to be wheeled out, carting must be resorted to, either by contract, as one of the conditions of the supply of materials, or, preferably, by the hire of a horse and cart; and it will be necessary to guard against waste by spreading too large quantities in one place, and carelessness in laying the materials.

When a hard and costly material is used in considerable quantities, it may sometimes be spread with advantage under the direction of a special man, instead of being left to the care of the road labourers. The latter, of course, assist in the spreading, and in this way one skilled man may superintend the spreading of materials over a long length of road.

The practice of picking up or loosening the surface of a road with a pick, sometimes called "stocking," in order to make the new materials unite more readily with the old surface, is one on which opinions have been divided since the days of McAdam, who appears to have recommended it, while Sir H. Parnell and Mr. Provis, speaking from the experience of the Holyhead road, condemned it as expensive, wasteful of the old materials, and of no good whatever to the road. On thin roads it is certainly almost impossible to pick up the surface without destroying the cohesion of the whole coat, thus doing far more harm than any benefit arising from it can compensate for. On thick roads with a hard surface, a proportion of stones may be crushed and wasted before they can be incorporated in the road, and picking up may be useful, but stones properly laid in moist weather generally bind sufficiently well on ordinary roads without any picking up, as the weak places, or hollows, where patches should be laid, have softness enough to render the working-in easy. At the most, a slight loosening of the surface round the margin of the patch is required to give the stones a hold, and hasten the setting.

On roads of considerable thickness, where the surface is hard and the material tough, there is no danger of breaking up the whole road, and a quicker consolidation may be worth obtaining at the cost of the extra labour, and even of some of the old materials. Loosening to about $\frac{1}{2}$ inch in depth, and rather more round the edges, is sufficient for small-sized metalling. The tendency of workmen is to pick up too deeply, and it is unavoidable when full-sized stones are disturbed in their bed.

Picking or stocking up the surface before laying fresh materials generally costs from $\frac{1}{2}d.$ to $1d.$ per square yard.

The use of a binding material in road maintenance, when materials are applied in thin coats and small patches, is seldom necessary or desirable. The road has already in it more than enough small stone and detritus to fill up all interstices, and in the damp weather in which stones should be laid there is generally little difficulty in getting a layer one stone thick to work in without adding any binding. On a road from which the mud is constantly removed, the places where fresh materials have been laid often appear, after the stones have worked in, as muddy places. So long as the materials remained unconsolidated, the mud forced out as the stones worked in could not be scraped off. It would evidently be a mistake to add unnecessarily to this excess of detritus in the road, and on the contrary it is generally right to scrape the road before laying down fresh materials, as a layer of mud hinders the incorporation with the road surface.

When large sheets of stones have to be laid in a street or road of great traffic, the use of a binding will ease the traffic and cause the new material to consolidate more quickly. A good clean binding material must be used, and evenly spread, and in dry weather watered. Too much binding, or a material of a muddy character, will make the road soft and weak until the excess has been removed by scraping or sweeping.

On a mountain road with light traffic, exposed to heavy rains and sweeping winds which remove all mud and detritus, a binding material may be used with advantage, especially with silicious materials.

The consolidation of materials after they are spread can be greatly aided by attention on the part of the roadman. The sooner they are consolidated the better they will wear, and a little care bestowed on newly laid patches will save much work and materials afterwards. If too many stones are laid down at once, the roadman cannot give them the necessary attention, and they do not become consolidated so quickly or so well as if they are spread in quantities that can be properly attended to. Ruts, which always have a tendency to form in freshly laid materials, especially if more than one stone thick, should be effaced by raking across backwards and forwards, and this requires more skill than may be thought necessary for such a simple operation. Everything should be done to distribute the traffic equally over the whole breadth, and prevent the formation of ruts by vehicles following in the same track. However carefully patches are laid, stones, especially round the edges, will be displaced; they should be put back, as single loose stones are dangerous to the traffic, hurtful to the surface of the road, and liable to be crushed and wasted as material. If consolidation does not appear to commence, a little small stuff from the clearing up of the side channels, or road scrapings, may be applied as a binding material, especially round the edges of the patch, where the old surface may also be slightly loosened with the pick.

It is the practice in France to aid consolidation by ramming the new-laid stones with a pounder, 15 or 20 lb. weight; the effect is good, and it is sometimes very useful, but it is not generally worth while to incur the cost of it.

In dry weather, when a dangerous hollow has to be repaired, and stones laid in the ordinary way will not set, a sort of concrete made of five parts of small stone and one part of road scrapings, mixed with water into a stiff paste, may be put on, after picking up and watering the old surface. When it has dried a little, the patch should be rammed or beaten, and be covered with a thin coat of dry small stones, over which detritus should be spread, and the ramming or beating should be repeated.

Smoothness of surface of a road is generally a proof that the materials have been carefully applied and raking in and scraping have been properly attended to, though hardness of material, and, above all, unequal hardness, will always tend to roughness.

The proper season for laying the bulk of the fresh materials, is in the autumn and early winter. The precise time at which it can be begun will depend on the climate, weather, subsoil, and the nature of the materials. As soon as the surface of the road softens from the wet, patching the hollows, wheel-tracks, and channels worn by water, should be commenced, the mud having been previously removed where necessary. The greater part of the new materials should be put on before the end of the year, so that they may be at least partially worked in before winter, when they are most required in the road, and before severe frosts come. Unconsolidated materials are more annoying to the traffic in frosty weather, and there is waste by the stones being crushed and scattered instead of being incorporated in the road. Stones laid late in the winter seldom consolidate thoroughly, and those laid in the spring hardly set at all, but work loose in the dry weather, if they are not of a binding nature. If a road from any cause shows weakness in the spring, and requires stoning, everything must be done to aid consolidation, and great attention to the newly laid materials will be required. All stones which do not bind must be raked off as the season advances and there is no longer any prospect of their working in.

On a road in good condition, of sufficient strength, and with ordinary traffic, by patching hollows as they appear, and by a careful attention to the surface, the materials consumed by wear can be replaced without difficulty, and the thickness of the coating can be added to if necessary. With greater traffic the quantity of materials laid and the size of the patches must be increased. After all hollows or slacks have been covered, or when there are no places which appear to require coating, the proper quantity of materials required to keep the road up to its full strength should still always be laid. This may be in sheets over the whole width of the road, up to, but not including, the water-tables, and in short lengths, with intermediate spaces free from stones.

The wear on a good road is often greater than appearances indicate, and if it be not replaced, although the surface may be kept in perfect condition, smooth and hard, and free from hollows, the road will be getting thinner and weaker, and at last will fail from having insufficient strength.

Experience has shown that this is no imaginary danger. In France the system of repairing by small patching and minute attention to the surface was strongly advocated by M. Dumas, and under some engineers was carried to an extreme. It was contended that the more perfect the surface of a road was rendered, the less was the resistance and shock to vehicles, and consequently the less the wear of the road, and that, therefore, roads with the finest surface were cheaper to maintain. To obtain this perfect surface the dust or mud was removed by continual sweeping, leaving a clean smooth surface, free from wheel tracks, over which the traffic was supposed to work evenly, and wear the road parallel to itself without forming hollows or ruts. The materials required to replace the annual wear were broken fine and applied in small patches. The outline of the spot to be covered was marked out, and in dry weather watered, the surface was picked up, the loosened materials were raked out and divided into coarse, middling, and small. The coarse was put back with new materials so as to cover completely the place to be repaired. The surface was then rammed lightly, and the middling-sized materials were spread over and rammed, and then covered with small stuff and detritus and again rammed. The sides of tracks formed on the new surface by wheels were rammed, and in dry weather the finished patch was watered daily till it set.*

The amount of manual labour was of course large, and more especially so when compared with the quantity of materials laid. On the roads of the department of the Sarthe it amounted to seven days' labour per cubic metre, where, before the adoption

* 'Annales des Ponts et Chaussées,' vol. viii. 1844, p. 273.

of the system by M. Dumas, it was only one day. On the other hand, a great economy of materials was claimed, and, on the whole, economy of maintenance was supposed to be obtained, as well as far better roads. The excellence of the roads was undoubted, but the economy, if any, was only obtained by not replacing the annual wear, which was greater than the fine surface indicated. The thickness of the roads gradually diminished, and at a certain point they went to pieces suddenly, keeping an admirable surface to the end.

The late Sir J. F. Burgoyne, then engaged on road works in Ireland, called attention to M. Dumas' system, in a paper written in 1843, and advocated its adoption. Constant attention, the prevention of the collection of mud or dust, frequent patching in small quantities with finely broken stone on the first appearance of inequalities, the use of a rammer, and artificial watering, were brought into practice to some extent on the Irish roads, without being carried so far as in France, and with good results.

*Repairs by Thick Coats and Rolling.*

When the traffic is very great, the quantity of materials required to replace the wear is so large that, if it is put on in patches and partial coatings, the road is always covered with newly laid stones. The plan of laying down a considerable thickness at once and consolidating it by rolling can then be followed with advantage. This mode of applying fresh materials has been practised in France since 1840, and since the introduction of the steam road roller it has been a good deal followed in towns in England. Instead of attempting to restore the wear annually, only such repairs are done as are sufficient to keep a good surface on the road, which is allowed to wear as thin as it can be with safety, having regard to its power to carry the traffic, and it is then coated with a thickness of materials sufficient to stand the wear of several years. The consolidation of this thick covering by rolling is of course an essential without which there would be nothing but a return to the old practice of road mending.

The advantages to the public of being spared the wear and

tear of vehicles, the excessive draught and labour, and perhaps injury to horses, resulting from the consolidation of large quantities of fresh materials by the ordinary traffic, and of having at once a road with a hard and smooth surface, are obvious. In many cases the question whether there is economy in the actual repairs will be a secondary matter compared with the indirect gain to the public both in money and in comfort.

The process of rolling has been already described in Chapter II. To make a coating of new materials unite with the old surface, the latter may be picked or stocked up before the fresh materials are laid, but it is not always necessary. The driving wheels of steam road rollers are provided with holes into which steel points may be fixed for the purpose of loosening the surface, and saving a good deal of the labour and cost of picking up by hand. Binding material must be used, and artificial watering, both of the old surface and of the new-laid stones, may be required. With the aid of the latter, fresh coatings of stone can be laid as well in the summer as in the wet season, and by some surveyors a better result is believed to be obtained. A less thickness than 4 inches of materials should not be laid down; the coating does not bind so readily, and the cost of rolling is not much greater with 4 inches than with a less thickness. It has been already stated that it is unnecessary to break materials which are to be laid with a roller to so small a size as would otherwise be required for patching. The greater amount of wear which always takes place in the middle of a road must be allowed for by making the cross section rounder than necessary at first, that it may not be too flat before the time comes for another coating.

A greater length of road than can be completed in one day should not be undertaken at once. The fresh materials may be spread one day, and the rolling may be begun and finished on the following day. On a wide road, one-half the width of a roadway may be coated and rolled and delivered over to the traffic before the second half is commenced. The inconvenience and loss of time experienced in turning a roller almost disappears when a steam roller is used, and short lengths, such as

30 or 40 yards, may be rolled at one time, and the roller may be used from side to side of the road. The area which can be rolled in a day will depend on the thickness of the covering, and on the nature of the material. A horse roller will complete a length of 300 yards on a wide road, and more on a narrower road, with a good binding material, and if the work can proceed without interruption, that is, at the rate of about 1600 square yards per day. The hindrances of street traffic may however reduce this to less than one-half. With a steam roller, Messrs. Mowlem, Freeman, and Burt state that they can roll 1000 square yards a day of the material used in the London streets. Other road surveyors and contractors give from 600 to 2500 square yards as a day's work. The steam rollers in general use are 10 tons in weight, rolling a width of 6 feet, or 15 tons, rolling a width of 7 feet. Heavier rollers, weighing 20 tons or 25 tons, are sometimes used, but the damage they do to pipes, drains, sewers, &c., is not compensated for by any increased utility.

Steam road rollers now work constantly in London and in many other large towns; and with ordinary precautions, such as blocking up entirely a short length of road, or diverting the traffic to one side while the roller is at work, or giving warning by a flag-man or other notice, little inconvenience arises from horses being frightened.

Economy is claimed for this method of repairs, both on the score of a large saving in road materials and in the cost of laying them down, and also because less after-labour is required for attending to the surface and removing mud and dust.

The result of observations made by M. Graeff in 1850,* on two of the national roads of the department of the Bas-Rhin, one of which had a traffic of 640 collars and the other of 280 collars per day, gave the following particulars of the average cost of the employment of a cube yard of materials spread in a coat about 4 inches thick, and rolled by horse power:—

* ‘Annales des Ponts et Chaussées,’ vol. ii. 1851.

|  | Road 4. Pence per cube yard. | Road 61. Pence per cube yard. |
|---|---|---|
| Delivery and spreading materials .. .. .. | 4·4 | 3·3 |
| Do. do. binding .. .. .. | 0·8 | 0·7 |
| Watering .. .. .. .. .. .. .. .. | 1·1 | 1·0 |
| Rolling .. .. .. .. .. .. .. .. | 4·5 | 3·4 |
| Purchase of binding material .. .. .. .. | 2·9 | 1·4 |
| Accessory expenses, maintenance and transport of roller .. .. .. .. .. .. .. | 0·1 | 0·1 |
|  | 13·8 | 10·0 |

This is 1$d$. to 1½$d$. per square yard for a coating 4 inches thick. Wages were 1·35 franc per day, and the above prices must be more than doubled to correspond with English prices of the present day.

The economy effected by this mode of maintenance was considered to be 20 per cent., not so much on the materials as on the labour, and in M. Graeff's opinion there was no economy at all when a 4-inch coat was required less often than once in seven years, or when the wear was less than ½ inch per year. In a subsequent memoir,* M. Graeff claims on roads of great traffic in the department of the Loire a saving of 30 to 40 per cent. on the quantity of materials, and another of 10 per cent. on the labour. Experienced surveyors in England estimate that there is a saving of one-quarter or one-third of the quantity of road materials, which, when the traffic is great and the wear rapid, is a considerable set-off against the expense of purchasing and working a roller.

The cost of steam rolling, when there is constant work for the machine, is far less than that of horse rolling, but the actual cost varies very much with the circumstances under which the work has to be done. The result of a comparative trial made in Paris between a horse roller, weighing 6¼ tons, and a steam roller, weighing 13 tons, was that, valuing the cost of the horse roller at 5$s$. per hour, and that of the steam

* 'Annales des Ponts et Chaussées,' vol. ix. p. 283, 1865.

roller at 7s. 6d. per hour, the cost of rolling per square yard was 1d. with a horse roller and ¾d. with the steam roller. Messrs. Aveling and Porter give the cost of continuously working a steam roller and rolling from 1000 to 2000 square yards in a day at from 22s. to 25s. a day, including wages of driver, coal and oil, and wear and tear of the machine, which is at the rate of a penny for from 3 to 8 superficial yards. In addition to the driver, two other men, or a man and a boy, are often necessary in towns ; and the cost of watering and of spreading and sweeping the binding material must be taken into account. When the working of the roller is not continuous, the interest and depreciation on the first cost of the machine is, of course, a heavier charge on the work performed. The engines are, however powerful enough to drive stone-breaking machines, and may be provided with arrangements for the purpose, and also with extra wheels for employment as traction engines to remove materials to the roads. By thus utilising them for other purposes when not wanted for rolling, the purchase-money may be not left entirely idle.

It appears from a table prepared by Mr. Lovegrove, which shows in detail the costs of repairs to roads with a steam roller in the Hackney district,* that the cost of laying coatings of granite from 2 to 3 inches thick, including wages, roller, watering, sharpening tools, and hoggin, was from about 2½d. to 5d. per square yard. The average cost of laying the 56,145 square yards in the twenty-one different streets included in the table is for the different items as follows :—

|  | | | | | Pence. |
|---|---|---|---|---|---|
| Roadmen and watchmen | .. | .. | .. | .. | 1·22 |
| Hire of roller | .. .. | .. | .. | .. | 1·50 |
| Water-carts and water | .. | .. | .. | .. | ·21 |
| Sharpening picks .. | .. | .. | .. | .. | ·20 |
| Surplus hoggin, &c. | .. | .. | .. | .. | ·51 |
|  | | | Total | .. | 3·74 |

or nearly 3¾d. per square yard.

The solidity and smoothness of a road thickly coated and consolidated with a heavy roller diminishes the wear from the traffic,

---

* Proc. Inst. C.E. vol. lviii. p. 63.

and consequently lessens the cost of sweeping, scraping, and removing dust and mud. It is a mistake, however, to leave a road so coated entirely to itself until it is so much worn as to require another thick coat of materials. Continual patching in small pieces should be practised, and this is as much or more required soon after the thick coat has been laid and rolled as later. The ordinary traffic searches out the weak places, which, from containing originally too much binding material, or from having escaped the weight of the roller, are less thoroughly consolidated, and a road on which a thick coat of stones has been recently laid with the aid of a steam roller often presents a more uneven surface than a road maintained by coatings one stone in thickness worked in by the traffic.

Unless the traffic and the wear are very considerable, say at the rate of $\frac{1}{2}$ inch of road surface in a year, there is no economy in adopting this method of road repair, whatever may be the increased comfort to the public, and the lessened draught and wear and tear of vehicles resulting from it.

On a thin weak road, the effect of the weight of the roller is destructive. A 15-ton roller, supposing it to bear equally over its whole width, may have no greater pressure on the surface of the road per inch of width than a cart wheel with three-quarters of a ton on it, and yet the load per square inch on the subsoil may be greater. In fact, however, the weight never is equally distributed, and the pressure is excessive at some points, while other portions escape. This is shown by the way in which the ordinary traffic of a road wears into hollows the smooth even surface left by a heavy roller.

The use of a roller to consolidate a coating one stone in thickness is not advisable on economical grounds, though it may sometimes be desirable for the comfort of the public. Unless the material be very hard, a good deal is crushed by the roller, even if the old surface has been first picked or stocked up. With the latter process, little or no binding material is required besides that derived from the picked-up surface.

## CHAPTER IX.

SWEEPING AND SCRAPING.    DRAINAGE.    WATERING.    REPAIRS
BEYOND ORDINARY MAINTENANCE.

*Sweeping and Scraping.*

In a good system of road maintenance the removal of the detritus resulting from the wear of materials holds an important place. It may be effected either as dust or as mud. In this country the removal of dust is only practised to a limited extent, and in towns; but in the drier climate of France it is considered to be attended with advantage on the roads in the open country, and dust is removed in the summer instead of mud in the winter, so that labour throughout the year is rendered more equal. When the materials of the road are silicious, and consequently disposed to lose coherence in dry weather, the removal of dust is liable to be injurious, by disturbing the surface, and exposing the loose materials to the wear of the traffic without the covering of dust which holds them in place and protects them. There is little danger of this on a calcareous road, which remains solid and united in the driest weather.

Dust may be removed by scraping, but sweeping is the more usual process. In France a long-handled flexible besom is used, with which a man placed in the middle can sweep from side to side of an ordinary road, and thus get over two or three miles per day of easy sweeping. Brooms fixed on a horizontal bar, and mounted on a wheel and handles like those of a wheelbarrow, and worked from side to side of the road, are also sometimes employed. In England a bass broom is generally used both for dust and mud, with which a man can sweep on an average about 2500 square yards per day. A good deal depends on the nature and condition of the mud. It is stated * that in the streets of Paris a man with a broom will sweep, without putting the mud up into heaps, 700 square yards per hour of macadamised road surface dry and slightly watered, 470 square yards when covered with liquid mud, and 350 square yards when the mud is sticky.

Sweeping machines are used in towns to remove both dust and mud. In one machine a revolving brush mounted obliquely sweeps a track about 6 feet wide, and leaves the dust or mud in a line along one side of it, to be afterwards gathered up. Whitworth's machine consists of a series of brooms, usually about 2 feet 6 inches wide, attached to an endless chain running over pulleys suspended in a frame behind a mud cart, the wheels of which give a rotary motion to the pulleys carrying the endless chain and the brooms attached to them. As the cart moves on the brooms are made to bear on the ground with a pressure that can be adjusted according to circumstances, and the mud or dust is swept from the surface up an incline into the cart. A machine with one man and a horse is said † to sweep 3 to 4½ acres of street surface per day, removing from 1 to 3 loads per acre, at a cost of from 10s. to 15s. a day for working. A good deal depends on the distance to which the stuff has to be carried, but allowing one-third of the day to be lost in going to and from the places of deposit, a day's work will be 14,000 to 20,000 square yards of sweeping.

A scraping machine drawn by a horse is also in use. The scrapers are mounted on a frame oblique to the direction in which the machine is drawn, which is along the road, and the mud is delivered at the hinder end of the oblique line of scrapers. A breadth of about 6 feet is scraped by the passage of this machine, which is, however, not so well able to follow the irregularities of the surface as the smaller hand machine.

These larger machines are little fitted for use on roads in the open country. They are costly, and therefore would, under any circumstances, be few in number, and they require the use of horses, whereas hand scrapers and hand scraping machines

---

* Homberg, 'Annales des Ponts et Chaussées,' vol. x. 1865, p. 263.
† Proc. Inst. Civil Engineers, vol. vi. p. 431.

can be kept in readiness at many points, and can be used at once by the roadman when the weather is suitable.

The ordinary hand scrapers are generally of steel, about 18 inches wide and 6 inches deep, with the ends bent backward to hold the mud. They are useful at times, when a machine scraper is not at hand, or when it will not act well, as when the road is littered with fallen leaves. Hand scraping is also considered to be more favourable to the road, and it certainly is so when the surface is tender or uneven.

Hand scraping machines have many advantages, the quickness with which they do their work being one of the chief. They consist of 10 or 12 scrapers 3½ or 4 inches broad, hinged to a horizontal bar, each pressed down by a separate spring to enable them to follow the inequalities of the road, and mounted in a frame on a pair of wheels, on which the machine can be pushed backwards with the blades of the scrapers clear of the road, and pulled forwards with the scrapers in action. They are worked from side to side of the road, the most convenient-sized machine scraping a width of about 4 feet at each passage. With such a machine a mile of road may be scraped in a day, two men being employed, one in using the machine, and the other making up the dirt into heaps, or depositing it on the sides. With a hand scraper not a quarter of this work could be accomplished. The best machines are those made of wood with steel-shod scrapers. They are liable to rot from the wet if they are not kept well painted, but they are less liable to damage, and are more easily repaired than those of iron, and they are also cheaper. A machine 4 feet wide costs between 2l. and 3l., and will last 15 years or longer if taken care of.

It is sometimes urged against scraping machines that they loosen the surface, drag stones from their places, and remove with the dirt materials useful in the road. This is to some extent true, especially if the surface is bad, or when scraping is done when the road is sticky or tender, and if the question were whether sweeping or scraping was the best mode of removing mud, it would be entitled to due consideration, but when it is whether mud should be removed by scraping or not at all, the slight injury that the scraper may do when used at improper times is not worth taking into account. The machine naturally tends to plane down inequalities, and thus gives an even smooth surface, which throws off the water, and dries quickly after rain, so that the removal of mud not only reduces the proportion of it in the road, but hardens the surface by promoting evaporation, and renders it far better able to stand the wear from traffic and the weather.

There is great advantage in scraping being done promptly, when the weather is favourable for the operation. This is generally after moderate rain, when the mud is soft without being too liquid. When it is still, the surface of the road is injured by the scraper, stones are loosened in their places, and useful materials are removed with the mud. If a favourable opportunity for scraping be allowed to pass by, the mud may remain on the road for a long time, preventing evaporation, and keeping it moist and soft, and, if frost comes on, causing far more damage in the thaw than would happen on a well-scraped road.

Scraping off a thin covering of mud takes almost as much time, and is, consequently, almost as costly as scraping a thicker coat, and this must be taken into account when, as usually is the case, economy has to be considered. About $\frac{1}{2}$ inch of mud is generally the thickness which it is best to scrape.

The dirt should not be scraped into the side channels, but should be at first drawn into long regular heaps, with openings at frequent intervals to allow the surface of the road to drain freely into the side channels. When sufficiently dry, the scrapings may be laid on the waste at the sides, or made up into heaps and carted away. It is a good plan to make it one of the conditions of the contract for the supply of road materials that the contractor shall take away the road dirt on receiving notice to do so from the surveyor or road labourer. The neighbouring farmers are sometimes ready to take the scrapings for use on their land, but they generally do it at their own time, and if the heaps are left on the road they get cut to pieces by the wheels, and washed into the side channels and outlets, and require clearing up a second time before they can be taken away. Under such circumstances it is better to go to the expense of cartage than to leave the dirt on the road. It is one of the advantages of having room outside the sod bordering that the scrapings can be deposited there, out of the way of all interference with the proper drainage of the road surface until they can be removed altogether.

The amount of scraping which roads require is very different, according to the material used and the traffic on them; and with the same material and traffic it varies a good deal with the situation. A hill requires little or no scraping compared with the flat ground at the bottom, and all damp and shady places need much more scraping than those that lie exposed.

It follows from what has been already said (p. 57) relating to road detritus, that if we suppose the exact amount of detritus resulting from wear on a road to be removed, and to be replaced by new materials, the quantity removed would be less in bulk than the materials applied, whether the detritus were removed as dust or as stiff mud, but that in the latter case the weight would be increased by the addition of about one third the bulk of water, or by about one-fifth; that is to say, on a road on which wear is exactly replaced, $1\frac{1}{5}$ the weight of materials worn out would be removed as a stiff mud. Actually however this is modified by several causes. Some detritus is washed away, and on the other hand the quantity is increased by horse droppings, rubbish from houses, &c., and also by dirt from fields or other roads, and the proportion of water is often greater. It is not, perhaps, far wrong generally to put the weight removed as mud from a well-maintained road at $1\frac{1}{2}$ times the weight of materials worn out.

When, from neglect in removing it, the road contains a large proportion of detritus, great quantities of mud can be scraped off in wet seasons, so as sometimes to lead to the belief that it comes from the subsoil. A thorough removal of the superfluous mud is what a road which has been neglected or improperly maintained often requires most. The coating may contain plenty of stone, but mixed with perhaps more than twice as much mud as it ought to have, and until this is reduced to a proper proportion by continued scraping, it is impossible to get a good road. In such a case laying more materials only hinders scraping, which cannot be done over unconsolidated stones.

With the autumn rains the results of wear through the summer months appear as mud in considerable quantities on the surface of the road. The early autumn is, therefore, the time when scraping is most necessary, and it should be done whenever the weather is favourable for it, so that it may not be behindhand when the time for laying fresh materials comes on.

The advantages of keeping the surface free from mud, and the body of the road hard, with no more than a proper proportion of detritus in it, are so great that there is generally no danger of scraping too much. It is, however, possible by over-scraping to increase the consumption of materials by removing stone of a size which would be still useful in the road, and also in some cases by increasing the wear of that remaining. On a good road in which the mud does not work up from the subsoil, and in which the amount of detritus is kept down by scraping to the proportion which is essential, the quantity of mud which appears on the surface and is scraped off is determined by the wear, and it should be replaced by an equivalent quantity of fresh materials. When, however, from want of funds or other cause, the new materials are insufficient to replace the wear, the road may get weaker in two ways. If the removal of mud is carried on to the full extent, the thickness of the coat will be reduced, while the proportion of mud and small stuff in it will remain the same. If the mud be only partially removed, the road coating will deteriorate by retaining a larger proportion of detritus. By which of these courses the strength of the road will be best maintained, whether by allowing the coat to get thinner with a smaller proportion of detritus, or by preserving thickness with a larger proportion in it, will depend almost entirely on the special conditions of the road.

It must be remembered that scraping must always remove materials more or less useful in the road, as well as mud. It has already been stated that scrapings from very good lime-stone roads were found to contain one-third of small stone that

could not be washed through a cloth having twenty threads to
an inch, and ranging to pieces ¼ inch or more in diameter,
when the roads were scraped under favourable conditions; and
it appeared that, of the whole coating of the same roads, about
one-third consisted of such stuff as would be removed by
scraping. These facts suggest caution in scraping when the
materials used by wear are not replaced. On the other hand,
a road containing a large quantity of detritus is more affected
by wet and frost, and wears more rapidly, perhaps by as much
as one-third more, than a road with a full proportion of stone
in it, so that, when a road is naturally wet, or the materials are
soon acted on by the weather, there is danger in allowing the
proportion of detritus to increase too much. A road of ample
thickness may safely be scraped thinner, and it will generally
be the best course where the subsoil is of a hard, dry, or rocky
character, or over a paved foundation.

### Drainage.

Attention to the drainage both of the surface and of the
subsoil of a road is a matter of great importance. The wear
of materials may be increased two or three fold on a badly
drained road, which, after all, will never be good; indeed, other
care is almost entirely thrown away on a road of which the
drainage is neglected.

The good drainage of the surface depends on the preservation of the cross section with sufficient and regular fall towards
the sides, so that water may not hang about in puddles. It
has already been pointed out (p. 12) that smoothness and
fairness of surface are more important than either extreme
convexity or any particular form of cross section. The latter
may often be varied with advantage within certain limits to
suit the situation; and it always will be so, more or less, as
maintenance goes on, but a fair surface to throw off the water
is essential. From the side channels, or water-tables, the
water should be passed at once by outlets, or gullies, to the
side ditches or other drains, and the course that it will take
from any part of the road should be well known to the road-

man. On a level, the fall in the water-table is but slight, and the wash from the surface of the best kept road will lodge in it, and afford a soil for the growth of grass and weeds, and hinder the flow of water. On steep gradients the outlets from the water-tables are more liable to stoppage, and when this happens the water runs down the side channel and scours it, and perhaps breaks out and damages the surface of the road. Slight but frequent attention is therefore required to maintain the flow of water from every part of the road, by removing obstructions both in the water-tables and outlets. The scouring of the surface on hills, which is often the cause of great damage, must be guarded against beforehand. Every beginning of a water-course must be checked, and all points where water usually breaks out from the side channels, or where outlets or drains get stopped, should be watched and have attention at once in heavy rain. Outlets and drains should always be cleared after a storm, as, if another storm finds them unopened, great damage often results from the neglect.

A thorough clearing out of both water-tables and outlets should take place in the autumn, as soon as the dry weather has passed. If all silt and road dirt is then removed down to the hard bottom, leaving nothing to give a hold to grass or weeds, this will generally be often enough for a general clearing up. The sod bordering should, at the same time, be trimmed with a spade by the aid of a line to fair curves. This, though very much aiding the flow of water, as well as giving a finish to the road, is not so essential as the opening of the outlets and the cleaning up of the side channels; and when time presses, it is sometimes necessary to open the outlets, and to trim the sod bordering and clear the side channels near them first before wet weather sets in, leaving the general cleaning up until afterwards. This, of course, involves some waste of time in the end, from going over the ground twice. Undue deepening of the water-tables in cleaning them, and thus converting them into steep-sided gutters, should be guarded against. There should always be a fair and gradual curved slope from the general surface of the road to the sod bordering.

Cleaning up the sides, trimming the sod bordering, and opening the outlets, is work which may be done by the piece, though it is doubtful whether there is any advantage in it. The work may be finished more quickly, from the men working longer hours, but there is the chance of its not being so thoroughly done, and if not, it will soon require doing over again. Under ordinary circumstances, a man can thoroughly clean up the water-table, trim the edges of the sod bordering, and open the outlets, of 6 to 10 chains of road per day. When there is little traffic, the work of cleaning the sides is heavier, and as little as 4½ chains of road is a fair day's work ; and in dry situations, or where a considerable traffic leaves less cleaning up to do, a man may get over 12 or 14 chains of road in a day.

Useful materials taken out of the water-tables can generally be disposed of on the road, or they may be laid aside for use with the fresh materials, and soil and dirt may be laid on the waste, or gathered in heaps for removal by farmers and others. Scrapings and dirt laid on the waste should be deposited quite away from the edge of the sod bordering, so that the latter may never be more than a few inches high. A steep slope of earth or scrapings, 9 inches or 1 foot high, is always mouldering away into the water-tables, and causing extra labour for clearing them.

All side-ditches, back-ditches, and drains, require to be cleared out periodically, and the best time to do it is in the spring and summer, the drier ones while the soil is moist and easy to move, and the wetter ones afterwards in the dry weather. Some ditches require to be opened every year, others far less frequently ; but they should always be kept clear. There are few things that show a neglected or badly managed road more than water standing in the side ditches or drains, and soaking up under the road. Whenever it is possible, the water level should be kept 1 foot at least, or even 2 or 3 feet, below the road, and to ensure this, the cost of additional drains or culverts would be often well incurred.

Covered drains require examination from time to time, and all blind drains, composed of loose stones, have to be renewed as they become choked up. Drains along the side of a road benched into a hill, to cut off the land water, should always be kept in good working order, and improved if the road seems to need it.

A surveyor has, under the General Highway Act, considerable powers with respect to the drainage of his roads. He has power to "make, scour, cleanse, and keep open, all ditches, gutters, drains, or water-courses, and also to make and lay such trunks, tunnels, plats, or bridges, as he shall deem necessary, in and through any lands, or grounds, adjoining or lying near to any highway, upon paying the owner or occupier of such grounds, provided they are not waste or common, for the damages he may sustain thereby, to be settled and paid in such manner as the damages for getting materials in inclosed lands or grounds are to be settled and paid," * and the owner or occupier may not alter, obstruct, or interfere with such ditches, &c., without the consent of the surveyor.

Whatever duty exists on the part of owners of lands adjoining highways to cleanse and scour ditches appears to extend only to the prevention of nuisance, or obstruction to passengers, and not to the drainage of the road.

Farmers are often willing to clear out the side-ditches for the sake of the soil obtained from them, and are apt to deepen them unduly where stuff fit for their purpose can be got, and neglect them in other places. It is better, therefore, that the work, if not done by the road labourers, should be done under their direction, so that the ditches may be regularly opened throughout, and when they require it.

On hills, side-ditches sometimes scour deeper and deeper till they become dangerous. This can be prevented by small weirs of fascines and stones, made by the roadmen at a nominal cost.

The effects of hedges and trees, especially on the south side, in keeping roads wet, and the injury thus caused, particularly on a clayey or imperfectly drained subsoil, have been already mentioned. The General Highway Act † provides that, if the surveyor shall think that a road is prejudiced by hedges or

---

* 5 & 6 Will. IV. cap. 50, sect. 67.      † Ibid., sect. 63.

trees, he may summon the owner to appear before the justices at a special sessions for the highways, and if they shall order the hedges and trees to be pruned and lopped, the owner shall do so within ten days, under a penalty, and the surveyor, in case of default, may do the same at the owner's expense. The term owner is made to include the occupier by the interpretation clause.

No person is compelled to cut or prune hedges at any other time than between the last day of September and the last day of March, and trees planted for ornament or shelter are excepted.

These provisions should be enforced, but with discretion and tact on the part of the surveyor, as there are few parts of his duties more liable to bring him into collision with owners and occupiers of land.

### Watering.

For the sake of the road itself, a road, except one of a silicious nature, seldom requires watering in this country. In very dry weather judicious watering binds the surface of a gravel or flint road, and lessens wear, but on other materials, even when done sparingly, it softens the road and increases the wear. In and near towns watering is necessarily practised for the comfort of the inhabitants, but it should be done in moderation, sufficiently to lay the dust without softening the road. The amount of watering required may generally be considerably reduced by preventing the accumulation of dust, by sweeping either combined with slight watering, or early in the morning while the dust is laid by the dew. By far the greater part of the nuisance from dust may be avoided by removing the mud. It is too often the practice to leave the mud on the road, and, when it dries to dust, to reconvert it into mud by copious watering. Watering is sometimes useful when mud is sticky, to prevent the tearing up of the surface by the wheels, and it may sometimes be advantageously combined with scraping or sweeping. The mud, when rendered soft and almost liquid by watering, is more easily removed, and grit of a useful size is left behind on the road.

Mr. Santo Crimp states * that a fall of ·04 inch of rain will lay the dust on a well-kept macadamised road, and also effect a very slight washing, and that that amount, or about one-fifth of a gallon per square yard is the usual quantity of water which he spread at one watering at Wimbledon, where the roads were watered on 132 days in a year. In the metropolis it is usual to allow for 130 days watering, and the records of rainfall at various places show that from 120 to 130 is generally the number of days on which less than ·04 inch of rain is registered in the six summer months in this country, the days on which no rain is registered being about 100. The total annual rainfall has some influence, but the number of days on which less than ·04 inch is registered appears to vary much less than the total rainfall.

Ordinary water-carts contain between 220 and 300 gallons, and deliver about half a gallon to the square yard of road, spreading it over a width of 12 to 16 feet. When watering is performed by contract, much more than this quantity is often delivered. Deluging the road prevents the necessity of frequent watering, and the sooner the cart is emptied the better for the contractor. The holes of the distributor have been found enlarged for a quicker discharge of water, and a thick cast-iron distributor has been used to prevent it.

According to a report of the town surveyor of Derby,† a superficial area of 23,849 yards can be watered by carts twice a day, being for a width of 4 yards, 5962 yards lineal, or for a double width, 2981 yards lineal, at a cost of—

|  | s. | d. |
|---|---|---|
| Horse, cart, and man .. .. .. .. .. .. .. .. | 8 | 0 |
| Maintenance of carts, harness, shoeing, &c. .. .. .. | 1 | 5 |
| Total .. .. .. .. | 9 | 5 per day. |

This is exclusive of the cost of the water. In Paris the total cost of watering with rather more than half a gallon to a square yard of macadamised road is said to be about $\frac{1}{8}d$. per square yard.

---

* Proc. Municipal and Sanitary Engineers, vol. xii. p. 235.

† A Report, &c., by E. B. Ellice-Clark, 1876, p. 25.

The old-fashioned water-carts on two wheels are now generally superseded by Bayley's patent hydrostatic vans, consisting of a wrought iron tank holding 450 gallons, mounted on springs and carried on four wheels, and drawn by one horse. They are no wider than an ordinary water-cart, but in consequence of improvements in the branch and distributing pipes they water a track 20 to 23 feet wide much more uniformly than a cart, and the outflow of water can be regulated by a valve. A great saving is effected by their use, as, in consequence of their holding a much larger quantity of water, less time is taken up in going backwards and forwards to refill. It is stated * that experiment has shown that a van will water an area of 161,000 square yards per day. The saving in London parishes by the use of the vans has been estimated at from 20 to 50 per cent. The first cost of a van is 60l., compared with 25l. for an ordinary water-cart.

In a trial in Regent Street a van holding 450 gallons of water spread it 23 feet wide over 6746 square yards, being at the rate of a gallon to 15 square yards; while a cart holding between 250 and 300 gallons of water spread it 16 feet wide over 2560 square yards, being at the rate of a gallon to 10 square yards. In each case the quantity of water delivered per square yard of surface was far less than is usual.

In Mr. Santo Crimp's experience a van holding 450 gallons waters a length of 480 yards of an average width of 5 yards, or 2400 square yards at the rate of ·192 gallon per square yard, and Mr. Ellice-Clark gives the length as 462 yards of an average breadth of 17 feet 9 inches, or 2733 square yards at the rate of ·165 gallon per square yard. The cost is stated by Mr. Crimp to be 1·92d. per 1000 square yards for water at 10d. per 1000 gallons, and 1·37d. per 1000 square yards for watering, together 3·29d. per 1000 square yards.

Willacy's watering machine is fitted with horizontal rotating spreaders actuated by the wheels. As the cart proceeds the spreaders revolve and throw the water to a width, it is said, of 33 feet. The machine is well spoken of.

Street watering is sometimes effected by a movable hose and

* Report by the Surveyor of the Parish of St. Marylebone.

jet, or by light iron pipes jointed together and carried on small trucks, in connection with the hydrants, and the system of Messrs. Brown and Co., by which the water issues in small jets from perforated pipes laid along the kerbs of the footway, has been tried in the City and elsewhere, but has not been much used.

In sea-side towns sea-water is used, the effect of which is to keep the surface moist, so that less than half the quantity of water is required to keep the dust effectually laid. A skin also forms on the surface which tends to bind silicious roads together. The only objection to the use of sea-water appears to be the injury that may be done to ladies' dresses, or coloured fabrics exposed for sale by excessive or careless watering.

A patent has been taken out by Mr. W. J. Cooper for mixing chlorides of calcium and sodium with the water for street watering, in the proportion of $\frac{1}{2}$ lb. or 1 lb. to a gallon of water. It is said that the surface of the road is not only kept moist by the deliquescent salts, but that they have an effect of concreting and hardening the surface of a macadamised road, so that little dust arises from it when dry. It has been found in Paris that the use of these chlorides produces a very good effect for the first twenty-four hours, after which slight additional waterings are required, and the process must be recommenced after the fourth day. Instead of moistening and refreshing the air as common watering does, the employment of deliquescent salts robs the air of the humidity which it contains.

### Repairs beyond Ordinary Maintenance.

On a bad road the ordinary processes of maintenance have to be applied to something beyond keeping up the condition of a road already in a good state. The first thing to do is to examine the road and find out the cause of its badness, and ascertain, by pitting or sounding, its composition and thickness. If the coating is thin and so mixed up with the subsoil as to have lost all consistence, it may be necessary to form a new coating on it of sufficient thickness to stand without being cut through and mixed up with the old surface; and it may be necessary to lay on a thickness of more than one stone at once. In many cases continual scraping combined with small patches of new materials to give form to the road is enough, there being sufficient thickness and plenty of stone, but, from neglect, too much mud. It may take several years to form a solid compact coating, and as the scraping reduces the thickness, large stones may have to be taken up, but the rest of the surface should not be disturbed if it can be avoided. The treatment which a bad road may require may range from ordinary maintenance to the reforming described in Chapter II. One thing, the drainage, will always be an important matter to attend to in any attempt to improve the condition of a road.

Besides the ordinary wear from the traffic and weather, there are damages which arise from unusual or accidental causes, which must be dealt with specially according to circumstances.

When a road has been broken up by frost and thaw, the best remedy is to consolidate it again by rolling. If this is impossible, it should be left to the traffic to consolidate it, with raking and attention on the part of the roadman. Spreading fresh stones on a surface already disintegrated only adds to the quantity of loose materials, and is rarely right, though patches may be useful here and there.

Holes are sometimes broken in the crust of a thin, worn road, under unfavourable circumstances of traffic and weather, and the subsoil works up and mixes with the road-coating, forming what is sometimes locally called a "mustard-pot," into which a horse's foot will plunge to a considerable depth. The cause is always water in the subsoil, sometimes from springs, and though drainage is the general remedy, coupled, on a bad bottom, with an increase in the thickness of the road-coating, the mode of promptly repairing these dangerous holes must depend upon the nature of the subsoil. If it be muddy or boggy, putting down broken stones is useless, as it soon works into the soft bottom. The whole, or a considerable thickness of the latter, must be dug out, and large stones, flat if possible, must be laid as a foundation for 4 or 5 inches of road materials. On a sandy bottom broken stone alone may often succeed. In any case the water must be tapped and led away by a drain.

The passage of exceptionally heavy loads, such as a traction engine and its trucks, sometimes breaks through the crust of a weak road, and makes a succession of holes of this sort, at points where the coating is thin or the subsoil soft. Repeated passages may form a pair of continuous tracks, 2 or 3 feet wide, in which the road coating is entirely destroyed and mixed up with the subsoil. It is useless to attempt repairs by adding more materials on the surface, as they are swallowed up and wasted. Everything, down to a firm bottom, must be dug out and removed, and the space must be filled in with stone, which may be of large size at the bottom. The drainage should always be looked to, and improved if it requires it. The stuff dug out of the road may be raked over when dry, to separate the useful metalling from the clay. Such repairs have sometimes certainly cost between 100*l.* and 200*l.* per mile, and it has been stated that in some cases the cost has been at the rate of as much as 500*l.* per mile.

The expenses incurred in repairing a road damaged by excessive weight or extraordinary traffic can be recovered by the road authority. By section 23 of the Highways and Locomotives (Amendment) Act, 1878,* " where by a certificate of their surveyor it appears to the authority which is liable or has undertaken to repair any highway, whether a main road or not, that, having regard to the average expense of repairing highways in the neighbourhood, extraordinary expenses have been incurred by such authority in repairing such highway by reason of the damage caused by excessive weight passing along the same, or extraordinary traffic thereon, such authority may recover in a summary manner from any person by whose order such weight or traffic has been conducted the amount of such expenses as may be proved to the satisfaction of the court having cognisance of the case to have been incurred by such authority by reason of the damage arising from such weight or traffic as aforesaid : provided that any person against whom expenses are or may be recoverable under this section may enter into an agreement with such authority as is mentioned in this section for the payment to them of a composition in

* 41 & 24 Vict cap. 77.

respect of such weight or traffic, and thereupon the persons so paying the same shall not be subject to any proceedings under this section."

The Act thus recognises the principle that those who damage roads by bringing upon them weights which they are not fitted to carry should bear the cost of the repairs, and if this could be enforced in practice, it would be a far better protection to the roads than bylaws regulating the width of the tires of the wheels.

Holes or trenches dug to get at or lay gas or water mains, and carelessly filled in, in wet weather sometimes cause troublesome places in a road. Properly ramming the stuff refilled in the hole or trench, and putting on a sufficient thickness of metalling at first, so that the wheels shall not cut through and mix it with the subsoil, will prevent this, and it is better not to raise the filling-in too much at first above the road surface.

In descending a hill, heavily loaded waggons, or timber carriages, are apt to keep one wheel in the water-table by way of a drag, often either breaking down the road-coating or bending it into a series of undulations. Fresh materials will not remain in the hollows thus formed so long as the heavy traffic continues, and it is of no use to lay them. Afterwards the sides must be levelled with a pick and coated.

Bridges, culverts, and drains, especially where they are exposed to the action of quickly running water, require watching by the roadmen, and examination from time to time by the surveyor. The scouring away of the bed of the stream and the undermining of foundations are the most frequent causes of damage where bridges or culverts have been built without an invert. The lower ends of culverts are particularly liable to be undermined. An invert, or a pitched apron with timber sills, is often required to protect foundations thus exposed, but a good deal may be done to prevent damage by checking the scour by weirs at the lower end, or by other suitable means. Obstructions generally occur at the upper ends of culverts, and they should be removed at once. A stoppage in heavy rain will be the cause of great damage from scouring the surface of the road, and in hilly countries the road itself may be washed away. In fine weather slight repairs can be done at a nominal cost which will prevent damage to the extent of many pounds in a storm.

## Obstructions from Snow, &c.

If any impediment or obstruction shall arise on a highway from accumulation of snow, or from falling down of the banks on the side, or from other cause, the surveyor is required,* from time to time, and within twenty-four hours after notice thereof from a justice of the peace, to cause the impediment or obstruction to be removed. Clearing away snow is on some roads almost an annual expense, and on some exposed places it is sometimes worth while to keep a snow-plough ready for use. This consists of two planks shod with iron and fastened together in a V, which can be drawn by a horse, point first, through the snow, clearing a track wide enough for a vehicle to pass along. A useful size is made of two 9-inch planks about 8 feet long spreading to a width of 8 feet, and joined by a platform which can be loaded with stones. Snow-ploughs can easily be improvised for use on an emergency. They are useless in heavy drifts, which must be cut through by men.

## Narrowing an Over-wide Road.

Considerable economy can often be effected in the cost of maintaining a road by narrowing it to suit the requirements of the traffic where it has fallen off. It is sometimes difficult to induce roadmen, and even surveyors, to give up excessive width in a fine broad road from which the greater part of the traffic has been diverted by railways. It is sometimes said that the traffic is the measure of the wear of the road, and that the result is the same whether it be distributed over a wide or a narrow road. But except in crowded thoroughfares, where the vehicles are obliged to use the whole width of the road, this is far from being the case. The traffic has a strong tendency to keep to one track, and the rest of the road, although it may be

* 5 & 6 Will. IV. cap. 50, sect. 26.

little worn by the passage of vehicles, is subjected to all the action of the weather, and requires almost as much labour for scraping, &c., as the part used by the traffic. The grassing over of the sides is a sure indication that the metalled surface is wider than necessary, and affords a means of judging to what extent it can be narrowed.

The new width should be regularly defined by a turf bordering, which will not prevent the passage of wheels over it on an emergency. Block stones may be used to protect the edges of the turf, but they should not project beyond the sod to form dangerous obstructions. Some attention to the new water-table will perhaps be required, and it is often best to leave the former water-table as a back drain, and connect the new one with it at frequent intervals by outlets through the turf bordering.

The result of narrowing the metalled surface is often not only a reduction in cost of maintenance, but an improvement in appearance, as a road too wide is generally irregular and dirty.

# CHAPTER X

## Manual Labour.

THE constant attention which a road requires to keep it in
good order is best secured by putting a labourer in charge of a
certain length. Road maintenance has been said to be an
incessant contest of a man aided by a few yards of broken
stone, and a few simple tools, against the constant action of
the traffic and the weather, and it is certain that in nothing is
the maxim, that "a stitch in time saves nine," more applicable.

In 1819 working foremen were placed in charge of lengths
of from four to six miles of the Holyhead road between
Shrewsbury and Bangor, having under them a sufficient
number of labourers to keep the road in proper repair.
Telford says :*—" A certain number of labourers ought always
to have the care of the surface of the road and never quit it
for a single day to do anything else ; they will always have
sufficient to do in spreading fresh materials in ruts and hollows,
in scraping the road, in cleaning out the side channels and
keeping open the water-courses, and generally in maintaining
the road in a clean and sound state. A few men constantly so
employed will do a great deal towards the preservation of a
road, while the greater number of workmen should be as
constantly employed in providing materials by contract work."

The duties of a constant road labourer could hardly be more
succinctly described.

The "General Rules for Repairing Roads," issued at the
same time by the Parliamentary Commissioners, to the turnpike
trustees on the Holyhead road between London and Shrews-

* Report on Holyhead Road, 1823.

K

bury, contain no such recommendation; but, on the contrary,
the discontinuance of all labour by day wages as much as
possible is insisted upon as essential. This was probably with
a view to getting rid of the old paupers then employed on the
roads, whose work was no doubt almost useless, and in the end
wasteful, but as these rules were published, and looked upon as
setting forth the proper principles of road maintenance, the
result appears to have been that the employment of men in
charge of a certain length of road did not become general,
though the constant attention given to the roads under both
Telford and McAdam was one important cause of their improvement.

In 1833* labourers called milemen had been for several
years in charge of one mile of road each, on the Windsor and
Bagshot roads, under Sir J. McAdam. They had assistant
labourers when required, and it was considered that two men,
working under a practical and skilful mileman, were equal to
three men working independently. Rewards were given every
year to deserving milemen, and a good deal of emulation was
produced among them, and it was found that a less quantity
of materials was consumed. The Committee of the House of
Lords before whom this was given in evidence reported that
"the measure of employing permanent milemen, with occa-
sional assistant labourers on the roads, has combined such
indisputable advantages that we do not hesitate to recommend
its more general adoption." This recommendation appears
not to have been much attended to, for in 1841 the successful
organisation of such a system in this country was claimed as a
novelty by Mr. Chaloner,† who appears to have become
acquainted with it in France, where "cantonniers" had long
been in charge of lengths of road.

At present in France each cantonnier has a portion of road
called a canton under his charge, and about six cantons compose
a brigade under a chief cantonnier who has a shorter length than
the others, and is expected to pass over his brigade once a week
at least. The men wear a distinctive dress, and they mark their

* Sir J. McAdam's evidence, Select Committee on Turnpike Trusts, 1833.
† Journal of Royal Agricultural Society, vol. ii. p. 353.

place of work by setting up a measuring rod surmounted with a mark showing the number of the canton. They keep a sheet on which they enter the work done by themselves and their auxiliaries, and a book wherein notes and orders are entered. A code of rules prescribes the conditions of service, the hours of work, and in some detail the manner in which work is to be done, and discipline is enforced by fines and rewards. A translation of these rules, which are for the most part applicable in this country, is given in Appendix I.

In 1845, when the system on which the county roads of South Wales were managed was organised by the late Sir H. D. Harness, R.E., constant labourers were put in charge of various lengths over the whole of the roads. The experience of forty-three years on roads of all sorts, from the streets of seaport and manufacturing towns to mountain roads, has fully proved the advantages of the plan. Skilful, practical, and industrious road labourers have been obtained, who take a pride in their road, and are capable of directing to the best advantage the labourers they have to assist them.

The constant labourer has entire charge, under the surveyor, of his portion of road, and is responsible for the work performed by the assistant or casual labourers employed under him. He also sees that the instructions given by the surveyor to contractors and others are properly carried out. It should be his constant care to prevent the formation of holes, ruts, or hollows in the surface, and thus prevent or lessen the wear from the traffic or the weather; and this forms quite as important a part of his duties as the application of fresh materials for repairs. He should be on his road all day, wet or dry, and no excuse should be allowed for absence. During rain it is particularly necessary that he should be on his road. He can then see where the water-tables need clearing out or lowering, where the outlets to the ditches require opening, or where a culvert or drain is choked; and a little attention on a wet day will often prevent much damage, and save much after labour and expense. Wet weather is often the most favourable time for scraping, and the unevenness of the surface is then also most apparent, and shows where patches of materials are required.

In storms of heavy rain the roadman should go at once to
any point likely to suffer from breaking out of water, but,
except in cases of emergency, he should go regularly through
his beat, giving to each part the time it needs.  Much time is
wasted in running from one point to another, and the road is
unequally attended to.  A good roadman soon becomes familiar
with the length under his charge, and knows what part will
require his attention under the various conditions of the weather,
and the best way of dealing with it, and he will keep his
road in a superior condition with far less materials and labour
than a less experienced man.  Without very good reason, a
man should not be moved from the road under his charge to a
fresh length.  When a man by his skill and attention has
brought his length to good condition, it is discouraging to him
and to other good men to move him, even should it appear to
be for the benefit of another length.

Considerable intelligence and aptitude, as well as the supervision of a surveyor who understands his work, are required to
make a good roadman.  Some men, however industrious and
well-trained, never become good roadmen, and the surveyor
should be allowed a good deal of liberty in his selection of
proper men, and in determining their wages.  It must be fully
recognised that the surveyor can be but seldom at hand to give
orders, and that much must be left to the initiative of the
roadman, who must day by day accommodate his work to the
weather, and to get and keep good men proper wages must be
paid.  The false economy of paying low wages to unskilled men
is evident.  A shilling a week in wages represents the value of
from 5 to 8 cube yards of materials, and it is certain that a good
roadman will save much more material than that out of the
200 or 300 cubic yards he may use on his length, which would
be absolutely wasted by an incompetent man.

The division of roads into lengths, each under one man's
charge, makes it easy to compare one man's work with another's,
and to excite emulation among them.  In some of the counties
of South Wales a sum of money was distributed annually as
premiums among the most deserving constant labourers, and
was found to be of value as an encouragement.  In other
counties it was found to provoke jealousy, and was either

abandoned or every constant labourer had his share, unless
there was special reason to the contrary. The general good
condition in which the road is kept, economy in use of materials
and casual labour, regularity and punctuality, should all be
taken into account in allotting the premiums.

The constant labourers should be required to keep books in
which to enter an account of how they occupy their time, and
the time of the casual labourers employed to assist them. The
pages may contain columns headed with different descriptions
of work, such as scraping, laying stones, raking, cleaning sides,
and other work, so that the labourer need enter only the time,
in days or parts of a day, under the proper heading. These
accounts are very useful as a check of the men's work, and as a
means of comparing constant labourers one with another; but
they should not lead the surveyor to slacken his personal
attention to the men. The form of a constant labourer's journal
is given in Appendix II.

The employment of constant labourers by contract or piece-
work in cleaning the sides, scraping, and spreading stone, is not
advisable. The interest of a constant labourer should be the
good of his road, and while a good man will work as well by
day-work as if he were on piece-work, another may be tempted
for his own interest to get over his piece-work in a superficial
manner, leaving it to be more thoroughly done when he is on
day-work. Such work as cleaning the side channels or water-
tables, and opening outlets, if not thoroughly done, soon requires
to be done again, from the growth of grass and weeds in the dirt
left behind. Any task work is best done by casual labourers
working under the eye of the roadman in charge of the length,
but even then spreading stones by the cube yard is very likely
to lead to a waste of materials, and entail more after-attention.

Working foremen are sometimes employed under a surveyor
to superintend the labour on the roads. A foreman should be a
skilful workman, able to show to others, tool in hand, how work
should be done. He may have a short length under his own
charge, but not too much to prevent his passing frequently over
the other lengths which he is to superintend. He should keep
a journal, and note in it what he does himself, and what he finds
the other men doing when he visits them. The drawback to

the employment of working foremen is that it lessens the
responsibility of the labourers in charge of lengths of roads,
and when they are well-trained and trustworthy men, any
other superintendence than that of a good surveyor is seldom
required.

The tools used by a roadman are, a wheel-barrow, spade,
shovel, mattock, pick, rake, scraper, stone hammers, and a reel
and line. Near towns brooms are required. It is usual for the
labourers to provide their own tools; but this has been sometimes found to lead to the use of inferior tools, and a waste of
labour. The men may with advantage be required to keep
their tools in repair, having an allowance for the purpose.
Blacksmith's bills for repairs of tools cannot be checked by the
surveyor, and are often considerable. The machine scrapers
are always provided for the men, and there should be a machine
in charge of the constant labourer on every length of road.
Wheelbarrows are sometimes provided likewise.

The tools of the country are usually employed rather than
the special tools for road work figured in the "General Rules
for Repairing Roads" issued in 1819, and copied up to this
time in treatises on road-making. It is, in fact, difficult to get
men to use tools they are not accustomed to. The pronged
shovel for laying stones is never used; it would leave behind a
good deal of useful material when the stone is broken to a
small gauge. The road level is not used in road maintenance;
and for forming and testing the cross section of roads, ordinary
levelling and "boning," supplemented by the eye of the workman, are generally found more convenient. The road level
resembles in general form the ordinary bricklayer's level, consisting of a straight-edge long enough to reach from the middle
to the side of a road, having an upright in the centre supported
by braces and carrying a plumb-bob by which the straight-edge is
set level. Gauges attached to the latter can be adjusted to
any offset from the lower edge to give the profile of the road.

With moderate traffic, such as on main roads in the country,
the length which can be most advantageously placed under the
charge of one man is that on which, when the materials are
supplied ready broken, the roadman's time will be fully utilised

all the year round, and which he can keep in good order with help from casual labourers during two or three months in the autumn and winter. This length will depend on many local circumstances, such as the traffic, breadth, situation, and materials of the road. Through a town or village the labour is much greater than in the open country, and on a hilly road the care of the water-tables, outlets, and side-ditches, to prevent water scouring the surface, may require, perhaps, twice as much attention as the same length of moderately level road. Soft materials, a bad or undrained subsoil, or a situation sheltered by trees, entail much more labour. Whenever possible, the length should be such that the roadman can go over it all daily, and he should do so twice a week at least. On a long length this leads to waste of time, especially if the length be a portion of one road only, and not made up of several pieces of different roads lying near together.

The length which may be best allotted to a man may, from these causes, be from two or three miles up to seven or eight, and it will always be a matter for the surveyor's judgment whether to give short lengths of road or longer lengths with more assistance from casual labourers when the work requires it. The work which casual labourers have to do is little more than an ordinary country labourer can perform, but they require the direction of the constant labourer how and when to do it, and they often waste much of their time when not working with the roadman in charge. It is therefore seldom well to have too many casual labourers, and two or at most three are enough to work to advantage under the direction of one constant labourer.

On roads on which there is a good deal of work to be done, a constant labourer may require the help of another man throughout the year, as well as additional men in the autumn ; while on unimportant roads the roadman may break stones during the summer months, or he may be permitted to do work not connected with his road. In such cases, however, he should always be considered to be in charge of his length, and ready to give his attention to it in any emergency, such as a heavy storm.

In France, where much more labour is given to the roads than is usual in this country, it is found that a cantonnier can employ about 260 cube yards of materials per year, and remove the corresponding detritus.*

There is sometimes considerable difficulty in keeping down the amount of surface labour to what is absolutely necessary. The roadmen are necessarily a good deal without supervision, and they may waste their time, or neglect their work, if they are not trustworthy. Even with a good roadman the cost of labour may be unduly increased. The pride of a man in his road's appearance sometimes leads him to devote time to work which is superfluous or ornamental, and he may in good faith believe that he has too long a length of road, when in reality he could undertake more, without the road being in any essential the worse.

The great difficulty in arranging labour arises from the inequality of the work at different seasons of the year. In the summer months the surface of the road requires little beyond the general attention of the man in charge, who may employ most of his time in clearing out side-ditches which are too wet to be attended to except in dry weather, regulating the wastes, cutting weeds, and doing such repairs to culverts, drains, and other works on the road as may be necessary. He may break stone by contract or otherwise, or he may be permitted to work away from his road.

The autumn work on roads is generally commenced after harvest, as the additional men which are required are then more easily to be had. Cleaning up the sides cannot be well done in dry weather, but the constant labourer should take advantage of suitable moist weather to get forward with it, so that the water-tables may be cleared, the outlets to the side-ditches opened, and the sod bordering trimmed before the wet weather sets in. If the manual labour be allowed to get behindhand in the autumn, there is often little chance of roads recovering it until the winter is over. Scraping is very necessary as soon as rainy weather commences, to get rid of the mud which then forms on the surface from the effects of the

---

* Debauve, Manuel de l'Ingenieur des Ponts et Chaussées ; Routes ; p. 191.

wear in the summer. As soon as the cleaning up of the sides is finished, and the scraping is well forward, the laying of materials in small patches should begin. The first patches should be laid in places naturally damp, and when the road generally begins to soften from the wet weather, spreading materials and scraping will take up all the constant labourer's time, and usually require casual labour besides until the middle of December, or even later. In the beginning of the year, after the great bulk of materials has been spread, less labour is necessary: only small patches to make good weak places which have shown themselves during the winter remain to be laid, and scraping is hindered by frost, and by the unconsolidated materials about the road. As the spring advances more scraping will be required in damp weather, and in dry weather the stones which have not worked in will require the roadman's attention, and must be raked off if they will not set. The spring and early summer is the best season for cleaning out side-ditches which are not too wet. The stuff is moved easier when still moist, and it is well to get forward with work of this sort in the spring, and not to leave it till the autumn, when there is so much other work to be done.

### *Proportion of Expenditure on Materials and on Labour.*

The outlay on manual labour and the proportion which it should bear to that on materials are important points for consideration both in preparing estimates and in regulating expenditure on roads. A certain amount of labour expended on laying stones, and in attending to them afterwards, and on sufficient care of the surface and under drainage, will be compensated for in the end by the saving in materials, and is therefore necessary for economy. The convenience of the public also has to be considered as far as possible, but while what is absolutely required for the good of the road is not neglected, labour should not be wasted, nor be employed on useless or merely ornamental work. This is more particularly necessary when the funds are limited. Spending too much on labour for unnecessary or ornamental work, instead of on materials, is

often a great cause of weakness in roads, and a surveyor cannot
be too careful in keeping the amount of labour down to the
lowest point consistent with real economy.

Of the manual labour employed on roads, one portion consists of work connected with the materials used, such as
spreading stones, raking and attending to them while consolidating, and removing the mud to which they are ultimately
reduced. On a well-kept road the amount and cost of this labour
depend almost entirely on the wear, the quantity of materials,
and the care with which they are used. It takes more time to
spread stones in small patches, with the care necessary for their
proper and economical use, than to lay them in large quantities,
or without after-attention ; and, if the traffic is light, and the
material hard, more after-care is required than where the traffic
quickly works in the stone. The removal of mud will also cost
more as the scraping is more frequent.

Another portion of the labour comprises work which is, to
a great degree, independent of the wear and the quantity of
materials used, such as cleaning the water-tables, trimming the
sod bordering, opening outlets, clearing out side-ditches, and
attending generally to the drainage. These naturally vary a good
deal in amount and in proportion on roads differently situated,
though they may be nearly constant on the same road under
ordinary circumstances.

Dividing thus the cost of labour, it appeared that on county
roads in South Wales on which 60 or 70 cube yards of materials
were laid annually per mile, the average cost under the first
head was from about 1s. to 1s. 7d. per cube yard, and that under
the second head, from about 3l. 5s. to 4l. 10s. per mile per year.
The total cost of manual labour thus approximately divided was
from 7l. 4s. to 9l. 1s. per mile of road per year, or from 2s. to
to 2s. 10d. to a cubic yard of materials laid. These may be
taken as the general averages for districts containing 70 to 90
miles of country main roads, on which the men were employed
all the year at wages ranging from 15s. to 18s. a week, and had
the materials delivered on the roads by contract, ready broken.
In districts where the labourers were not employed on the roads
during the summer, or were preparing materials by contract,

the labour was sometimes as low as 5*l.* per mile per year, and in more populous districts it was as high as 15*l.* per mile per year. In and near towns, the additional expense of frequent scraping, sweeping, and removing mud, more than counterbalances the saving in the labour of spreading when materials are laid in large quantities, and the cost of labour per mile is far greater.

On the above roads, the cost of manual labour was generally from 30 to 40 per cent. of the combined cost of labour and materials, and sometimes a larger proportion when the state of the finances demanded retrenchment in the amount of materials. When a large quantity of materials is laid down the cost of labour is sometimes less in proportion.

On parish roads in a highway district where the roads were well kept on the same system under a good surveyor, the manual labour cost about 4*l.* or 5*l.* per mile per year, which provided sufficient labour for the economical use of materials, and for the care of the surface of the roads according to their relative importance, and the proportion spent upon manual labour was from 37 to 42 per cent. of the combined cost of materials and labour.

The returns of expenditure on turnpike roads and highways in England and Wales have not hitherto afforded trustworthy data from which either the actual or relative cost of manual labour and materials can be obtained. Other partial and scanty particulars appear to confirm the conclusion, to which observation leads, that the road surveyors of this country generally trust to quantity of materials rather than care in their employment.

On the national roads of France, M. Dupuit estimated the manual labour connected with a cube yard of material at, on an average, rather more than one day's work. Other authorities give from ¾ day to 1⅓ day per cube yard, and on the roads of the department of the Sarthe, under the system adopted by M. Dumas, which has been before alluded to, the labour on a cube yard of materials reached 5½ days' work.

In a circular issued in 1850, fixing the bases on which the estimates for the national roads of each department were to be framed, and which was probably founded on the averages of all

France, the labour relative to the employment of a cube yard
of material was given as 1·46 day's work, and the labour on
accessory work as 64 days per mile, making together, for a road
on which 60 cube yards of material per mile were used, a total
of 152 days' manual labour per mile, which, at 2s. 6d. per day,
would amount to 19l. per mile.

In 1860 it appears* that, on the departmental roads, the
maintenance of which cost on the average of the whole of France
28l. per mile, the proportion per cent. of the cost of labour was
44, of materials 42, and of accessory works 14 of the whole.
The labour per mile thus cost about 12l. 6s. when wages were
about 1s. 6d. per day, equal to 20l. 10s. per mile with wages
at 2s. 6d. a day, and a larger amount was spent on labour than
on materials.

From a report presented in 1879† it appears that in 1877 the
mean amount of the labour employed on a cube yard of
materials on the national roads was 1·17 days, ranging from
½ or ¾ days to as much as from 1¾ to 3 days in different departments. On maintaining the sides, ditches, slopes, &c., the mean
amount of labour was 62⅓ days per mile, ranging from 24 to
46½ days in some departments, to 85 and 137 days in others.
It is not evident to what these large differences, both in the
amount of labour connected with the material, and that on sides,
ditches, &c., are due. With reference to the latter it must be
observed that much more work is generally done on the sides of
the roads, which are often very wide, than is usual in this country.
Other particulars of the actual and relative cost of manual labour
will be given in the following chapter on the cost of road maintenance.

It is evident that very different results may follow according
to the manner in which a given sum is expended on the
maintenance of a road. Observation and local experience will
guide an intelligent surveyor in partitioning the expenditure
between materials and labour, but there are certain general
principles always applicable. The chief care should be to
replace the wear by a sufficient quantity of fresh materials, and

---

* Documents statistiques sur les Routes et Ponts, 1873.

† Annales des Ponts et Chaussées, 1879, vol. i., p. 316.

so preserve what may be called the "capital value" of the road. When the funds are sufficient the only difficulty in maintaining this capital value lies in estimating the amount of wear which has to be compensated for by fresh materials, and this is generally done by experienced surveyors by observation and comparison, without the elaborate process of measurement before described. Roads are, however, to be seen, with ample funds for their maintenance, and already quite strong enough, on which materials are laid year after year far more than sufficient to replace the wear, while the necessary labour is neglected. In such cases, while the thickness of the coating is increasing, the surface is often full of holes and muddy, or covered with unconsolidated materials and loose stones, and a better road might be obtained by employing more manual labour judiciously, and reducing the quantity of materials, in most instances with a saving in the total cost of maintenance.

It generally happens that a limited amount has to be expended which must be apportioned to the best advantage. As a general rule, the greater the traffic is, the larger should be the proportion of the expenditure devoted to materials. Where the traffic is heavy, the full quantity of materials should be laid, even if the amount of labour has to be reduced to pay for it. The stones can be laid in larger sheets, and they will work in quickly with less attention than under lighter traffic. If, however, the quantity of materials be unduly increased at the expense of the manual labour, the spreading will be done without the proper care, and the surface work will be neglected, so that, while the road is getting thicker and stronger, it will also get rough and out of shape. The consolidation of the materials becomes besides a serious inconvenience to the traffic when more stones than can be readily worked in are spread without an adequate amount of labour.

If, after the labour has been reduced as much as possible, the amount to be expended on materials is so small that the quantity will be insufficient to replace the wear, the road must of course get weaker, either by losing thickness or by containing a less proportion of solid stone. But if the labour remains enough for the care of the surface, the road may even improve in appearance while it is getting weaker, because there will be less materials to work in.  Under the usual traffic, and with judgment on the part of the surveyor, this state of things may go on for several years without danger, more particularly if the road was originally strong.  Thus take for instance a road on which the wear has been exactly replaced by 75 cube yards of materials to a mile.  As 300 cube yards will coat a mile of road 5 yards wide one stone in thickness, 75 cube yards will coat one quarter of this surface, giving about $\frac{3}{4}$ inch in thickness of consolidated road, which in the case supposed must represent the wear of four years, since the same part can only be coated once in four years, if the wear be supposed to be uniform over the whole surface ; $\frac{1}{4}$ of $\frac{3}{4}$ inch, or $\frac{3}{16}$ inch, will therefore be the annual wear of surface, which has been replaced by 75 cube yards of materials per mile in the case supposed, the composition of the road remaining the same, and thickness only being lost by wear.

Suppose now that necessity causes the materials to be reduced from 75 to 60 cube yards per mile : then only one-fifth of the surface, instead of one-fourth, can be covered each year, and it will be five years instead of four years, before some part is coated, and in that time it will have lost $5 \times \frac{3}{16}$ or $\frac{15}{16}$ inch of thickness, which will be replaced by $\frac{3}{4}$ inch of consolidated road ; $\frac{3}{16}$ inch of thickness, or one year's wear will thus be lost in five years, supposing all the detritus resulting from wear to be removed, and the composition of the road-coating to remain unaltered.  If scraping be not carried to this extent, the same amount of thickness will not be lost, but the road will contain more detritus.  In practice the wear will not be uniform over the whole surface, and the materials will be laid by a good roadman where the surface shows signs of weakness ; but it is evident that for several years there will be no appreciable deterioration in the road.  Nevertheless, it must not be lost sight of that the capital value of the road has been drawn upon to cover insufficient revenue, and if it be not replaced, the increased wear of materials which always takes place in a weak road will certainly begin to tell sooner or later, and a general break up under some extra traffic or unfavourable weather may happen when not expected.

# CHAPTER XI.

THE total cost of maintaining roads ranges between very wide limits. A road with little traffic, well drained, and exposed to the sun and air, with tolerably good materials at hand, can be kept in good order at a yearly cost of little more than a few pounds per mile for labour ; and a suburban road, or macadamised street, may cost many hundred pounds per mile per year. Unless the quantity of materials used, their price, and other particulars be taken into account, the cost per mile at which a road is maintained affords little real information, and may be misleading.

The following particulars of the cost of maintaining macadamised roads are given with such details as are obtainable.

In 1856 it was stated* that the yearly maintenance of the road over Westminster Bridge cost at the rate of 3300l. per mile per year, the average wear of granite being 5¼ inches. Regent Street is stated to have cost at the rate of from 3400l. to 3600l. per mile per year, and the City Road 2300l. per mile, with an average wear of rather less than 3 inches of granite per year. The wear, however, was probably not measured, and what is given as such is most likely the thickness of the materials laid down.

The cost of maintaining the macadamised roadway of Parliament Street was, for 1877, 2s. 9¾d. per square yard, and for 1878, 3s. 1d. ; Whitehall cost 2s. 10d. per square yard in 1877, and 3s. 2½d. in 1878. The average cost of maintaining King's Road, Chelsea, and Sloane Street, was stated to be at the same time 2s. 11d. per square yard per year, and in one portion which

* Select Committee on Metropolis Roads ; Mr. Browse's evidence.

is narrow as much as 6s.   On the Chelsea Embankment, where the macadamised roadway is laid on a concrete foundation, 12 inches thick, the cost was said to be 1s. 4d. per square yard per year.* The cost of the macadamised roadway in Park Lane and Knightsbridge is given as 3s. 6d., and Grosvenor Place and Buckingham Palace Road as 3s. per square yard.† In these cases Guernsey granite, at 16s to 18s. per cube yard, was the material used, and the cost of maintenance was exceptionally great.

In a recent report by Mr. Santo Crimp the annual cost of the maintenance of the Victoria Embankment is stated to be :—

|  | Pence per sq. yd. |
|---|---|
| Granite .. .. .. .. .. .. .. .. .. .. .. | 9·00 |
| Picking up, rolling, &c. .. .. .. .. .. .. .. | 4·40 |
| Cleansing, and removing slop .. .. .. .. .. .. | 9·43 |
| Watering 1·00, Water 0·62 .. .. .. .. .. .. | 1·62 |
| Sanding .. .. .. .. .. .. .. .. .. .. | 0·55 |
|  | 25·00 |

or 2s. 1d. per square yard, and the annual cost of seven other macadamised streets is given as from 1s. 8¼d. to 2s. 6¼d. per square yard.

The cost of the macadamised surface of 13 of the Brighton streets, including some of the principal thoroughfares, was ascertained by Mr. Lockwood to be, in 1887, per square yard :—

|  | d. | d. |  |  | d. |
|---|---|---|---|---|---|
| Repairs .. .. | 0·69 to | 13·42 | .. | average | 7·11 |
| Scavenging .. | 2·78 ,, | 9·88 | .. | ,, | 5·23 |
|  |  |  |  |  | 12·34 |
| Watering .. .. | 0·57 ,, | 2·03 |  | ,, | 1·11 |
|  |  |  |  |  | 13 48 |

The total cost of repairs, scavenging, and watering ranged from 7·27d. to 24·07 per square yard in different streets.

The 11 miles 5 furlongs of the Metropolis Roads, north of the Thames, on the London side of the toll-gates, in 1856 cost at

* Stayton.  Proc. Inst. Civil Engineers, vol. lviii. p. 74.
† Ellice-Clark    ,,          ,,          ,,      p. 92.

the rate of 1350*l.* per mile per annum; the 53 miles within the limits of the Metropolis Local Management Act (including the above 11 miles 5 furlongs) cost at the rate of 761*l.* per mile per year; and the 68 miles beyond the same limits cost 268*l.* per mile per year, exclusive of management, establishment charges, and toll-house repairs.

It appears, from the annual reports of the commissioners, that the ordinary maintenance of the Metropolis roads north of the Thames, including water and watering roads, salaries, and establishment charges, was from 490*l.* to 620*l.* per mile previous to the abandonment of the roads within the district of the Metropolis Local Management Act, in 1864, when from 470 to 580 cube yards per mile, principally of granite and hard stone, were used annually. Afterwards the annual cost for the remaining roads was 373*l.* to 408*l.* per mile, when from 380 to 470 cube yards of granite, hard stone, gravel, and flints per mile were used.

The following are the details of the ordinary expenditure per mile of road in the last year, which included the maintenance of the roads within the Metropolis Local Management Act district, and in the last year in which the roads outside that district remained under the charge of the commissioners.

COST OF MAINTENANCE OF METROPOLIS ROADS PER MILE.

| | 1863–4. | | 1871. | |
|---|---|---|---|---|
| | £ | s. | £ | s. |
| Day labour, including men at the pumps during the watering season | 93 | 3 | 71 | 13 |
| Digging gravel, and preparing materials by contract | | | | |
| Team labour, including watering | 133 | 6 | 65 | 8 |
| Materials, including freightage, wharfage, &c. | 274 | 2 | 177 | 9 |
| Tradesmen's bills | 16 | 4 | 12 | 15 |
| Rents of wharves and depots, taxes, water, lighting gates, drain-pipes, and incidentals | 25 | 8 | 14 | 3 |
| Establishment, salaries, printing, stationery, advertising, office expenses, &c. | 32 | 12 | 31 | 3 |
| Total per mile | £574 | 16 | £372 | 11 |

L.

TURNPIKE ROADS IN THE COUNTY OF EDINBURGH.—COST OF MAINTENANCE PER MILE, 1877.

| District. | Quarrying, Breaking, and Carting Stones. | Day Labour: Spreading Stones, Scraping and Cleaning Sides, Drains, and Ditches. | Carting, Scrapings, Repairs, of Bridges, &c., Footpaths, Tools, Rents, Cutting Snow, Incidentals. | Total Repairs. | Improvements. | Salaries and Management. | Total. | Cube Yards per Mile. | Labour: Spreading, Scraping, Ditches, &c. Per Cube Yard. |
|---|---|---|---|---|---|---|---|---|---|
| | £ s. | £ s. | £ s. | £ s. | £ s. | £ s. | £ s. | | s. d. |
| Lasswade and Wrights-houses, 186½ miles | 13 14 | 6 11 | 2 7 | 22 12 | 1 19 | 2 13 | 27 4 | 39 | 3 4¾ |
| Dalkeith and Post Road, 85¾ miles | 29 12 | 14 2 | 5 3 | 48 17 | 9 16 | 7 7 | 66 0 | 100 | 2 9¾ |
| Cramond, 29½ miles | 42 6 | 17 2 | 5 10 | 64 18 | 33 12 | 13 3 | 111 13 | 170 | 2 0 |
| Calder, Slateford, and Corstorphine, 139 miles | 16 17 | 9 15 | 1 15 | 28 7 | 1 7 | 3 12 | 33 6 | 76 | 2 6¾ |

In the former year, 1863–4, an average of 550 cube yards of materials per mile was used; and in the latter year, 1871, an average of 413 cube yards per mile, the total quantity consisting of 17,195 cube yards of granite and hard stone, 3781 cube yards of flints, and 6699 cube yards of gravel.

The labour per cube yard of materials laid amounted in different years to from 1s. 7d. to 3s., including men employed in pumping during the watering season, but not including those digging gravel and preparing materials.

The cost of maintenance of the macadamised national roads of the department of the Seine may be given here for comparison. In 1876 it was, for :—

|  | £ | s. |  |
|---|---|---|---|
| Materials .. .. .. .. .. .. | 167 | 14 | per mile. |
| Manual labour.. .. .. .. .. | 134 | 19 | ,, |
|  | 302 | 13 | ,, |

The quantity of materials used was 390 cube yards per mile. Wages were 2s. 11d. a day, and manual labour cost on the average 7s. to a cube yard of material, and 2¼ days' labour was spent on the maintenance of the surface of the road for each cube yard of material used.

The annual reports on the state of the turnpike roads in the county of Edinburgh afforded information of the cost of maintenance in considerable detail. The opposite statement of the cost per mile under different heads of expenditure has been prepared from the report for 1877, and may be taken as a fair average of the annual expenditure.

In each district the roads extended from Edinburgh to the boundaries of the county, so that the costs per mile are the averages of rates varying widely with the traffic and the situation of the roads.

The wages were about 18s. per week, and the materials cost from 4s. 5d. to 7s. 1d. per cube yard on the average. Manual labour cost from 30 to 36 per cent. of the combined cost of materials and labour.

The published abstracts of the expenditure by turnpike trusts do not give the lengths of the roads, but, deducing the total mean length of turnpike roads in England and North

Wales from the figures given in the Seventh Report of the Local
Government Board,* the following statement of the average
cost per mile in 1874 and in 1875 under the different heads in
the abstracts is arrived at.

TURNPIKE ROADS OF ENGLAND AND NORTH WALES.—AVERAGE COST PER
MILE, 1874 AND 1875.

|  | 1874. | 1875. |
|---|---|---|
|  | £ s. | £ s. |
| Materials, team labour, statute duty .. .. .. .. | 10 12 | 10 11 |
| Manual labour .. .. .. .. .. .. .. .. .. | 13 11 | 12 18 |
| Tradesmen's bills, incidental expenses .. .. .. .. | 2 15 | 2 12 |
| Improvements and land .. .. .. .. .. .. .. | 0 14 | 0 15 |
| Repairs .. .. .. .. .. .. .. .. .. | 27 12 | 26 16 |
| Salaries and law .. .. .. .. .. .. .. .. | 4 2 | 4 0 |
| Total cost of maintenance according to abstracts .. | £31 14 | £30 16 |

There is no information as to the quantities of materials used,
and unfortunately the relative cost of materials and of labour
are not truly stated, as under the head of manual labour are
included large sums paid for repairs by contract, and payments
for quarrying and breaking materials. Neither is the entire
cost of maintenance included, as in many cases highway
districts and parishes partially or entirely repaired the turnpike
roads lying within them. The repairs of turnpike roads by
highway districts alone appear to have cost 25,193*l.* in 1875,
and 27,484*l.* in 1876, when only about three-fifths of the total
length of highways were included in districts.

In 1876, when roads formerly turnpike were repaired out of
the common fund of highway districts, the cost per mile of the
disturnpiked Metropolis roads in the Edgware district of
Middlesex was 296*l.* 1*s.* per mile. In other counties the average
cost ranged from 9*l.* per mile in Suffolk to 75*l.* 18*s.* per mile in
Lancashire, the mean of the whole, excluding the Edgware roads,
being 30*l.* 1*s.* per mile.

These amounts are for repairs alone, exclusive of salaries, etc.,

* P. 245.

a proportionate share of which would be about 1*l.* 7*s.* per mile more, on the average.

Here, again, there is no information as to the quantities of materials used, nor of the true cost either of materials or of labour.

The cost of the repairs of the main roads constituted under the Highways and Locomotives (Amendment) Act, 1878, in highway districts, rural sanitary districts, and highway parishes, has been given since 1880 in Parliamentary returns. From them it appears that the average cost from the year 1881, when the system of main roads had been fully established, to the year ending 25th March, 1889, when the main roads came under the management of the County Councils, has been as shown in the following table. Roads situated in districts of urban sanitary authorities are not included in the returns :—

AVERAGE COST OF REPAIRS PER MILE.

| Year ending 25th March. | Main Roads in | | South Wales County Roads. |
|---|---|---|---|
| | England. | North Wales. | |
| | £ s. | £ s. | £ s. |
| 1881 | 36 12 | 21 9 | 22 4 |
| 1882 | 37 19 | 21 11 | 20 13 |
| 1883 | 38 1 | 21 7 | 20 13 |
| 1884 | 37 6 | 22 13 | 21 0 |
| 1885 | 39 8 | 20 19 | 21 13 |
| 1886 | 39 16 | 22 0 | 21 7 |
| 1887 | 41 6 | 20 7 | 21 14 |
| 1888 | 42 17 | 19 1 | 22 17 |
| 1889 | 42 18 | 19 0 | 21 7 |

In different counties the cost per mile in 1881 ranged from 4*l.* 8*s.* in Merioneth, and 11*l.* 4*s.* in Westmoreland, to 148*l.* 17*s.* in Middlesex, and in 1889 from 7*l.* 15*s.* in Merioneth, and 18*l.* in Westmoreland, to 240*l.* in Middlesex. Neither the quantities of materials used, nor the cost of materials and of labour are given.

In Herefordshire, where the main roads were maintained by

SOUTH WALES COUNTY ROADS—COST OF MAINTENANCE PER MILE, 1877.

| District | Miles | Materials £ s. | Labour £ s. | Miscellaneous £ s. | Total Repairs £ s. | Salaries, Management, and General Superintendence £ s. | Cube Yards per Mile | Labour Per Cube Yard s. d. | Labour Per Centage of Cost of Repairs |
|---|---|---|---|---|---|---|---|---|---|
| Glamorgan, Eastern District | 80 | 19 0 | 9 14 | 0 16 | 29 10 | 5 4 | 95 | 2 0 | 32·9 |
| Northern ,, | 73 | 23 17 | 10 15 | 2 14 | 37 6 | | 91 | 2 4 | 28·8 |
| Western ,, | 72 | 43 8 | 14 13 | 7 2 | 65 3 | | 130 | 2 3 | 22·5 |
| Carmarthen, Carmarthen District | 94 | 12 8 | 8 7 | 0 15 | 21 10 | 2 16 | 67 | 2 6 | 38·9 |
| Three Commnotts ,, | 108½ | 16 11 | 8 3 | 1 3 | 25 17 | | 70 | 2 4 | 31·1 |
| Llandovery ,, | 87½ | 13 5 | 7 7 | 1 6 | 21 18 | | 68 | 2 2 | 33·5 |
| Pembroke, Haverfordwest District | 40 | 8 12 | 7 0 | 0 9 | 16 1 | 3 14 | 48 | 2 10 | 43·6 |
| Narberth ,, | 45 | 10 11 | 6 14 | 0 10 | 17 15 | | 63 | 2 1 | 37·7 |
| Cardigan, Upper District | 65½ | 9 18 | 5 4 | 0 8 | 15 10 | 3 1 | 60 | 1 9¼ | 33·5 |
| Lower ,, | 68½ | 8 13 | 5 3 | 0 10 | 14 6 | | 58 | 1 8¾ | 36·0 |
| Brecon, | 127 | 11 15 | 7 7 | 0 12 | 19 14 | 3 2 | 51¾ | 2 10 | 37·3 |
| Radnor, | 130 | 6 5 | 5 1 | 0 11 | 11 17 | 2 7 | 39 | 2 7½ | 42·6 |
| Average | 991 | ... | ... | ... | 24 5 | 3 10 | 68⅕ | ... | ... |

the surveyors of highway districts, at first under the author's supervision, and afterwards on the same system under Mr. J. Kirk, the cost of repairs per mile was, in 1880–81, 35*l*. 2*s*., and in 1887–88, 34*l*. 6*s*., the average of the eight years being 34*l*. 3*s*., including roads in urban sanitary districts and short lengths of town streets costing in one case 113*l*. per mile on the average. Excluding streets, the roads cost from 20*l*. to 49*l*. per mile per year in different highway districts, the materials being Clee Hill stone, limestone, and pebble stone.   Labour cost 28·3 per cent. of the whole cost in 1881–2, gradually falling to 24 per cent. in 1887–88, when it was 8*l*. 2*s*. per mile.   It ranged from 20·4 to 30·8 per cent. of the whole cost in different districts, the latter rate being in the district in which the roads were best and most economically maintained with Clee Hill stone, costing about 10*s*. per cube yard.   The quantity of materials used varied in different highway districts from 32 to 45 cube yards per mile of Clee Hill stone, to 72 cube yards per mile of limestone, and in urban districts from 80 cube yards to 127 cube yards per mile of Clee Hill stone, and higher rates in streets.

The average cost of the South Wales county roads, which represented the main roads in England and North Wales, as given above from the Parliamentary returns, is the cost of road repairs only, as in the case of the main roads.   In 1877 the average cost of these roads, exclusive of salaries, management, and general superintendence, which averaged 3*l*. 10*s*. per mile, was 24*l*. 5*s*. per mile, where an average of 68½ cube yards of material per mile was used.   The table opposite gives the cost of maintenance per mile for each county and district under the different heads of expenditure, together with the number of cube yards of materials laid, the cost of labour corresponding to a cube yard of materials laid, and the proportion of the cost of labour to the total cost of repairs.

It will be observed that, comparing whole districts, the average cost of maintenance varies considerably, and if single roads, or parts of roads, were to be taken, the difference of cost would be far greater, some being as little as 5*l*. per mile, while others with heavy traffic cost upwards of 350*l*. per mile for short lengths.

The wages were from 15s. per week in the cheaper counties, to 18s. or more in Glamorgan, and the cost of materials per cube yard ranged from 2s. 6d. in some parts of the cheaper counties to 8s. near Swansea.

In France, in 1876, the maintenance of the macadamised national roads cost on an average 33l. per mile, of which 18l. 6s. per mile, or 55½ per cent., was for materials, and 14l. 14s. per mile, or 44½ per cent., was for labour. The average quantity of materials used was 78 cube yards per mile, and the total labour per cube yard of materials cost on the average 3s. 9d., being at the rate of 1⅓ day per cube yard for the maintenance of the surface, and 64 days per mile for the labour on ditches, sides, etc. The mean rate of wages was 1s. 10d. per day ; taking wages at 2s. 6d. per day, the cost of labour per mile would be 22l. ; and per cube yard of materials used, 5s. 1d.

The cost of maintenance of course varied a good deal in different departments, the average in some being as low as 15l. or 16l. per mile, but in the majority the cost was not very far removed from the average.

On the national roads of the department of Calvados, having an average traffic of 207 collars per day, in 1880, flint, sandstone, and quartz, having a mean coefficient of 13·9, were employed, at the average rate of 86 cube yards per mile. The materials cost 30l. 16s. per mile, or 7s. 2d. per cube yard on the average. The labour in spreading and attending to them cost 1s. 6d. per cube yard, and in removing mud and dust 1s. 11d. per cube yard ; together 3s. 5d. per cube yard of materials spread, or 14l. 14s. per mile. The labour on ditches, sides, etc., cost 7l. 14s. per mile. The total average cost of maintaining the roads was thus 53l. 4s. per mile, of which labour cost 22l. 3s., or 42 per cent. of the whole.

# CHAPTER XII.

## Road Surveyor's Duties.

THE general duties of a road surveyor will have been, to a great
degree, gathered from what has preceded. The length of road
that a surveyor can properly superintend depends upon many
circumstances—the extent of country covered, the facilities for
getting about by railway if he keeps no horse, and the amount
of personal attention he is expected to give to details. If
materials are supplied by contract ready broken, the surveyor is
relieved of the superintendence of quarrying, carting, and
breaking them, and has only to measure them, and see that they
are properly broken after delivery on the road. He is thus able
to superintend a greater length of road, but at the cost of the
contractor's profit on the materials. If he has working foremen
under him, or assistants, he can of course take charge of more
road.

Mr. McConnell, a gentleman of long and wide experience in
superintending roads, gave it as his opinion* that a surveyor in
charge of a district of roads so concentrated that he has not to
go more than 10 miles from home, and requiring for their maintenance an expenditure varying from 5l. to 40l. per mile per
annum, having neither foremen, nor contractors, but himself
letting work in detail to working men, ought not to have under
his charge more than 60 miles of road, or 100 miles if he keeps
a horse. In making this statement, a system of close superintendence is calculated on, and it is considered that the surveyor
should inspect the greater part of his charge once in every week.

* Letter from Mr. McConnell, Appendix to Report on Public Roads in
Scotland, p. 80.

A surveyor who keeps a horse can do his duties much more effectually than without one, and more economically if his district can be proportionally enlarged. Thus, if a surveyor without a horse be paid 100*l.* a year, his salary on 60 miles of road will be 1*l.* 13*s.* 4*d.* per mile ; with 50*l.* more for the keep of a horse, he can look after 100 miles for 1*l.* 10*s.* per mile.

In South Wales the county road surveyors superintended 86 to 145 miles of roads, keeping horses, and having materials supplied by contract ready broken. The constant labourers, in permanent charge of their lengths of road, being generally long-tried and trustworthy men, were in some cases left to themselves more than would otherwise be desirable.

The lengths of roads under one surveyor's charge in highway districts are generally from 100 to 200 miles, and sometimes as much as 300, or even upwards of 400 miles. Such long lengths as the latter cannot be properly looked after by one man, if much work is done on them, unless they are concentrated in a small area, and it is probable that many miles of the more unfrequented roads get little attention. Other circumstances than the length of roads in them govern the extent of highway areas, but whatever be the mileage put under the charge of one surveyor, the supervision should be effectual and constant, by the aid of assistants or working foremen if required. Great loss is sustained both in materials and labour by neglect, or the unwatched performance of the daily work on roads, and more especially so when there are not trustworthy constant labourers in charge.

Surveyors of highways are required by the General Highway Act to keep accounts of the money received by them for the purposes of the highways, and of the manner in which they apply it, and they are liable to penalties for neglecting to do so. Under other circumstances a system which relieves the surveyor from payment of money gives him more time to attend to the work on his roads, and has other advantages. It may be arranged that all payments, whether wages or bills, shall be by drafts attached to vouchers prepared by the clerk from particulars furnished him by the surveyor, and signed by the chairman of the board, or other person authorised. Vouchers for payment

of bills are received by banks as cheques, and for the wages of
labourers cheques or pay lists are sent either to the men or to
convenient places for payment, and each man signs a receipt for
the amount credited to him opposite his name in the sheet. No
money thus passes through the surveyor's hands, and the clerk,
if he does not actually keep the accounts, is responsible for them,
and sees that no unauthorised payment is made. Fraud or
peculation is impossible without collusion between the clerk and
surveyor, and the keeping of proper accounts is rendered easier.

A surveyor should always enter on the spot, with the date, a
clear and distinct measurement of any work or materials which
are to be paid for by measurement. A proper book should be
kept for the purpose, to be produced, if required, in case of
dispute.

To carry out a systematic renewal, year by year, of the
materials worn out and removed as mud or dust, with strict
accuracy, the amount of materials consumed, and the quantities
supplied to replace them, must be known. The difficulties in
the way of ascertaining the amount of wear of materials in a
road have been noticed, and the surveyor must generally rest
content with such an estimate of the amount required to replace
it as observation and comparison may enable him to form. It is
however, a simple matter to keep an account of the quantity of
materials spread, and unless this be done, no intelligent system
of maintenance is possible. The proper quantity to be included
in the estimate for any one year, depends on that which has
been spread in several previous years. The wear must be replaced,
and the capital value of the road must be maintained, and if not
to the full extent one year, it must be made up sooner or later,
or the strength of the road will suffer. It often happens that
the intentions of estimates are not carried out, materials destined
for one road or portion of a road may be used elsewhere, or a
reduction of the total quantity may become necessary for financial
reasons. Comparisons of the amounts spread on various lengths
of roads are also most useful and instructive. The excessive
quantities of materials required to keep a badly drained piece of
road in even tolerable condition, compared with other lengths
exposed to the same traffic but more favourably situated, or the

contrast in the condition of similarly situated lengths of road with the same quantities of materials, when one is well attended to and another ill-kept, are thus made evident.

As far as circumstances permit, account should be kept of the actual quantities of materials spread on every mile or short length of road. The road may be divided into well-defined sections of known length, each as far as possible of a uniform character throughout as to traffic, situation, &c., and the contracts for materials may be made with reference to these lengths. When the heaps of stone are measured by the surveyor after delivery on the roadside, their position should be noted, and the quantity delivered on each mile or short length may be recorded. When this has been done, it is easy to arrive at the quantity used. The road labourer may keep an account, which can be checked by the surveyor from the quantity delivered and remaining unexpended. The quantity used on each length should be reduced to cube yards of materials per mile of road, that comparison of one length with another may be easy.

Statements of the quantities of materials received from contractors, or prepared under the surveyor, the quantities laid, and remaining, should be prepared every quarter. The account of the quantities laid in the year may be conveniently made up for the financial year ending 31st March, as little material should be laid in the spring after that date. Records of materials used may be conveniently kept in the form of a diagram, the number of cube yards per mile being plotted to a suitable vertical scale along a horizontal line on which the years are marked. The history of a piece of road for many years is thus seen at a glance.

An account should be kept of the tools, machines, and other property belonging to the road authority, showing where and in whose charge they are, and a statement of this account should be prepared annually.

Annual estimates of the cost of road maintenance should be made in detail, showing the number of cube yards, price per cube yard, and the total cost of the road materials intended to be used, the cost of labour, and any miscellaneous expenditure that may be required beyond the ordinary maintenance, for every mile or less length of road. When the miles are not marked, the road should be divided into short well-defined sections of known length, which can be grouped together into larger divisions for recording the materials actually used.

The form of estimate used for the county roads of South Wales is given in Appendix III.

A summary of the cost of different roads or lengths of road included in the estimates may be afterwards prepared for general use, but detailed estimates should always be made in the first instance, whether they are required by the authority under which the surveyor acts or not.

The estimates for the French national roads are prepared with an elaboration not attempted in this country. The coefficient of quality of each kind of material used, and the quantity used per kilometre, and per 100 collars and 100 tons of traffic, are stated as well as the total cost when delivered on the road. Manual labour is dissected so as to show the amount and cost of it per cube metre for spreading and attending to the materials, and per kilometre of road for maintaining the sides, ditches, &c.

The expenditure set forth in the annual estimate may be considerably modified by the state of the weather during the year. A wet season may demand a greater outlay, both on manual labour and on materials, and tax the skill of the surveyor to use the means at his disposal to the best advantage. A dry and favourable year, on the other hand, may allow of a considerable saving, or the full amount of the estimate may be spent on a reserve of materials.

The accounts of expenditure should be kept in such a form as will show plainly what is spent on road repairs, i.e. on materials, on manual labour, on miscellaneous repairs to culverts and other works; and what on salaries, law, management, and other establishment charges. The annual statements of expenditure on the South Wales county roads recorded this information for 40 years, giving the cost of road repairs under the separate heads of materials, labour, and miscellaneous repairs in each county and district, and on ninety separate lengths of road, apart from salaries and other establishment charges, and any special expenditure on improvements. There is no such record of the cost of maintenance of either turnpike roads or highways in England, as from the manner in which the returns and abstracts were made they are useless as information regarding road maintenance. In the turnpike accounts under the head of "manual labour," payments to parishes, materials, and repairs by contract, were often included ; and under the head of "materials for surface repairs," contract work, team labour, &c. ; "tradesmen's bills," comprised repairs to works connected with the roads, tollhouses and gates, as well as stationery, printing, &c.; and "incidental expenses" were made up of items of all sorts, whether road maintenance or establishment charges, watering and lighting, compensations, losses, &c. A similar confusion existed in the statements of the expenditure on highways.

Surveyors of highway authorities are now required to keep accounts according to a prescribed form, which seems to have been framed for the convenience of audit rather than with a view to any useful statistical information. It is, however, quite possible, while keeping the books in the prescribed form, for a surveyor to embody all the information that will enable him to record for any length of road the quantity of material used, the cost of it when delivered on the road, the cost of manual labour on surface work, and of any miscellaneous expenditure not connected with the maintenance of the surface or works. This information is quite essential for maintenance on a proper system.

## Repairs by Contract.

The ordinary surface repairs of roads are sometimes let by contract, under the belief that men on day wages, and necessarily without close supervision, do not work as well as under a contractor. The advantages of repair contracts are doubtful, except in special cases, such as an outlying piece of road. Materials will often be carelessly used, and harm will arise from neglect and in other ways, unless the supervision is as close as a good roadman in charge of a length of road would generally require. Small contracts are the best, the roads being divided into sections of such a length that the contractor can himself superintend the work, acting as foreman over his men. The contract should be for a term of three to five years, terminable at the end of any year by three months' notice to the contractor, and in case of neglect to carry out the contract, the road authority should be empowered to perform the work and deduct the cost from the sum to be paid to the contractor. The contractor should be required to find sureties for the proper fulfilment of his contract. A specification of the work to be done and the mode of doing it must be prepared, setting forth the quantities of materials to be provided on each length of road, the nature of the stone, the size to which it is to be broken, and how it is to be spread. The contractor should be required to keep open and in good repair all drains and ditches, side channels, footpaths, mounds, borders, &c., and to scrape the road and remove the scrapings. It may be specified that the road shall be scraped whenever there is $\frac{1}{2}$ inch of mud on it, and that the side channels shall be cleaned out after every scraping. Payments should be made periodically, by instalments, according to the work done, on the certificate of the surveyor.

## Road Management.

Large areas of road management have been often advocated, and they are attended with many advantages. Uniformity of system and maintenance on correct principles under the superintendence of persons of wider experience than the ordinary road surveyor tend to economy in road repairs, and if the expenses of management are not less in proportion, as is usually the case, the total cost of maintenance is generally lower in large areas. There are facilities for generalising any improvement of practice, and it is easier to purchase machines, such as steam road rollers, horse scraping and sweeping machines, or stone-breaking machines, and to use them to advantage.

A well-know instance of road management on a large scale is that of the Administration des Ponts et Chaussées in France. The opportunities which such an organisation affords for investigation, and for collecting and generalising information, are shown by the documents issued by it, and by the many valuable memoirs on the subjects connected with road maintenance contained in the 'Annales des Ponts et Chaussées.'

Management by county areas has been general in Ireland since the Grand Jury Act of 1836, and with the best results as to the excellence and economy of road maintenance. In many of the counties of Scotland both turnpike and statute labour roads were under one management for many years, and by the Roads and Bridges Act of 1878 the system of county management was extended to all parts of Scotland.

In the Isle of Wight all public roads were for many years previous to 1889 under one management, with good results.

In South Wales the turnpike roads of six counties were managed from 1845 to 1889 by county roads boards, aided by district boards for local purposes, and the whole of the roads, nearly 1000 miles in length, were, until 1882, under one general superintendent. A uniform system was thus established, combined with the advantages of local management, under which the roads compared very favourably, both for excellence and economy, with other turnpike roads. The advantages of county management were in a measure extended to the ordinary highways. Under the South Wales Highways Act of 1851, the whole of South Wales was divided into districts by the county roads boards, in whom were vested the appointment and dismissal of the surveyors of the highway districts and the fixing of their salaries. Thus, the county roads boards had a certain control over the highway surveyors, which proved very beneficial.

The Highways and Locomotives (Amendment) Act, 1878, enlarged the areas of road management in England in several important respects, and gave the county authority a control over the authorities of the highway areas, while leaving to them the duty of repairing the roads within their district.

By Section 7 the repairs of all roads within a highway district were made a common charge on all the parishes in the district, instead of being, as before, a separate charge in each parish. The enlargement of the area of chargeability was equitable, and there was a provision that a district might be divided with the approval of the county authorities into parts upon which to charge the expenses of the roads within them. The relief to parishes with more than their fair length of roads was great, but it was otherwise with parishes with few roads in them, and they, to escape the increased highway rate, succeeded in some counties in breaking up the highway districts, of which there are now 56 less than in 1878. This retrograde step was possible because highway districts in England were not made general.

By section 10, power is given to the county authority to enforce the performance of duty by defaulting highway authorities.

By section 13, roads which, within the period between December 31, 1870, and the date of the passing of the Act, ceased to be turnpike roads, and any roads which had afterwards ceased to be such, are to be deemed main roads, and by section 15 the county authority may make an order declaring certain other highways to be main roads. It was further enacted that one-half of the expenses incurred by the highway authority in the maintenance of a main road should be paid to the highway authority by the county authority "out of the county rate, on the certificate of the surveyor of the county authority, or of such other person or persons as the county authority may appoint, to the effect that such main road has been maintained to his or their satisfaction."

The power thus conferred upon a central authority in each county had, when properly exercised, considerable influence over the maintenance of the main roads. The cost of such superintendence on the part of the county as would ensure maintenance on proper principles and check improper charges, was generally recouped by the saving effected in the moiety of the cost paid out of the county rate, while economy of maintenance was accompanied by improvement in the roads.

The duty of maintaining the main roads of the county was, by the Local Government Act, 1888, transferred to the County Councils, except with respect to such roads as urban sanitary authorities claimed to retain. An opening for road management on a wider scale than has hitherto been possible in England is thus afforded, and one which, for the sake of economy and efficiency, it is to be hoped will be taken full advantage of. To do so it will be necessary to employ a staff of surveyors specially for the main roads, acting under the superintendence

M

of a county surveyor who would be responsible for the annual estimates of expenditure, and should besides carefully analyse and digest the actual expenditure, and record the quantities and nature of materials used on different roads or lengths of roads. The objection is sometimes raised that with one set of surveyors in charge of the main roads, and another set in charge of the ordinary highways, there would be two sets of surveyors going over the same ground, but this arises from an imperfect acquaintance with a road surveyor's work. He can only attend properly to such a mileage of roads as he can travel over often enough for proper supervision, whether they extend over the country or lie within a small area, and there need be no conflict of authority between the two sets of surveyors. There is none in France, where the national, the departmental, and the local roads have different organisations; and there was none in South Wales where there were separate surveyors for the highways and the county roads from the constitution of the highway districts in 1851 down to 1889. There was indeed a distinct advantage to the highway surveyors in having before them a pattern of good maintenance, and the highways benefited by it. The same result would follow in England.

Instead of themselves maintaining the main roads, the County Councils may contract with a highway authority to perform the work, and they may require any highway authority to undertake the maintenance of the main roads, for a payment to be agreed upon or to be determined by arbitration. In either case the payment is to be made on the report of the county surveyor that the roads have been properly maintained and repaired. Contracts of this sort, whether entered into voluntarily or on the requisition of County Councils, will, the author believes, prove unsatisfactory. In rural districts it will be almost impossible for the county surveyor to regulate, or even to know, what quantity of materials have been used on any road, and with parish surveyors the case will be still more hopeless. In urban districts contracts may prove more practicable. There must be a specification of the quantity and the nature of the material to be used on each length of road, of the manual labour, and all other work to be performed, and the amount to be paid for the specified work must be agreed on beforehand. But there must be also provision for the employment of an extra quantity of materials and of labour, should the circumstances of the year demand it, and this will require very careful arrangement.

The necessity for records of annual expenditure, other than those required to be kept for the purpose of a money audit, has been pointed out. It is very desirable that counties should adopt some common form, showing plainly the cost of materials, of labour, and of any miscellaneous expenditure connected with the maintenance of the roads. Comparisons of the total cost of different roads, and of the proportion of expenditure on materials and labour, and on other things, would be facilitated, and a step would be taken towards gathering statistics relating to road maintenance which are at present wanting in England. Surveyors and others interested in road management would then have the means of knowing how roads were maintained in other counties and districts, and of intelligent comparison of the cost. The effect would certainly be to promote economy of maintenance.

# CHAPTER XIII.

## RECAPITULATION.

IT is evident that the maintenance of a road already in good condition and of sufficient strength, if properly carried on, is almost entirely a question of wear. With greater traffic, or a softer material, the wear will be faster, but with good maintenance there need be no deterioration. The problem is to reduce the wear, both from the traffic and the weather, to a minimum; and to substitute other materials for those which are unavoidably worn out, and to do so in the most economical manner.

The conditions under which the wear will be reduced to a minimum under a certain traffic are: good drainage of road and subsoil; materials sufficiently hard to resist the traffic without undue wear; a coating without an excess of detritus; a well-cared-for surface; and sufficient strength to bear the loads to which the road is subjected, so that wear may be confined to the surface.

On very few roads are these conditions to be found, but their attainment should always be kept in view, and it is certain that in proportion as they are attained will be the economy of maintenance.

Drainage almost always requires attention, and there is generally a good deal that can be done to improve it at a slight expense, and nothing pays so well in the end. Proper care of the surface is generally all that is wanted to prevent the water hanging about on the road, or in the side channels; but a dry surface alone is not enough. On a flat, water may often be seen standing in the side-ditches up to within a few inches of the surface of the road, in which case both the subsoil and the road-coating are softened by the soaking of the water, and remain so long after the water in the ditches has fallen. A deeper ditch, a larger or a new culvert, or a drain cut through adjoining land, is generally sufficient to remove a cause of great mischief. Springs under the road, and land water from the side of a hill when the road is situated on a hillside, not properly cut off and led away, can often be thoroughly dealt with at a trifling cost compared with the expense they cause.

There is generally some choice of road materials to be had even from local sources of supply, and if that at hand is not strong enough to stand the traffic to which it is exposed, it will always be a question whether it will be more economical to go farther for a better material at an increased cost.

The road-coating may often be improved in composition and rendered harder by scraping, and a tolerably good surface can be obtained under almost any disadvantages by proper attention to it. The influence which a good surface has in keeping down wear is greater than might be supposed with materials of all sorts, but particularly with those that are weak.

Everything should be done to render a road strong enough to bear the traffic to which it is subjected, without wear from bending or cross-breaking, and a reserve of strength is always of advantage. Fluctuations of traffic are most trying on roads which have no reserve of strength, and whenever there is reason to expect a large increase of traffic over a road, it should be strengthened beforehand for it, by adding materials. Otherwise, a larger quantity of materials will be required when the heavy traffic comes, which may cease before they are consolidated, and leave the road covered with loose stones, which will take a long time to work in under the usual traffic.

A road may be strong enough for its ordinary traffic, and even have a considerable reserve of strength, and still be quite unable to stand the loads that may be brought upon it. When a road is thus broken down or cut into by excessive weights, it is no longer a matter of replacing wear, but of serious repairs, and it may be almost of reconstruction. It may be desirable that all roads should be rendered strong enough for

any traffic that may come upon them; that will be a question
of expense, but until they are so, it is unfair to expect a road
to bear heavy loads which it is not intended for. It is as
unreasonable to suppose that a road which is only moderately
strong, though good, is fit to bear the traffic of a traction
engine and trucks, or heavy timber hauling, as it is to think
that a heavy locomotive could be run on a light railway
without seriously damaging it.

To replace the wear which is unavoidable, economically,
materials must be applied only where they are wanted, and
with sufficient care both in spreading them and in attending
to them afterwards, to ensure their being usefully employed.
When the quantity to be laid is small, they must be applied
in small patches where hollows or slacks of the surface show
where they are required, and in thin coats. As the quantity
to be spread is greater, so must be the size of the patches
or sheets, but they should never be more than one stone in
thickness when applied in this manner. After attention, to
ensure the consolidation of the materials, will comprise raking
and re-arranging stones, and, it may be, the use of binding, or
even picking up round the edges in unfavourable circumstances;
and if, owing to the lateness of the season when they were
spread, the stones will not set, economy of materials as well
as public convenience may require that they should be raked
off the road.

If the wear be very large, say more than $\frac{1}{2}$ inch of consolidated road surface in a year, materials may be economically
applied in thick coats with the aid of a roller, a thickness
of 4 inches being laid down at once; and this method, even
when not economical, recommends itself to the public, because
it spares them the annoyance of having to work in the stones
by the ordinary traffic, and gives them at once a perfectly
smooth road.

There is perhaps nothing which is generally more neglected
than the removal of the worn-out materials from the road.    It
appears to be often looked upon merely as a clearing of the
surface from mud, and as such an unnecessary expense, while
in reality it affects the composition of the whole road-coating,

and unless the mud is washed away naturally from the surface, scraping or sweeping is quite necessary to preserve the proper proportion of solid stone in the road. Experiment has shown, what might have been expected from other considerations, that from one-fifth to one-fourth of the whole bulk of a road-coating must necessarily be small stuff under $\frac{1}{6}$ inch in diameter, which moisture will convert into mud, and it is certain that, as this proportion is exceeded, so will the road be soft, easily acted on by traffic, wet, and frost, and wasteful of materials.

An adequate amount of manual labour in laying materials, scraping, and attention to the surface, is quite necessary. It is no real economy to save in labour, while more is spent on materials with a worse result. At the same time there is always the danger of too great an expenditure on manual labour. Work may be performed which, without being altogether useless, is unnecessary or not worth its cost, or much time may be absolutely wasted. Experience shows that the expenditure on the manual labour employed on surface work under ordinary circumstances may with advantage amount to 30 or 40 per cent. of the combined cost of materials and labour, but no fixed proportion can be laid down, and the employment of the proper amount of labour, and its economical adjustment to particular circumstances, will always require considerable care.

The advantages arising from having men in charge of certain lengths of road cannot be too much insisted upon. Even if a man is not constantly employed on the surface work of the road, but is engaged in stone-breaking or harvest-work during the summer, he becomes familiar with the peculiarities of his length, and with the best way to deal with them, and if he is a good workman, he soon learns to take an interest in the road which it is his business to keep in order. It is in vain to expect the same skill or industry from men employed by the job, or having no interest in the goodness of the road, or in making the most of the means at their disposal.

Expenditure on road maintenance has often to be reduced below what is desirable that it may not exceed a certain amount, and skill and judgment are then required to use the limited amount to the best advantage. Manual labour must be reduced, that sufficient materials may be employed, and if materials enough to replace the wear cannot be afforded, it must not be forgotten that the strength of the road is being drawn upon, and that in however good a state it may be, it will certainly deteriorate to a condition which will demand extensive repairs, unless the loss of materials be made good in time. It has been shown, however, that the process of deterioration is a gradual one in a road originally strong enough when it is skilfully managed, and a careful surveyor can therefore tide over several years of reduced expenditure without much danger to his roads. He will watch how far different portions are losing strength, and to what extent wear is consequently augmenting, and he will not let matters go too far. In more favourable times a reserve of strength may be laid up by adding more materials than the wear consumes, which, by increasing the strength, will also lessen the wear of the road, and in the end tend to economy.

Care in the preparation of estimates, and in accounts of the actual expenditure on different roads, year by year, are both equally necessary. A good deal of examination and comparison of expenditure under different heads, on different roads and portions of roads, will be found useful. All expenditure on road repairs should be kept distinct from the cost of management, and the manual labour employed on the surface work of the roads should, as far as possible, be separated from that which is properly a part of the cost of materials, such as stone-breaking or quarrying.

A careful account of the quantities of materials spread year by year on each road and portion of road, is essential to systematic road maintenance. It constitutes a record of the strength of each road, and when reduced to the rate of cube yards per mile of road, the quantities used on different roads are readily compared. Comparisons of traffic and wear are much easier than absolute measurements, and it is by such comparisons, and records of the quantities of materials used, and of the expenditure on manual labour, &c., on various roads, that an opinion must generally be formed of the economy with which they are maintained, and of the requirements of any particular road. Due allowance must, of course, be made for difference in materials, situation, and other conditions, and regard must be had to the state in which the roads are kept, but when comparisons are possible over considerable areas, they are less influenced by minor differences.

Hitherto the materials for an intelligent comparison of expenditure on road maintenance have been wanting in England, but it is to be hoped that one effect of county management of main roads will be to provide them. That good results, both as to economy and efficiency, would follow cannot be doubted.

# APPENDIX 1.

## PONTS ET CHAUSSÉES.

### REGULATIONS FOR CANTONNIERS.

#### *Art. 1.—Definition of the Work of Cantonniers.*

The cantonniers are charged with the manual labour connected with the daily maintenance of the roads, over a definite length of road called a *canton*.

They must obey, in everything relating to their work, the engineers, foremen, and other agents of the administration of roads and bridges.

#### *Art. 2.—Nomination of Cantonniers.*

The cantonniers are nominated by the prefect, from a list submitted by the chief engineer, containing three times, or at least twice the number of candidates required to fill the vacancies. They are dismissed by the prefect on the proposal or advice of the chief engineer.

#### *Art. 3.—Conditions of Admission.*

To be nominated a cantonnier it is necessary (1) to have fulfilled the laws relating to service in the army, and to be not more than 45 years old ; (2) not to be subject to any infirmity which may hinder daily and diligent labour ; (3) to have worked on the construction or repair of roads ; (4) to have a certificate of good conduct from the mayor of the *commune* or the sub-prefect of the *arrondissement.*

Candidates who can read and write will be preferred.

#### *Art. 4.—Chief Cantonnier.*

The cantons of the roads in a department shall be grouped in districts containing at least six cantons; the six cantonniers will constitute a brigade : one of them shall be chief cantonnier ; he must be able to read and write, and shall be chosen from the cantonniers distinguished for zeal, good conduct, and intelligence.

The chief cantonniers shall have a shorter length than other cantonniers, so that they may be able to attend to special duties allotted to them. They shall accompany the foremen in their rounds, and note the orders which may be given to the cantonniers of their brigade, and see that the orders are carried out. They shall accordingly go over the whole extent of their district at least once a week, varying the days and hours of their visits, to satisfy themselves of the presence of the cantonniers, and to direct them in their work; they shall report to those under whose orders they are more particularly placed, and shall furnish to the engineers all the information that may be required of them.

They may be temporarily employed in superintending and keeping account of the works of re-dressing the paved causeways, and in directing itinerant gangs of workmen.

### Art. 5.—*Distinctive Marks of Cantonniers.*

Cantonniers shall wear a blue jacket and a leather hat, round which shall be a band of copper 0·28 m. long, and 0·055 m. broad, with the word "cantonnier" cut out in it. The chief cantonniers shall wear besides on the left arm an armlet of the prescribed pattern.

There shall be given besides to each man a mark consisting of a staff 2 metres long, divided in decimetres, shod with iron, and furnished at the top with a strong iron plate 0·24 m. wide, and 0·16 m. high, on each side of which shall be shown in letters 0·08 m. high the number of the canton. This mark must always be set up on the road at less than 100 metres from where the cantonnier is at work.

### Art. 6.—*The Work of the Cantonniers.*

The work of the cantonniers consists in maintaining and repairing the roads daily and constantly, so that they may be dry, clean, and smooth, safe in times of hard frost, and of a satisfactory appearance at all seasons.

To effect this, they must, subject to the orders and instructions which may be given them in case of need :

(1) Insure the flowing off of water by cleansing the gutters, pipes, &c., by making small drains for the purpose wherever they may be necessary, taking care that these drains should never be made in the body of the road.

(2) At suitable times open and maintain the ditches, regulate the sides, throwing the surplus earth on the neighbouring ground, if there is no objection, or putting it together to facilitate its measurement or removal.

(3) Remove as soon as possible with a scraper or shovel, all liquid or soft mud from the whole breadth of the road, even if there be neither hollows nor ruts, and collect the mud in regular heaps on the sides to be measured, if there is room for it there.

(4) Spread the mud, when dry, on the sides which have lost their shape or have a slope of more than 1 in 25 from the road, and throw the surplus on the neighbouring fields, if not objected to.

(5) At the approach of winter redouble attention to all which is prescribed in the two preceding paragraphs, to prevent lumps of frozen mud.

(6) In dry weather, remove the dust and deposit it on the sides.

(7) Clear away the snow from the whole breadth of the road, or at least from the middle, particularly at places where it accumulates and obstructs the traffic; throw it immediately on the neighbouring fields if possible, or collect it in heaps on the sides, so as to show drivers of vehicles where the road is.

(8) Break and remove ice from the road, and scatter sand and rubble, especially at the sides and at sharp turnings.

(9) Also break the ice in the ditches and remove it where it accumulates so as to threaten flooding of the road in the thaw.

(10) In the time of thaw assist the flowing off of water and remove pieces of ice, mud, and dirt, so that the effects of the thaw may prejudice the traffic and the road as little as possible.

(11) Collect, break, and stack in separate heaps and in a particular shape, all loose stones, and those projecting or only just showing if too large, and those near in the neighbouring fields which can be used for the purposes of the road. Break the materials intended for maintenance if the breaking is not done by the contractor.

(12) Cut or dig up thistles or other weeds, especially before their flowering season.

(13) Clear away loose stones from the road and every thing which may hinder the traffic.

(14) Clean and clear away earth, plants, and extraneous matters from the plinths, string courses, and parapets of bridges, &c.

(15) Look after the preservation of mile stones, sign posts, and bench marks on the road.

(16) Cultivate and look after plantations belonging to the State,

see to their preservation and to that of plantations of private owners, straighten provisionally all young trees bent by the wind, and do generally all that the welfare of the road demands, conformable to more particular instructions given by the engineers of the district for carrying out the above general orders.

### Art. 7.—Employment of Materials.

On roads in a state of repair the road labourers shall conform to the following rules for employment of materials.

The materials shall be made use of as they are required, always choosing damp weather for their employment, avoiding wholesale coating and throwing down stones at random.

To proceed regularly, care should be taken to observe in time of rain the hollows and tracks of vehicles which perceptibly alter the shape of the road.

These worn parts should be cleaned and picked, particularly at the edges, but only to the depth necessary to insure the binding of the materials. The materials arising from the picking should be cleared of earth and broken if necessary before being used.

The filling up of the hollows or wheel tracks should be effected with the debris and with the necessary quantity of new material received through the engineer. It must be carefully beaten so as to incorporate it with the lower layer, and then made even with the form of the road. The parts thus restored should be maintained with particular care until they are completely consolidated.

With respect to roads which are not in a good state of repair, and which nevertheless are open for traffic, one should endeavour to keep them in as good a condition as possible by employing with the care which has just been indicated the materials available.

All stones too large or projecting should be taken out, as they cause damage, and they should be broken to a proper size before being used again.

The coatings more or less extensive to be made on worn roads will be prescribed by the engineer, who will also decide on the materials to be used. The hollows and ruts to be filled up must first be cleared of mud and earth, and their surface then picked to a depth of from 4 to 5 centimetres (1½ to 2 inches). The materials should not be spread except in layers of from 5 to 6 centimetres (2 to 2½ inches), which should be carefully beaten and consolidated.

### *Art. 8.—Task Work to be Performed.*

To excite and maintain the activity of the cantonniers, the engineers, inspectors, and foremen shall assign them work to be performed in a given time, whenever local circumstances permit it. A summary of information on these tasks shall be entered in that part of the cantonnier's book reserved for the orders of the service.

Works thus prescribed shall be one of the principal objects of supervision by the immediate head of the cantonniers, as well as by the mayors and road commissioners.

### *Art. 9.—Determination of Working Hours.*

From the 1st of May to the 1st September, the cantonniers shall be on the roads, without quitting them, from 5 o'clock in the morning to 7 o'clock in the evening. The rest of the year they shall be there from sunrise to sunset. They shall take their meals on the road at hours fixed by the chief engineer. The total duration of meals shall not exceed two hours, but during great heat it may be prolonged to three hours.

### *Art. 10.—Removal of Cantonniers.*

Cantonniers may be moved, either singly or in brigades, when the needs of the service imperatively require it, to be directed to points indicated to them. These displacements shall not take place except under an express order from the engineer.

### *Art. 11.—Compulsory Attendance of Cantonniers in time of Rain, Snow, &c.*

Rain, snow, or other inclemency of the weather shall not be a pretext for the absence of cantonniers ; they must, in such times, redouble their zeal and activity to prevent damage and keep the road in good condition for the whole extent of their cantons ; they are, however, authorised to make themselves fixed or portable shelters, which shall not interfere with the public way or adjoining property, and which must be in sight of the road, and less than 10 metres off, so that the presence of the workmen can always be ascertained.

### Art. 12.—Gratuitous Assistance to Travellers.

Cantonniers must render gratuitous aid and assistance to drivers and travellers, but only in case of accidents.

### Art. 13.—Surveillance over breaches of Highway Law.

To prevent as much as possible breaches of highway law, the cantonniers shall warn frontagers who may be disposed to commit them. They shall consequently keep an eye on repairs, building, deposits, encroachments, and planting which may take place without leave on the highway. They shall report any such breaches to the surveyor, either when he makes his rounds, or at once by letter or by message through the chief cantonnier.

### Art. 14.—Tools with which Cantonniers must be provided.

Every cantonnier shall be provided, at his own expense, with a wheelbarrow, an iron shovel, a wooden shovel, a road-pick, an iron road-scraper, a wooden road-scraper, an iron rake, an iron crowbar, an iron sledge-hammer, and a line 20 metres long.

The head cantonniers must besides be provided with three boning rods, with a level graduated to indicate gradients, and with a double metre measure.

### Art. 15.—Tools of a particular kind to be furnished by the Administration.

Each cantonnier shall be entrusted with an iron ring, 6 centimetres (2¼ inches) in diameter, so that he may ascertain if the stones which he has to spread on the road, have been broken according to the specification.

### Art. 16.—Providing Tools in advance to Cantonniers.

Cantonniers who have no means of procuring them, can have any tools they require supplied in advance. The repayment of the cost of these tools will be insured by the administration, by stoppages, which, except in cases of dismissal, shall not exceed one-sixth of the monthly salary.

### Art. 17.—Keeping Tools in Repair.

Cantonniers shall keep their tools in a good state of repair. If they become negligent in this respect it will be done by the administration, and the expenses will be repaid as stated in Art. 16.

Tools must not be taken to be repaired during working hours. Excuses for absence based upon the necessity of getting tools repaired will never be accepted.

### Art. 18.—Cantonnier's Books.

Every cantonnier will be provided with a book similar to the one annexed to the present regulations. This book is intended to receive notes on the work and conduct of the labourers, any orders and instructions given them, and information of the work which has been assigned them. It must be presented by them to the agents charged with the supervision of the road, every time they are required to do so, under penalty of the stoppage of a day's pay for every time they neglect to produce it, or of three days' pay in the case of having lost it.

### Art. 19.—Means of verifying the Absence of Cantonniers.

The absence and negligences of cantonniers will be verified by the engineers and the agents of the administration employed under their orders, who will make a note of them in the books just spoken of. Absence can also be verified by gendarmes on their rounds, by mayors of the parishes in which the cantons are situated, and by road commissioners.

### Art. 20.—Leave of Absence at Harvest Time.

At harvest time, when the road is in good condition, cantonniers can obtain leave of absence from the engineer in ordinary, when authorised by the engineer in chief. They will receive no salary while on leave of absence, at the expiration of which they must returned punctually to their posts, or they will be immediately superseded.

### Art. 21.—Surrender of Book and of Distinctive Badges on Dismissal of a Cantonnier.

When a cantonnier is dismissed, he must surrender to the engineer his book, his staff, his ring, and the distinctive badges which he wears on his arm and cap. Failing to do this, double the value of these articles will be retained from that which is due to him for salary at the time of his dismissal.

*Art. 22.—Classification and Salary of Cantonniers.*

Cantonniers of each department will be divided into three classes of equal number, whose salary, for each class, will be fixed by the prefect, on the proposal of the chief engineer.

The classification will be made each year by the chief engineer, on the report of the engineer in ordinary, and according to the services of the cantonniers during the preceding year.

The chief cantonniers will be divided into two classes, likewise of equal number.

Their salaries will be fixed, like those of the ordinary cantonniers, by the prefect, on the proposal of the chief engineer.

*Art. 23.—Indemnity for Removal.*

Cantonniers who leave their cantons by order of the engineer will receive an indemnity of one-fifth more than their salary, and three-fifths for every day they sleep out.

No indemnity for removal will be allowed to head cantonniers except when they go out of the district of their brigade. In this case, the indemnity to which they are entitled will be regulated in the same way as those which are paid to ordinary cantonniers.

*Art. 24.—Annual Gratuities.*

Every year, on the report of the engineer in chief, the prefect may grant to the most deserving cantonnier in each district of the engineer in ordinary, a gratuity, which shall not exceed a month's salary.

A similar gratuity may also be awarded to that one of the chief cantonniers of the department, who shall have rendered the best service.

*Art. 25.—Fines on Account of Absence.*

Every cantonnier who shall not be found at his post by one of the agents having a right of supervision on the road, shall be subject to a fine of three days' pay for the first time, of six days' in case of a second offence, and be dismissed the third time.

Those who, without being absent, shall not have done enough work during the month, or who have neglected the duty entrusted to them, will be fined enough to pay for repairing any damage resulting from their negligence.

A part of these fines may be granted by the chief engineer, on the report of the engineer in ordinary, for the benefit of those cantonniers who by their zeal and work have deserved encouragement.

N

# APPENDIX II.

## (Form of Road Labourer's Journal.)

_____ Roads, _____ District.

Diary of _____, Constant Labourer, for week ending Saturday, _____ 18 .

Open to the inspection of every member of the County or District Roads Board.

| Date. | Description of Work. | | | | | Surveyor's Minute of his Visit, and the Work he found the Labourer engaged on. |
|---|---|---|---|---|---|---|
| | Spreading Stones. | Raking Stones. | Scraping. | Siding. | Other Works. | |
| M. | | | | | | |
| T. | | | | | | |
| W. | | | | | | |
| T. | | | | | | |
| F. | | | | | | |
| S. | | | | | | |

# APPENDIX III.

## (FORM OF ANNUAL ESTIMATE.)

Roads.

Estimate for the Year ending March 25, 18 .

| Line of Road. | Length of Portion. | | | Materials. | | | Labour. | | Miscella-neous. | Total. | REMARKS, and Report respecting the Casual Labour, and Miscellaneous Expenditure anticipated. (As full explanation as possible should be given of the reasons for which the several sums are required.) |
|---|---|---|---|---|---|---|---|---|---|---|---|
| | Miles. | Furlongs. | Chains. | Cube yds. | Price per Cube yd. | Amount. £ s. d. | Constant. £ s. d. | Casual. £ s. d. | £ s. d. | £ s. d. | |

N 2

# INDEX.

LONDON: PRINTED BY WILLIAM CLOWES AND SONS, LIMITED,
STAMFORD STREET AND CHARING CROSS.

# SPONS'

# TABLES AND MEMORANDA FOR ENGINEERS.

Selected and arranged by J. T. Hurst, C.E., Mem. of the Society of Engineers, Mem. Phys. Soc. of London, Surveyor War Department, Author of 'Architectural Surveyors' Handbook,' 'Hurst's Tredgold's Carpentry,' etc., 64mo, roan, gilt edges, eleventh edition, 1s. In cloth case, 1s. 6d.

CONTENTS:

This work is printed in a pearl type, and is so small, measuring only 2½ in. by 1¾ in., by ¼ in. thick, that it may be easily carried in the waistcoat pocket.

"It is certainly an extremely rare thing for a reviewer to be called upon to notice a volume measuring but 2½ in. by 1¾ in., yet these dimensions faithfully represent the size of the handy little book before us. The volume—which contains 118 printed pages, besides a few blank pages for memoranda—is, in fact, a true pocket-book, adapted for being carried in the waistcoat pocket, and containing a far greater amount and variety of information than most people would imagine could be compressed into so small a space. . . . . The little volume has been compiled with considerable care and judgment, and we can cordially recommend it to our readers as a useful little pocket companion."
—*Engineering.*

*Crown 8vo, cloth, with Illustrations, Price 5s.*

# Workshop Receipts,

### FOR THE USE OF

## Manufacturers, Mechanics, & Scientific Amateurs.

## BY ERNEST SPON.

### CONTENTS :

Bookbinding—Bronzes—Candles—Cement—Cleaning—Concretes—Dyeing—Electro-Metallurgy—Enamels—Engraving—Etching—Firework Making—Freezing—Fulminates—Furniture Creams, Oils, Polishes, Lacquers, and Pastes—Gilding—Glass Cutting—Glass Making—Graining—Gums—Horn Working—India-rubber—Ink—Japans—Lacquers—Marble Working—Matches—Mortars—Paper Hanging—Painting in Oils—Photography—Polishes—Pottery—Silvering—Soap—Solders—Taxidermy—Treating Horn, Mother-o'-Pearl, and like substances—Varnishes—Veneering—Whitewashing, &c., &c.

---

*Crown 8vo, cloth, 5s.*

# WORKSHOP RECEIPTS
## (SECOND SERIES).

### By ROBERT HALDANE.

Devoted mainly to subjects connected with Chemical Manufactures. An entirely New Volume. Uniform in Size, Style, and Type with the Original 'Workshop Receipts.'

### CONTENTS.

Acidimetry and Alkalimetry—Albumen—Alcohol—Alkaloids—Baking Powders—Bitters—Bleaching—Boiler Incrustations—Cements and Lutes—Cleansing—Confectionery—Copying—Disinfectants—Dyeing—Staining and Colouring—Essences—Extracts—Fireproofing—Gelatine—Glue and Size—Glycerine—Gut—Hydrogen Peroxide—Inks—Iodine—Iodoform—Isinglass—Ivory Substitutes—Leather—Luminous Bodies—Magnesia—Matches—Paper—Parchment—Perchloric Acid—Pigments—Paint and Painting—Potassium Oxalate—Preserving.